Praise for *Angel de la Luna ar*

"Guaranteed to tug at your heartstr
adult novel is just what the doctor ora
—Shondaland

"Adolescence, family issues, music and revolutionary politics all sink sharp hooks into a Filipino teenager at the beginning of the twenty-first century." **—Kirkus**

"*Angel de la Luna* is a beautifully told, and at times heartbreaking, coming of age and coming to America story. M. Evelina Galang is a masterful storyteller, and through her brilliant voice and craft, Angel and her family become ours too." **—Edwidge Danticat**

"A story of teenage rebellion, *Angel de la Luna and the 5th Glorious Mystery* is also a novel of adult grace. Its particular triumph is to give an intimate voice to radical themes: a young woman sees the immigrant's American dream through the lens of Third World activism and gives us startling ways of looking and words for seeing the world." **—Gina Apostol**

Praise for *Her Wild American Self*

"Stirring debut collection of stories. . . . All are told in an elegant, mesmerizing style. . . . The brief, chantlike monologues that frame the collection are as lyrical as prayers." **—New York Times Book Review**

"An honest and insightful look at the experiences of Filipina American women who 'grew up hearing two languages.' . . . A meaningful contribution to the growing chorus of Asian American voices." **—Ms. Magazine**

"Through these richly drawn women, we experience what it might mean to be a Filipina American woman. . . . [Galang] shows us how we might find in art, dance, play, family, friendship, or community that which can save us from our cultural scripts." **—Review of Contemporary Fiction**

Praise for *One Tribe*

"Galang infuses her novel about Filipino Americans with a sense of urgency by crafting it around the lives of a group of troubled teenagers struggling to find their way in both their ethnic and geographic communities. . . . The danger teens face and the concern Galang expresses are real, and she demands that readers acknowledge just how difficult it can be to straddle two ways of life while seeking your own place in the world." **—Colleen Mondor, *Booklist***

"*One Tribe* is political without being preachy, and in the end is a layered story about survival, especially for the young women caught up in this violent struggle (a veritable culture war) over affirmations of power and territory—a paradigm that mirrors the conflicted history of the Philippines." **—Rigoberto González**

"*One Tribe* is ambitious, beautifully paced, ingeniously constructed, a multi-layered novel in which virtuosity is a vehicle for wise, deeply compassionate storytelling." **—Stuart Dybek**

"M. Evelina Galang's *One Tribe* is a bold, ambitious, moving, and deeply surprising novel about the necessity and dangers of the human need to belong to other people. Galang writes beautifully and precisely about the world of her wonderful main character, Isabel Manalo—her students, her lovers, her parents, her fears—and in doing so has written a universal book about teaching, fear, parenting, and love."
—Elizabeth McCracken

"Reading *One Tribe*, I entered a strange, feminine world—the Yin mind of a caring teacher. A teacher myself, I identify with Isabel Manalo, whose students dwell in an alien country. A poetic book."
—Maxine Hong Kingston

"This novel deftly navigates the tension over being American and yet not quite so; the conflict between race and personal relations; and the contradiction between the reality of history and that of the present. It adds to the growing body of literature about Filipino presence and experience on this continent." **—Ninotchka Rosca**

When the Hibiscus Falls

When the Hibiscus Falls

M. EVELINA GALANG

COFFEE HOUSE PRESS
Minneapolis
2023

Copyright © 2023 by M. Evelina Galang
Cover design by Christina Vang
Book design by Rachel Holscher
Author photograph © Isabella Cendan, Bella Rosa Productions

Coffee House Press books are available to the trade through our primary distributor, Consortium Book Sales & Distribution, cbsd.com or (800) 283-3572. For personal orders, catalogs, or other information, write to info@coffeehouse press.org.

Coffee House Press is a nonprofit literary publishing house. Support from private foundations, corporate giving programs, government programs, and generous individuals helps make the publication of our books possible. We gratefully acknowledge their support in detail in the back of this book.

LIBRARY OF CONGRESS CATALOGING-IN-PUBLICATION DATA

Names: Galang, M. Evelina, 1961– author.
Title: When the hibiscus falls / M. Evelina Galang.
Other titles: When the hibiscus falls (Compilation)
Description: Minneapolis : Coffee House Press, 2023. |
Identifiers: LCCN 2022050185 | ISBN 9781566896795 (paperback) | ISBN 9781566896801 (epub)
Subjects: LCSH: Filipinos—Fiction. | LCGFT: Short stories.
Classification: LCC PS3557.A375 W47 2023 | DDC 813/.54--dc23/eng/20221206
LC record available at https://lccn.loc.gov/2022050185

PRINTED IN THE UNITED STATES OF AMERICA

For Miguel Trinidad Galang, MD,
Anna Karina Bate Lopez-Tan,
Giovanna Pompele,
and all our ancestors.
For your wisdom and guidance from the other side.
In gratitude, in love, in remembrance.

"We were born matter and spirit. Once we pass on, we become pure spirits, able to assist and provide guidance to humans who are blanketed by material needs. We can become guardians, as well as teachers of future generations, translating for them the true meaning of life. The problem, however, is that most people today, including baylans or indigenous spiritual functionaries, have lost their connection to ancestral guides. They have also not given much importance to where we are going. We need to know what world we are moving towards, to avoid losing our way. Without this knowing we cannot possess the true meaning of a complete existence."

—Datu Migketay Victorino Saway

TABLE OF CONTENTS

STRENGTH IS THE WOMAN   3

I.

America, Still Beautiful   7

Drowning   16

The Typhoon Is a Hurricane   28

The Esguerra Sisters   39

When the Hibiscus Falls   45

II.

Foodie in the Philippines   67

Hilot of Parañaque   94

Loud Girl   103

Holy Thursday   123

Hot Mommies   137

III.

Deflowering the Sampaguita   161

Fighting Filipina   171

The Kiss   183

Imelda's Lullaby   199

Labandera   206

ISLA OF THE BABAYLAN   225

When the Hibiscus Falls

STRENGTH IS THE WOMAN

• • •

Strength Is the Woman

No one ever gets the story right.

Malakas and I lived in the hollow of a bamboo reed. We were lost, tangled up in a thicket of long thin shoots, when a bagyo— heavy with rain and wind—swept us away. The islands were just forming. There was nothing but sea and sky, and these bamboo stalks knocking into one another like tribal drums. During the monsoon, the bamboo circled us, swallowed us up whole.

Malakas said he'd find a way to get us out. But all he did was whine. He was cramped. He was hungry. He had to relieve himself. He could not see for the dark.

But we could hear the ocean beating on our bamboo pole. We could hear wind sweeping across the sky. We could hear the cries of a prehistoric bird caterwauling like it too was lost. Malakas wept, bathed me in his tears.

We drifted in the current, spinning like a compass, never settling on a direction. We were always moving.

I liked the dark. I liked the cool shade. I liked the lull of the tide. I found it soothing. And the silence that came when he slept was so peaceful. My body fit right next to his, and if he'd just learn to relax, we could have been together like that forever. My arms stretched high above our heads. Fingers poking out the end of the bamboo like leaves, wet when it rained, warmed in the sun, salty.

Most days I closed my eyes and breathed. I used to meditate a lot back then and if I listened very carefully, I could almost hear a flute-like melody swirling around us.

"Why aren't you freaking out?" he wanted to know.

"Over what? It is what it is. Just chill."

And then the bird flew past us, heard Malakas say, "Anybody out there? Help!"

"Hush," I told him. "Breathe," I said. "Relax."

But he kept yelling, like the world was on fire.

And so, the bird swooped down and kissed the tips of my fingers. Cawed.

"We're stuck. We're hungry. We can't breathe."

"Quiet," I told Malakas.

That's when the bird struck the reed, slashed the bamboo right in half. And there we were, naked, brown, thin from the narrow bamboo.

"You are beautiful," said the bird, reaching its wings to touch me.

I gave him the evil eye, and the bird, perched on the edge of the bamboo, lost his balance just as the sea rose and swallowed him up.

"No, you stupid bird," Malakas said. "She is strong."

And that was the beginning of everything.

I

America, Still Beautiful

Faustina leaned back in her recliner, feet twitching. Her toes were dry and itchy. Her knees ached. Outside the sun had set early, even for November. She turned the television up.

"Lola, you want company?" Mahal stood in the doorway, holding out a bowl of popcorn.

"Sure," Faustina said. "Halika."

If Orlando were alive, his old body would be perched on the edge of the recliner, rooting as if at a boxing tournament. She'd beg him to come to bed. And he'd wave her away.

Music from the news program scored their conversation. A white image of Illinois filled the screen. "Too close to call," said the commentator.

Mahal sat on the rug next to her lola, offered her the popcorn.

Faustina sighed. Declined.

"I miss him too," Mahal said. The sixteen-year-old leaned on her lola.

Faustina ran her hands through the child's hair, felt the coarse strands weaving through her fingers. Mahal's devotion to politics reminded her a lot of Orlando.

Mahal took a handful of popcorn. "Democracy!" she said, mimicking her lolo. She gestured her finger to the ceiling.

The old woman wrinkled her brow, envisioned him, a young man standing before Malacañang Palace with his batch mates. He wrote about it. Published the story in the *Collegian*. Was labeled a communist.

Faustina pointed to the screen. The lady waved from a platform. Balloons the color of the flag fell around her. "Walang hiya," she said. "She hasn't even won and see how she acts?"

"She's not perfect," Mahal said, "but she'd be our first female president."

"Everyone says she is a liar."

"And you know," Mahal said, "if that guy wins, he'll deport immigrants."

"Stop, iha." Faustina put her hand up.

❂

After being blacklisted, Orlando could not find any work as a journalist. He insisted Manila was no place to raise a family.

He left the Philippines months before the dictator proclaimed martial law. Their son was not even a year old. Before their families, she stood in support of the move. Toasted him at his despedida. Kissed him on the tarp of Manila International Airport. But between them, in their bedroom, she was against it.

In Milwaukee, he got a job as a bellman at the Pfister Hotel. He rented a room with a busboy and an elevator operator. Between shifts, he took classes. Her husband saved every paycheck for almost ten years before he moved into his own place, before he could sponsor Faustina and their son, Boy. It took another fifteen years of catering out of their kitchen before they bought the shop.

Back home, they would have been surrounded by their big families. Cared for. Pampered.

Held hostage, she could hear him saying, his body pacing circles in their bungalow back home.

❂

The television glowed a winter blue. The blonde commentator called the states like a teacher taking attendance. Faustina closed her eyes.

In her dream, Orlando was a young man with hair greased back and parted to the side, chiseled jaw and a smile that still made her feel weak. "How we doing?" he asked her. "America still beautiful?"

"Ano'ng beautiful?" she answered.

"Come on," he said. He lit a cigarette, and she pushed the smoke away. She noticed her wrinkled hands, spotted with grease burns.

"Why am I old and you are not?" she asked him. "Why are you still smoking?"

He took a drag. Squinted. "Boy still traveling?"

"Ever since."

"Mahal okay?" he asked Faustina.

She nodded. "A little moody." She ran her hand along his arm. "Like you."

"Nako. More like you."

"Ikaw," she whispered, closing her eyes, wishing the dream was not a dream, but a message.

"And you, mahal ko? Okay ka?"

She waved him away. As the states went red, she fell asleep.

●

They bought a storefront in 1996, even though the neighbors were not so friendly. Even though at first, they lost money on the shop, giving away egg roll gift baskets, raffling off free dinners at community meetings. "Faustina's Homemade Lumpia" was twenty-four years old now.

Orlando would have voted for business. "Protect the shop, mahal," he'd tell her. "Guard our apo with all your might." He would have made Faustina stand in line with him no matter how cold. He would have said the woman running for president was a liar. All you had to do was watch the news, he'd say. Just look at her.

Faustina liked the way the woman stood tall even after the husband cheated on her. Liked the way the woman let the insults roll past like rain clouds in April. She thought about voting for her. Too liberal for Orlando.

After he died, she could not bring herself to fold his clothing into cardboard boxes, to give his things away. She couldn't stop watching his news shows either, though the anchors talked as if they were always angry. "Ang pangit naman," she used to say to him. "All they know is bad news."

The noise from the television irritated Faustina. "Turn it off," she'd tell her husband. "Give me peace."

But after he died, the silence suffocated her.

The newscasters called the lady candidate terrible names. Why would they do that if it weren't true? Weren't they journalists? Faustina wasn't sure when, but she stopped liking the lady too.

Last week her son called to instruct her who to vote for and why. "Don't campaign me," she said. "Don't tell your mother what to do."

Her words cut him off. Reminded her of how mad she was. A husband dead. A disrespectful son, never home. A dalagang apo, so emotional.

If today she were back home, they would be in the ancestral house, surrounded by family, cared for by a cook, katulong, a driver, an infinite number of nieces.

Was it worth it? she says to him now. Every limb ached for him.

◊

She didn't like the other candidate either. The man. He gesticulated at cameras, clumsy as a drunk on New Year's Eve. His face a permanent scowl. Like a bully on the playground, he called people names. "I don't like the look of him," she whispered to Orlando. But all the journalists said he was a successful billionaire genius who was going to let people run their own businesses. Not the government. Was she not a businesswoman too?

She weighed the candidates, slipping their campaign promises into her pockets and rolling them like loose change. Maybe she'd vote for the lady, a woman like herself, a self-starter, the mother of an only child. But then again, she could not stop hearing those voices from the cable channel. She could not stop thinking that her husband was somehow still with her, hovering over her and telling her to listen not with her heart but her head. The business.

In her dreams, young Orlando co-anchored the news with an older White gentleman. Bill was Orlando's favorite. "He tells it like it is, Faustina," he often said. The two men sat before a map of the United States, pointing to the colors as they turned. Red. Blue. Red. Red. Blue. Red. Red. Red.

•

Faustina walked the house, checking each room, locking windows, securing doors. When she neared her granddaughter's room, she stopped. The girl was weeping as if someone had died.

"Ano'ng nangyari?" Faustina called, opening the teenager's door. "Mahal, why?"

The girl sprawled on her bed, wailing into her pillow. Faustina kicked off her slippers and climbed next to her. She pulled Mahal to her chest and sniffed the top of her head. The girl smelled of the wind. Her hair carried traces of cigarette smoke. "It's okay, anak," she whispered. "You're okay."

Mahal cried louder.

Faustina brushed the girl's tangled hair, rocked her, hummed to her. She could not imagine what had set the girl to crying. Is she pregnant, Faustina thought. It would be okay no matter what. She waited for the girl to speak.

"Oh, Lola," she said, "what are we going to do?"

"About what, anak?" Faustina asked.

The question triggered sobbing. Uncontrollable. Loud.

Faustina explored the girl's face, the soft contours and the lips, like fallen petals. Her only grandchild. She fell asleep cradling Mahal. The girl's cries seeped into her dreams that night, and though she didn't know what was wrong, Faustina felt the grief too. The child's sadness came over her in waves.

•

The man had won and Mahal refused to eat. Faustina pushed a plate of garlic fried rice and eggs toward the girl. "Sunnyside up. It's your favorite," she told her. "You have to eat or your father will be mad at me."

Mahal collapsed, her body hunched over the table, her arms sprawled like spider's limbs.

"Oh, come on, it's not the end of the world," Faustina said, wiping the kitchen counter with a wet rag. Mahal's face was swollen from the crying. Her lips were fat. Her eyes, tiny little raisins. Faustina continued. "We have our health. We have our house. We have the lumpia shop."

Mahal sighed and her thin body shivered.

"You are a sorry loser," Faustina told her. "If your lolo were here, he'd tell you to be gracious."

"Like he was when Obama won?"

The girl had a point. Orlando stormed around the house that year, muttering to himself. Arguing with Mahal, who was only a little girl then. There was door slamming and a lot of pounding on tables.

"Sige," Faustina said. "Come to work with me today. You can roll egg rolls. I'll make you noodles."

"My teacher told Amna they were going to deport her dad."

"Ridiculous. Who?"

"The government."

"Isn't her dad American?"

Mahal nodded.

"So, impossible."

❂

They waited for the bus. The sky hung before them like a dirty curtain. The winds spat rain at their brown faces. Wiping tears from her face with the back of her hand, Mahal stared at the sidewalk. Faustina ignored her. The child was too emotional. Faustina regretted not sending her to school. It was only an election. The man would not change anything. She had been in this country long enough to know that politics was all talk. Mahal would get over this like the breakup with that boy last month.

The bus rolled to a stop. Exhaust sputtered into the air. Faustina nudged her granddaughter to move. She watched the teenager step up. She's too skinny, she thought. She needs to eat. Faustina placed her hand on the railing and pulled herself up step by step. She had not slept very well in the child's twin bed.

Every seat was taken. Men. Women on their way to work. Teenagers off to school. Old ladies like Faustina. But mostly the bus carried construction workers who had parked their trucks at a nearby lot. Mahal walked to the back, her head bobbing left and right in search of a seat. As they passed down the aisle, the people grew silent. All Faustina could hear was the rumble of the engine.

Mahal stopped in front of a boy. "Would you mind giving your seat up for my grandmother?" she asked. He wore a ski vest and a backward baseball cap. His eyes were so blue. His skin, the color of eggshells.

Faustina put her hand on Mahal's sleeve. Held her breath. The boy stared at them. No expression. "H'wag na. I can stand," Faustina said.

"Come on, bro," Mahal said.

The boy looked the girl in the eye. Then turned and stared out the window.

"Seriously?" she said.

Faustina sent a prayer to her husband. "Protect her, ha?"

The boy grunted and stood up and shouldered past Mahal.

"Hey!" she yelled.

He pulled the string above them, one hand in his pocket, his hip cocked to the side.

Faustina smelled the exhaust from the belly of the bus. The stench made her queasy. The bus drifted to a slow crawl, paused. The boy scuttled past them.

"Fucking foreigners," he yelled back, leaping off the steps and into the cold.

"What a jerk," Mahal said. "You okay, Lola?"

More people boarded as Faustina sat herself down. And the passengers began talking. Their words fell on her like flames. Singed her from the inside out. She held her head up.

"It's a new day," someone said.

Faustina turned to find the voice. A woman wrapped in a thick wool sweater stared at her two seats back. Her cheeks were red from the cold, her nose too. Her hair piled high upon her head.

Faustina did her best to disregard them. She imagined holding fire in her hands, balancing flames on her head. As if she were young and this was Pandanggo sa Ilaw. She wore a deadpan face, concentrating, careful not to stumble. Not to drop a single ember.

When she was a girl in the province of Quezon, she mastered the dance of fire. She knelt and steadied the flame on the crown of her head. She slid her elbows to the ground, the palms facing up, cradling the fire. She turned her body in circles. She never dropped the flame. She never let on how much she hated the dance. Now all of it came back to her. The fire burned through her. Why did Orlando leave her like this?

"That's right, lady," said the White woman. "We won. He's deporting all of you. Comprehendo?"

Faustina looked past the woman. She too had words that could burn, a fire coursing inside of her, heavy and hot and all in Tagalog. But she would not be a sorry loser.

She turned back to Mahal who stood with her legs apart, one hand on the silver pole, the other on a hip. Mahal cocked her head. Threw the woman a look.

"You okay, Lola?" Mahal asked again.

Faustina nodded. Looking out the window, she counted the shops along the boulevard. The traffic moved in starts and stops. The grimy air colored everything like day-old snow. She shut her eyes and tried to imagine Orlando sitting next to her, reading the news. She could not locate him anywhere—not the shape of him, not the scent of him, not the words that he spoke over and over again.

When she glanced at Mahal she had to look twice. They were so similar. Never quiet. Never still. Always pushing. She pursed her lips, kissed the air, gave another nod.

"Kumusta ka?" Faustina mouthed.

Mahal threw her hand up and flashed her grandmother a peace sign. Faustina smiled. The girl's body took up the entire aisle, small and dark and visible.

Drowning

I hear my sister, a siren with blue fins and skin the color of palm trees, skimming coral reefs, sighing to herself. She floats east. Her spirit hums alongside tropical winds, breathes cool and high-pitched arias. Tokens of minor discord. Some nights she caws in between the buzz of ambulance horns, whistles, cop cars, and fire engines. My mother is the only one who drowns my sister's presence with her moaning, low and steady, sending my ate's blue scales swimming east to the islands of Mindanao. Even then, Ate Lourdes stays with me, always. And when I try to forget, to ignore her sitting to my left or floating just above me, she beckons me, tugs at my sleeve, mews in my ear, an alley cat forever lost.

◉

One week after the drowning, my family visits Chick's Beach, as if to see her there, as if to bring her home for dinner. I try to imagine her very last moments of breath. I walk along the bay, its shoreline stretching out like arms, welcoming the swell of saltwater. My eyes strain to see just beyond the horizon. The place where her giant milk crate, her life-size balikbayan box, crammed with my sister and her two best friends, fell off the edge of the earth.

Today the sky is as gray as my mother's hair. My mother cries every day. Her voice wafts above the waves, snakes its way to the sky where it is carried off by winds. Mommy clings to my baby sister, Riza, looks small against the sky, as if she herself were a girl, holding onto her doll. My little sister squirms to get down. My mother won't let Riza run on the beach. Won't let her roll in the sand and tease the tide.

Daddy sits apart from them. Far to the left. He has grown silent these last few days. Rarely speaking. He disappears. Lets my mother grieve aloud for both of them.

The day must have been as dismal as this. The wind snapping at my big sister's hair, wrapping against her face, her body. The waves must have been taller than the battleships resting in the shipyards of Newport News, Norfolk, and Chesapeake. The beach must have looked ugly, just like this. Nothing but sand, driftwood, and gray sky. This ocean waiting to devour them.

When I was six, the waves swept me up, and all I could see were brown patches of ocean, sky, and a thousand bubbles. I still think of the sound of water hiccupping through my body, the salt stinging my nose, my tongue, burning my eyes like acid. The deeper I fell into the mouth of the sea, the calmer I felt; the calmer I felt, the less I struggled, the deeper I fell. I almost settled down at the bottom of that sea, except that Ate Lourdes swam out to me and hooked her elbow around mine like one of those plastic monkeys in a barrel. She saved me. She saved me exactly the way I didn't save her.

◆

The last time she saw me, I was digging through her closet, looking for her burgundy scarf made of chiffon, light as air and the color of blood. I wanted to wrap it around my neck, tie it in a loose bow. Pretend I was seventeen. I liked the way the fabric felt against my skin, the way it held the scent of her, a perfume of citrus and spice braided into its fragile weave.

She screamed at me, her face turning the color of the scarf. Her eyes mean as monsoon skies. She pulled me out of the closet, flinging me like a rag doll onto her bed.

"Stay out, Nightmare," she screamed at me. She pinched me to make sure I would understand. Then she stormed out of the room, her blue windbreaker sailing from the palm of her hand.

At the funeral everyone had nice things to say about Ate Des. How the last time they saw her she was so beautiful or pretty or kind. The last time I saw her, she said she hated me.

●

Ate Des used to sneak out her bedroom window. It was her habit, like brushing hair a thousand strokes before sleeping, painting lipstick onto her full mouth every time she was irritated, or praying at the end of her days. She crawled out her window to do everything my parents warned her not to do. On that roof, she smoked skinny cigarettes rolled in leaves brown as coconut, smelling of cinnamon and orange tea. Against the roof, she lay down with her pimple-faced boyfriend, Ramon, and kissed.

Their soft moaning floated down and into my bedroom window, kept me wondering what it might feel like to lay underneath a boy. She'd crawl out the ledge and take off with Las Dalagas, wandering Tidewater, looking for something, I don't know what. She was good at sneaking about, nimble little street cat, living against our parents' rules and swearing me to secrecy.

"Quiet, huh, Nightmare—or I'll spank you."

I never told on her, but sometimes they found out. The house ached whenever she got caught. The voices—Mom's, Dad's, and hers—like water bubbles in a kettle, rumbling against one another. Baby Riza joined in—throwing a tantrum—shrieking—warning them to stop. My father listed grievances—school and boys and tsismis and how she might go right ahead and kill herself with all her careless antics.

"Then what," my father would shout, "what do you think that would do to your mother? What kind of example is that for your sisters? Think, anak, think!"

When my parents yell at me, I crumple up, small like a scrap piece of paper. I close my eyes and I let the words wash over me.

I disappear. I wish I was dead and I swear never to repeat my mistakes.

But not my ate. She screamed back. She ran circles around them and dodged their words, which were sharp as darts dipped in poison.

"I don't care what your kumpare think! Tsismis—gossip? That bullshit?"

The walls trembled like they understood the power of her anger. The windows even cracked once, as if the house could not contain her.

◊

The day her best friend Marilena got her license, Ate Des was gone. She joined every function—community, school, church—just so she, Mercedes, and Marilena could cruise Tidewater with permission. She wore butterfly-sleeve dresses at picnics and parties, stepping high between the clapping bamboo lights on top of her head and fans waving from her hands. Some events required her to wrap brightly colored muumuus—yellow and mango cottons—around her slight body. She met people as she swung coconut husks from her hip, Tahitian humming her way around town.

She stayed after school and helped Ms. Manalo come up with dramas for high schoolers. She invented stories about Filipino Islanders, the Igorots, and the tribes of Mindanao. She'd spend a day painting props, canoes, huts, and rubber plants in Technicolor fuchsias, aquas, and tangerines, and two more days wandering the shops at Military Circle and the beach. She'd tell our mother she was doing volunteer work. Then, never one to lie, she'd spend an hour at the hospital carrying flowers to patients' rooms and two hours sitting at the 22nd Street Beach Dairy Queen, smoking cigarettes and hanging on the boys.

She came home to eat. To sleep. To bathe. She came home to haunt the house with her things—trails of clothing, of books and phone calls, traces of perfume, cloves, and nasty old bags of chips. She was moving away from us, spinning in larger circles where brothers and sisters meant something more than blood. No one spoke of it; in fact, my parents used to ignore it. What did matter to them was who she was running with—they knew the parents, other Filipinos, other good families.

I took over her chores. I watched Riza, changed her diapers, and washed green pea soup from her face and hands, or followed her around the house and pulled her off the stairs, the dining room table, my father's speakers. We never saw Ate Des. She only came around long enough to stare my parents down and trick them out of grounding her.

In death, she lives with us the way she never could in life. An angel shifting among us, she lays her hands on our shoulders at dinner, slips into our beds and naps next to us, visits our thoughts, our nightmares. She has become a fairy of sorts, playing favorites with Mom, Dad, Riza, or sometimes me.

I catch her looking at me across the room, a breeze blowing through the window or a light dancing across the floor. Sometimes the scent of her perfume is so strong, especially late at night when the house is dark and the muffled voices come from my mother and father's room. My parents lament how little they knew their daughter. Mostly it's her voice I hear, singing and sighing and humming low.

Sometimes from my window, I climb up to her roof to watch the full moon, and I think of how she must have loved that. The color of midnight draped in silver light. I can smell the saltwater from the roof. I can hear the water pulsing up and down the shore. It is the tide I hear, coming and going, taking with it everything in sight.

◊

Riza doesn't understand. At the funeral home she pushes her way through a forest of pant legs and high-heeled ladies. She slips in and out of different drawing rooms, sometimes finding herself at some stranger's casket. She stares at all the grown-ups, her dimples creasing into a slow smile. Thinks they're playing with her, pretending to cry, and moan, and sigh.

Riza knocks at our sister's casket, runs her hands along the railing of the other girls' coffins—the other girls, Ate Des's street sisters. Then grabs up our sister's photo. Our ate dressed in native costume, a straw hat in her hand, winks from underneath the paper roof of a fake nipa hut, sometime in July.

"Ate Des," she says, pointing to the photo. Then she speaks her baby gibberish. Holds the frame up to her ear. "Hello? Ate Des?" She frowns. Listens. Answers back, staring at the photo intently. Her eyebrows go up.

"But Ate Des," she says. As if Ate's explaining—I am dead, you are not. This is how it is now. "Nah, nah, nah," Riza screams.

"Give it to me, Nightmare," I say, taking the picture from her. "Put it back."

She bears down. "Ate," she tells me and then pointing she says, "Baby too."

"No baby," I tell her. "Only Ate Des. See?"

I run my fingers along the photo, my older sister's memory caught in a silver frame, her eyes shining at me. "Not you, Baby Nightmare, only Ate Des."

She shakes her head, speaking rapidly in a language all her own, insisting, "Baby too, baby too, baby too."

My mother forgets who is in the room with her. She forgets about the baby. When Riza's hungry or wet. When she needs her nap. My mom's busy thumbing through Ate Lourdes's life, flipping through pictures and newspaper clippings and construction paper projects from her days of elementary school. She holds my ate's sketches up against a window so that light shines through the paper and brightens the images. Black and white drawings from the past year. Mom's looking for answers. "Where did I go wrong," my mother wants to know.

The newspaper printed a photograph of my sister and her best friends dancing at the multicultural celebration. The girls have bodies different from one another. Mercedes oozes out of her terno, all curves and cleavage. She is a glamour queen and the reigning

Miss Virginia Beach—dash—Philippines. Marilena, tall and lanky, stretches her body across the photo, her arms held up above the two and pointing east and west. She sways, a long stalk of bamboo floating in the wind. Ate Lourdes peeks out from behind the two of them, small in their largeness.

"Debutantes Drown in Gang Ritual" bleeds across the top of the photo. The paper looks for reasons and thinks my sister and her friends were going through some initiation rite.

"They have no proof!" my mother blurts out to no one in particular. She shakes a painted fingernail at the page. Carefully, she unfolds the paper, flaps its corners up wide and high like a beautiful paper butterfly.

"Why do they have to say this?" my mother says. "What gang?" The paper asserts they may have been high or troubled with pregnancy, suggests a shared suicide.

Mom stays up, rattling through my sister's life. I am the one who picks up after the family—the dishes and breakfast. I do the laundry. She sometimes looks at me, whispers something, calls me iha. But I think she's seeing not me but my older sister. I think she holds me only because she's thinking of Ate Lourdes.

My father keeps to himself. Enters the house, patting me on top of the head. Late at night I hear their voices through the walls. He's telling her she's still the mother. "You have two daughters more," he tells her. "You can't stop now."

I have one sister left. A little one. Two parents. But only one who sees me. This week, we are living in separate rooms. We are on the lookout, searching from each window, waiting for Ate Lourdes to come home.

◆

I used to hide underneath Ate Des's bed, spying on her. I loved the way she used to take a paintbrush, dip its tail into a bottle of eyeliner and ink her way across her eyelid, or the way she'd define the arch of her brow, or fade the color of pumpkins and autumn leaves onto the apple of her cheek.

She was as beautiful as I hope to be. I understand why her pictures mesmerize our baby sister. Ate Des's body was small and the curves were beginning to find their way along her torso, her waist, the flesh of her hips and thighs. I want to be who she was becoming, even if she hated me.

Sometimes when I'm brushing my teeth and looking straight into the mirror, I feel her standing there, and I look, and I am not so sure the mirror is reflecting me as much as it reveals the shadow of her ghost. I see what Riza sees. Baby too, I think, baby too.

*

We eat dinners sent over to us by the Kapampangan Women's Auxiliary. They take turns making chicken adobo, rice, and pansit. The Kapampangan aunties leave meals wrapped in cellophane on our back porch. I am the one who retrieves them and pops them into the microwave just before my dad gets home. I don't think these women, who mean well, speak to one another. I don't think they realize they are bringing us the same meal over and over again. In the end it doesn't matter. We eat them anyway.

*

In school we simulate Filipino burial jars, clay pots shaped like genie bottles. Our ancestors painted the bones of the dead the color of fire and moss, the color of wild birds, tropical flowers, and mango. They celebrated the spirits' travel—this side to over there—gave them food for the journey, gave them coins for the tollways, combs to decorate the hair, and mother-of-pearl for their bony wrists. They packed all this, including the painted bones of their dead, into genie bottles and sent them floating in the sea.

I imagine my sister's bones, caught in the spurt of growth—long legs, slim rib cage, hard head. No painting her bones, no beautiful send-off. No wishing her well on the other side; we are too busy drowning.

At her wake, my classmates brought several burial jars and lined them along the windows of the funeral home. They painted them in tempera colors—royal blue, true red, sun-bright yellow—and glued all kinds of gold and silver and metallic-colored glitter along the surface of the jars. Mine was the color of iridescent oyster. I pasted a collage of broken shells, old sea bones, along the jar's mouth. I found a six-armed starfish, the tail of a sea horse, the house of a ghost crab, and I arranged them like ornaments at Christmas.

Inside the jar I placed her favorite lip balm, a raspberry gloss the color of bruised plums, her Wu Tang and Boyz II Men CDs—the ones that used to keep me up at night, blaring from the roof of our house—and a handful of uncooked rice and her set of house keys—just in case.

*

The burial jars go against our religion, contradict the novenas we recite each night, but they were a gift from our community, so my mother thanks the children and my teacher, Ms. Manalo. Sometimes the class comes over with their mothers and fathers, and we kneel on the cold basement floor while my mother leads us in prayer. A painted statue of the Virgin Mary stares down at us, and the prayer beads bang up against our hearts like penance.

The drone of the prayers scares me. The words uttered over and over lose meaning and fall into a hypnotic chant. Every now and then my mother, no longer able to contain the grief, lets out a howl, as if someone has ripped her open and is pulling at her stomach, her lungs, her heart, taking out all the things she needs to go on living. At that moment, one of the other mothers of the dead— Marilena's or Mercedes's—picks up where my mother has left off. My father, who continues his vigil of silence, wraps his arms around my mom and takes her up the stairs and lies with her in their king-size bed.

We continue reciting—Hail Mary, Full of Grace—Our Father who art in repossession of my sister's soul—and underneath our voices, my mother's wailing sings forth. I see how strong the other mothers are, how they lead the prayers with authority, how their voices sally forth without any fear, and I wonder why my mother is so different.

My knees wear down, the bones of them scraping against our wall-to-wall carpet, sense the concrete underneath.

I leave our guests and climb the stairs to find my parents lying long and fitted just so, in each other's arms. They are lost among the blankets, the comforters, the pillows; they are small and slipping deeper into the mattress. I see them and what they must have been like as children. Fragile and well behaved, nothing like us. We are loud, almost too loud. My sister was a tomboy; my baby sister is only one and a half and bossy. My parents listened well to their parents; I can see it in how they collapse in each other's arms, holding each other up against the clatter of the rosary beads below.

My father's face swells, tears washing over the two of them. "You act like you're the only one," he whispers. He moves the blankets over their bodies, embraces my mother with his whole self, and she struggles, trying to free her body from his. She is not interested in calming down. She has no use for it.

●

I steal my way into my sister's locked bedroom. I commit the crime she has accused me of over and over again. I search her drawers, find old notes from her girlfriends, a sheet of forgeries. My mother's signature, my father's. A copy of *Cosmopolitan*—the one where an Asian American woman with her hair teased round and high like the halo of a nasty saint straddles the cover in a sequined kimono, complete with *Cosmo* breasts.

I dabble at her vanity, testing perfumes, eye shadows, lipsticks, and blushes. I try on her dresses and slip my small feet into her clogs and platform shoes. I shift the burgundy scarf around my neck, hold it to my face, and breathe.

Deep in her sock drawer, I find her sketchbook and a packet of colorful oil pastels. The oils are untouched, perfectly shaped reds, greens, and blues. Only the black is worn down to a stub, its paper wrapping peeling in strips of gray confetti. Her drawings are etched in heavy charcoal. The strokes of her pencil, loud and wild, dart across the page. There are several self-portraits—dark sinister poses—the lips full and wide, the high arch of a brow, and the black shadows rubbed under the circles of her eyes.

◉

My teacher brings us rice cakes, their tops burnt with sugar and coconut milk, their bodies textured with cassava root and ginger. Her face is flushed. Red and blue veins crack the wildness of, the brightness in, her eye.

She holds the rice cakes out to my mother, her hands shaking, her chest heaving. I go to her, run my hand along the muscles of her back, which are lean and well defined.

She's come over to comfort us, wonders why the girls headed out in the crate, knowing Hurricane Emilio was on his way.

"They must have known," she says. "Wouldn't they have seen him coming?" She searches my mother's face, then turns to Dad and me. Picks up Riza in her arms. Riza pulls at her dangling earrings, giggles into her chest. "Why did they go?" she asks Baby as if there is an answer.

"Foolish accident," my father tells her.

"Gang ritual?" she asks. "Were they in trouble? Could it be drugs?"

Here my mother grows silent and it's my father who answers. "They were good girls," he shouts. "Lourdes was a good girl."

◉

I have stolen Ate Lourdes's drawings. I keep them under my bed now and when my parents slip into a state of mourning I shut the door and crawl under the bed. I turn the portraits over, page after page, the charcoal smudging my fingers, blurring the images of my older sister. In one of the drawings, her face is fuller. Her eyes a little rounder. The hand of the pencil feels lighter. It takes me a while to realize the picture isn't of Ate Des, it's me.

The paper feels raw, smells of pencil grease and lemon eau de toilette. I hold the drawing up to the mirror. I suppose it doesn't really look anything like me.

On paper, thick as cardboard, oceans roll moody and uncontrollable, white water crashing onto shore, frenetic strokes swirling skyward. Silhouettes of slender girls with pouting bellies drape themselves along the rough textures of the page. At the corners she's scribbled symbols of Las Dalagas—the blue fin of a mermaid sewn onto the torso of a beautiful girl.

Underneath several heavy marks, an image floats up at me. The bottom of the sea fills the page. Five floating bodies of different shapes and sizes scatter themselves upside down and sideways. I count a mother, a father, three girls, each a little longer and a little closer to womanhood than the next. Except for the biggest girl, the bodies stretch their legs, their arms, their fingers out, spin in circles, one living far away from the next. The biggest girl blossoms—two breasts, a set of hips, figure eights flipping from a tail just below her torso. She floats an irregular-sized belly, swollen like a loaf of rising dough. Below her tummy, she's sketched an array of scales, a hippy fish, wide and womanly.

I pull the colors from the box—the browns, the blues, the sea greens, and fierce fuchsias, and slowly I color the pictures. It is my newfound prayer. Each night before I close my eyes, I wish my sister home. Pulling out her sketchpad and her oils, I fill the drawing out a little more. I start with the mother and work my way to the little baby swimmer. I color life into the face, a little blush on the cheeks of the floating bodies, a little melon in the skin to keep the family Brown, a wash of blue drowning out the black lines.

I outline the bodies, making them bigger, pulling them closer to the center of the page. Eventually I cut the figures from the sketchbook, I free them. I hang them from silver threads along the windowsill, let the sunlight bleed through their paper bodies, watch them spin, colliding with the wind and knocking into one another, breathing.

The Typhoon Is a Hurricane

Celit pushed the cart, pulling tins of sardines, Vienna sausage, and Spam from the shelves. She took the last carton of saltine crackers and grabbed several liters of cola. She looked for peanut butter. The flashlights were all gone. She rummaged through batteries scattered on tables like dominoes. "D," she said out loud. "D. Saan ba ang mga D?"

"Can I help you?" asked the manager as she walked by.

"I need D batteries," Celit said.

"That's it right there," said the manager.

Celit felt her way through the pile. There was one more. Two more.

Down the water aisle, she saw wooden pallets where bottles of water had been stacked hours ago. Her shift at the hospital had kept her from shopping any sooner. She found two gallons of distilled water hidden behind the paper cups.

At checkout, carts lined up, bumper to bumper, weaving in and out of lanes. The waiting made her think of Manila traffic, long lines of cars traveling three slow hours to get ten kilometers across town. Checking out of Publix today was just like that.

When her cell phone rang, she rolled her eyes and answered it.

"When are you coming home, na?" she asked her cousin.

"Celit," Gina said. "We been trying to get a flight back. Walang flights."

"What do you mean, no flights?" The cart behind her rolled into her ankle. She turned and smiled at the Cuban vieja.

The old woman grinned back at her. "Permiso, China," said the lady.

"We can't get in. No flying into Miami. Not until after the storm."

"I told you," Celit said. "She's gonna hit hard. Sabi nila cat five. She has a temper."

The Cuban lady tapped Celit on the shoulder and pointed at the conveyor belt. She made a face with her lips, eyes wide, eyebrows up. Celit nodded and pulled items from her cart.

"Don't worry," Gina said. "We'll be back before you know it. Make sure you give my papa food with his meds, okay?"

"Did you hear what they named her?" Celit asked. "Irma. Like Irma from St. Scho, that bitch. Remember her?"

"The one who broke your heart?"

"As if," Celit answered.

"Just take care of Papa. Il'wag kang makulit."

Celit said nothing.

"You hear me?" Gina asked. "Don't agitate him."

"I know," Celit said, grabbing a candy bar from a nearby bin.

"How is he?" Gina asked.

"Tito Pat? He's the same."

"Good."

●

The news said Irma was on her way. Celit pushed her cart through the parking lot beneath cloudless skies. The sun was hot. The winds were soft like kisses. Celit could tell Irma was coming by the way people crawled all over town like ants on brown sugar, hunting for hurricane supplies, cutting each other off at gas stations, covering windows with sheets of plywood. All of Miami had gone mad and Tito Pat was her charge.

The townhouse in North Miami had hurricane shutters— accordion wings made of sharp metal. Celit heaved the shutters closed, placing one foot on the ground and the other pushing at the side of the house. The metal was rusty, stiff, and stubborn. She jiggled the key inside the locks and the shutters rattled as if to say, no, not today.

As Celit secured all twelve windows, the winds picked up. Palm trees dipped and bowed. Avocados from the neighbor's tree fell like softballs. Debris from the streets swirled. Every now and then a chorus of wind chimes sang and light rain fell from the cloudless sky.

◉

Inside, Tito Pat sat in front of the television. Men and women, with pink powdered faces and high-teased hair, barked weather updates and flashed maps with hurricane cones the size of Florida across their picture frame. The shutters blocked light from entering the house. It was dark and the screen was like the sun. But noisy. And angry. And everything that Celit hated about living with her cousin.

"Nighttime comes too soon," he said.

She picked up the remote and lowered the volume. "Po, it's daytime pa." She handed him a glass of water. His medication was in her hand, a small array of red and blue and yellow pills. "We're preparing for the hurricane."

"A typhoon?" He placed a pill on his tongue, took a swig of water and tossed his head back.

"No, po. A hurricane. Sa Pilipinas, typhoon."

"Same thing."

"Si Irma."

His eyes were gray and vacant. "Irma, is that one of Gina's friends?"

"No, po. That's the hurricane." She handed him another pill. "You have five more pills, po."

"What time will Gina be home?" He pushed her hand away.

"Remember Frankie and Gina are out of town?" She handed him another pill. He gave her side eye, but swallowed the medication anyway. "They'll be gone for a while."

"Who are you?" he asked.

"Your favorite niece, Celit."

"Are you a boy or a girl, I can't tell."

"Po, I'm your niece."

"You should dress like a girl, then."

Celit held her breath. Counted to ten.

When Celit was a girl, she could feel a typhoon coming weeks before the wind picked up, before the clouds formed dark swirls over the barangay, before palm trees lay flat to the earth, only to rise again. She could smell the rain coming. She dreamed it.

Tito Pat squinted at her. Shook a finger at her. "I remember when you were little, so pretty!" He nodded. "Penelope's girl, di ba?"

"Opo," Celit said. "Do you want to have your lunch? It's ready."

"Not hungry. Bring me a San Miguel."

"Po, you have to eat. You just took your meds." She gave him her hand. His was soft and knobby, white ash covering brown, wrinkled skin. "We'll have to put lotion on, po."

"Your hair is like a boy."

She sat him down before a bowl of tinola, the steam rising in small, savory puffs, pieces of chicken swimming in a broth along with potatoes, carrots, and spinach leaves. They ate in silence, mostly.

"How will you ever find a husband if no one can tell if you are girl or boy?"

"Tito, eat your soup before it gets cold." She put a plate of rice before him. "You want Coke?"

"Gusto ko ng serbesa. How about San Miguel?"

"I'll get you Coke."

She watched him slurp his soup up with a spoon and fork, the way his mouth moved in circles, the way the chicken slipped off the side of his lip.

"Tito, where are your teeth?" she asked him.

He winked at her and she smiled.

"I guess I forgot to put them in again."

She took a deep breath. "I will get them for you."

●

Celit searched the old man's bedroom. Ran her hands along the side tables, crawled under the bed. She went into his bathroom and rattled the cup he kept them in. "Shit," she whispered. "Lost again."

She called to him as she went into the kitchen. "Po, look in your pockets."

"What?" he answered, reading last Sunday's paper. "What am I looking for?"

"Pustiso mo, po."

She helped him stand and watched him jiggle his pant pockets, pat his shirt down. "Nothing!"

"Po! Ano yan?" she asked him, patting a bulge in his khaki pants.

He pulled a wad of tissue out, opened it like a gift wrapped in gold. There they were. A set of coffee-stained teeth. Tops and bottoms. He raised his shoulders like a question mark. "I forgot I put them there."

He smiled, mouth wet and gummy, his unshaven face spotted with whiskers. She laughed and kissed his cheek. "Tito Pat! Ano ba yan?"

⬦

The rain came down on Friday in rounds. Pissed off, violent, nasty, Irma screamed all night long. Sometimes she was high pitched and shrill. Other times she growled, running at trees and buildings, turning over loose pots, untethered lawn furniture, branches that had snapped in her horrific yawp. The worst moments were when she quieted down.

Celit slept on the chair in Tito Pat's room and listened to Irma throw a witch's tantrum. Tito didn't move. His slumber was deep, and his face slackened. Celit stood over him. She tried to imagine him in his younger days, when they were living in a fishing village, swimming in the dagat with the whole family on a Sunday. The other cousins used to gang up on Celit. She was too quiet, for one thing. They talked too much, she thought. Too frivolous and plastic, always talking about boys.

One Sunday, only Celit and Tito Pat remained in the fishing boat, while the others had leapt into the sea.

"Anak," he said, tugging at her ponytail, "why aren't you swimming?"

The cousins swam like minnows. "Ayaw ko," she told him in a whisper.

"Why not?" he asked. "You don't want to play with your pinsan?"

He picked her up and held her on his knee, looked into her eyes, said nothing. He was a handsome man then with a full head of wavy black hair, and a smile of big white teeth. Finally, he said, "It's okay, child. You stay with Tito Pat. Help me with the boat."

●

She leaned over now and kissed his weathered hand.

The wind picked up again, howling, yelping, calling all the aswang to run the boulevards with their wicked hands and webbed feet, shoving banyan trees out of the way. One by one they fell like giants. The world collapsed in grunts and sighs, too exhausted to go on. The old man snored through most of it, didn't even notice the lights flickering in the house, the television going silent, the darkness filling every room. The air con stopped humming. Celit felt the storm around them, banging on the shuttered windows, threatening to come in.

●

Irma left as suddenly as she came. She took with her the winds, the banging, the night. She took with her electricity—air conditioning, overhead lights, access to the stove and microwave. Heat seeped into the tiny house, sneaking in through the vents, rising up from the floorboards. It warmed the darkness like the hot breath of a sleeping lover.

When Celit was in nursing school and Manila was knee-high in baha, she waded through the streets in rubber boots, wearing garbage bags for ponchos. These things were not new to her, and she was not afraid of the rain—nor the brownouts, nor the tropical heat in a room hot as a tinderbox. Still, Celit stayed awake through the storm, sitting at her uncle's bedside, pulling at her fingers.

Tito Pat cried out only once during the storm. He sat straight up and spoke to his parents. Talked as if they were standing near his bedside.

Celit put her hand on him. Rubbed his arm. "Po, you are dreaming again." The room was dark. The heat, rising.

He pulled his arm away from her. "Don't interrupt. Inay is talking. Listen."

"Po, wala na si Lola Emmy. Panaginip lang yan." She put her hand on him again. "You are dreaming about your inay, but she is gone."

Celit tried to think of him as one of her patients. She tried her best to be clinical, but his dreaming scared her, made her think of ghosts and aswang stealing pieces of her—little bit by little bit.

●

The next morning, Celit worked the keys through every rusty lock and wrenched the metal sleeves back, let the sunshine through the house. She picked her way around fallen palm fronds and unripe fruit to get to all the shutters. Across the street, a neighbor's house was crushed under the weight of a hundred-year-old banyan tree. The sun baked the earth hot and steam rose from the ground. Inside, the house was like a pressure cooker. Heat sucked all the air from the rooms.

Tito Pat sat in his chair, waving a newspaper. He called for Tita Aida, his beautiful dead wife. He called to her as if she were in the other room, making soup for breakfast. Celit heard him, but she didn't have time today. She wanted to bring light back into the house. She wanted to conjure up a breeze. To give some semblance of order before Gina and Frankie got home.

When Celit finally stepped through the doorway, he cried like a baby.

"Iniwan niya ako?" he asked Celit. "Why is she not answering?"

"Po, wala na si Tita Aida," Celit told him, handing him a bowl of sardines over cold rice. "She died ten years ago."

"What? Dead?" He placed his hands to his face and cried. He tossed the bowl to the floor.

"Po, you have to eat something," she said. "You have to take your meds."

◈

Heat slipped into the house in waves, penetrated the windows, and sank through the curtains like fire. Celit picked up the landline, called the power company, and sat on hold. She wanted to talk to a person, but what she got was a robotic voice reciting a litany of addresses where the electricity had gone cold. Finally, an operator, from a call center. She could tell from the accent the woman was Filipina.

"A crew will be out in your neighborhood tomorrow. Thank you for calling."

"Celit!" yelled Tito Pat from his recliner. "What's wrong with the television?" He waved a remote at the screen like a magic wand, his skinny arms bent like chicken wings, his face distraught. He wiped his brow with a hanky.

"Sandali, po! I'm on the phone," she whispered.

To the voice on the phone, she spoke slowly. "Every day you say you are coming."

"There are many neighborhoods without power, ma'am."

"But you don't understand, my uncle is old. He can't take this heat. He's not eating right."

Tito Pat pushed himself up off his recliner, nearly losing his balance. Celit put her hand up as if to catch him. "Po, sit down!"

He whacked the television with the palm of his hand. "Punyeta!"

◈

Tito Pat refused to eat. To drink water. He refused everything. He woke up later each day, which worried Celit. It was nearly noon and he had not gotten up. She cooled his face with a moist hand towel, humming a Philippine folk song. She bathed his arms and shoulders, cleansed the sweat from behind his neck. He continued to sleep. She combed his hair, thinking of the night before when he called her a stranger. He thought she was a boy stealing pesos from his pockets.

A murderer, torturing him with fire. He would not eat the can of sausages she had sliced and placed on crackers. "Nilalason mo ba ako?"

"Poison?"

"What have you done with my daughter?"

She hated him. The weight of him. The sounds he made. Garbled. Off-color. She knew he was her blood. She knew she loved him, but in those moments, her stomach curled into itself and she wanted to spit.

❡

Celit walked up and down their street, stepping around debris, slipping under eaves of broken branches. She saw no sign of the crews—not working on her neighbors' houses, nor on the apartment buildings a block over, not fixing street lamps on the boulevard around the bend. Seven days without electricity.

The heat was Manila heat. Piles of garbage, broken furniture, and storm debris were stacked along the sides of the road. Unbearable sunshine made everything stink. Back home, near Dagat-Dagatan, there was a trash heap called Smokey Mountain. Celit used to ride past on her way to nursing school and see the wisps of smoke trailing from different parts of the hill. Now, palm fronds and trunks of fallen mango trees were pulled to the side of the road. Banyan trees tipped to their sides, exposed gnarly roots, fifteen feet in diameter, their branches reaching up like arms in motion. The old trees were dying. The lushness of Miami had grown brown and crisp as autumn.

Celit made her way to the nearest Publix, hoping the store would be open. With Tito Pat sleeping most of the day, she thought she might steal a moment to replenish their supplies. She walked past other people who seemed lost in their own neighborhood. She pulled out her cell phone. Still no signal.

At the grocery, she walked the aisle and saw nothing on the shelves. It was as if Irma had made it into aisle nine, swept through ten, torn down eleven, twelve, and thirteen. People pushed empty carts past her, as if they were shopping. But there was nothing.

Outside, she hiked her way around the block and saw a young woman handing out containers of water.

"How much," Celit asked.

"Just take it," said the woman.

Celit took three gallons of water and carried them home.

At the front door, Celit placed the jugs on the welcome mat as she dug for keys. She unlocked the bolt, then the lock, and pushed the impact-resistant glass door open. Inside, hot air rose up in rays of dust and swirled before the living room window.

"Tito Pat," she called. "Gising ka?" He should be awake by now, she thought. "Uncle, you awake?"

When she got to his bedroom, the covers were thrown to the ground and the pillows were cocked to the side of the bed like dog ears. She smelled urine coming from the bed and saw the stained sheets crinkled and damp. She tossed them as if to find him there, hidden at the foot of the bed.

Celit knocked on the bathroom door. "Tito Pat?" she called. When he didn't answer, she barged in. She drew the shower curtain. Light from the bathroom window streamed into the small room. Made everything hot to the touch.

Her heartbeat was loud in her ear. She ran from room to room, calling his name, beseeching him to answer. But there was only silence.

"Don't agitate him," Gina had said. "Make sure he eats when you give him meds."

And when the old man refused to come out, Celit thought Gina was there, saying, "You hear me, ha? You hear me, Celit? H'wag kang makulit!"

She moved through the house like a hurricane, pushing furniture aside, looking behind doors, hunting under tables. When she couldn't find him, the tears began to rise up out of her, a kind of rain, spilling everywhere.

And then she heard him crying. Celit ran out the back door and found her uncle sitting in the grass, bent over like a child. His teeth were in his hand and he was calling for his mother. For the first time in days, Celit saw him in the light, and he was small and bony. He had lost weight since Irma. When Tito Pat saw Celit running toward him, his eyes went wide.

"Inay?" he said. "Inay?"

Celit put her arms around her uncle, answered him yes, yes, yes. She wiped the tears from his face.

"I couldn't find you," he said. "Inay, where did you go?"

She looked into his eyes, but still could not find him. "I went to the store."

"And where is Papa?" he asked.

"You know where he is."

Celit embraced Tito Pat, humming in his ear. He smelled of old cigars and perspiration. He smelled of urine. He felt small and tired in her arms. She held him tighter even as he squirmed.

She closed her eyes, pictured the fishing village where she grew up. The blue-green sea. The boats. The cousins in the water. She was singing now. She held him close. Rocked him. Waited. Held him until the wind came rushing through, until a cloud swooped in to shade them and then, the rain.

The Esguerra Sisters

When my twin and I turn sixty-five, the women in the city begin coming out of their houses. One at a time, we hear their stories. We hear them speaking on the radio. We hear them on the news. Sometimes, on our way to the market, we see the old women lined up and carrying placards, wearing purple scarves and kamiseta two sizes too big, with angry letters scrawled across their chests. Today the women are marching. "Laban!" scream the women. "Laban!" call the protesters. "Laban! Laban! Laban!"

Flora looks at me and shakes her head. "What do they think they're doing?" She wants to know. "Walang hiyang mga babae!" She spits on the ground and keeps walking. I want to stop her and say, "You know the story, Flora. You know it's not their fault." But she is moving quickly through the heavy crowd, weaving her way around the people like a needle sewing stitches. I can barely keep up with her.

We lost everything in the war—our parents, all our siblings, our house, and all our possessions. We have never talked about it. It's easier that way. Almost fifty years ago, Flora and I moved to the city and we began all over again, the Esguerra sisters on a new adventure. I met Pepito on a pier one day, and Flora has been chaperoning us ever since. We have never been apart. Not in all these years. And when the children came, my twin was the one who delivered the babies and nursed me back to health. She cooked the meals and bathed the little ones while I slowly made my way out of the bedroom and back into the kitchen.

We were so busy. Flora never left my side, never married. "When would I leave you," she asked me once. "There's barely time to sleep. How can I go?" So, she was always there.

The women spread their stories, cast a haze upon our city, and I forget to sleep for all the thinking that I do. I go back to the war. I hear bombs coming down, lighting the night like fireworks at Christmas. I remember every little thing. Could I ever stand on the streets like that? Could I ever shout in front of all the world? Then everyone would know, I think. They'd know.

Once I asked Flora, "Should we?"

"Don't be ridiculous. You have a husband. Your children are old enough to have children. So tell me, should 'we' what?"

"So you've forgotten?" I asked.

"Have you?"

These conversations keep me up until the skies grow light and our cock crows and Pepito has left for the fishing boats. The children get up. They are the ones frying rice, preparing milkfish, eggs, and fresh-cut tomatoes. A little something for the belly before the day begins and I still have not slept.

◉

Flora screams in the middle of the night. I stumble through the house and find her rolling about the bamboo cot, clawing at her nightclothes, pulling at her hair.

I tell her it's okay. "You are only dreaming, Flora." When she doesn't wake, I shake her bony shoulders. "Sige, Flor, enough now. Wake."

Sometimes she sleeps so deep, she swings her arms at me as if I am the enemy. "Gising na, Flor!" I shout. "Gising na!" And other times, she snaps right out of it, straightens her hair, and throws me a dirty look. "What are you doing here? Can't I get any peace?" As if I am the enemy.

The next morning, while scrubbing the kitchen floor, I say, "Are you remembering?"

"What?" She pours soap into a bin of water.

"At night, Flor. Are you remembering?"

She says nothing. She balances her body on the husks of coconut shells, polishing each square tile of the linoleum. "Too much work for two of us. You should get the girls to help."

"They have their own jobs, Flor. They are supporting us in other ways."

"They could help a little more."

Pepito doesn't know. By the time we met, the war had been over for years. Why tell him? Why ruin love? None of the children know. Lately he's saying to me, "Mahal, bakit gising ka? Sleep already!" When I don't answer him, he asks, "May nagawa ba akong hindi mo nagustuhan?"

No, I think. You do everything for us, I think. You are kind. He is so brown and his face is young, though his hair is as silver as the moon. Pogi pa rin. If he knew, he'd leave me. And where would I be. Would he leave me?

These days, I look for signs. I listen to the air and I wait to hear the women chanting when I take the jeepney down the boulevard just past EDSA. I know I shouldn't look, but I can't help it. I want to know if the women look like me. I want to know if they are older or younger or richer than me. I want to know if their children are marching with them. Or if their husbands still think they're beautiful. I sometimes scour the pages of the paper just looking for something about their fight against Japan.

Late one night as we are washing dishes, I try again. "Maybe we should find out more about mga lola," I whisper to Flora. "Maybe we can join them."

"Leave it alone, na!" she snaps at me.

"But don't you ever think that maybe if we had this justice, things would change? You might have been able to love a man?"

"Stop. What's that got to do with it?" The more she shouts, the quieter I get, but I don't stop asking.

"Baka your nightmares would stop?"

"What nightmares?"

◊

She stops talking to me for almost two weeks. She moves about the house, banging dishes and pans. She lets the cock into the house and shouts at him for sneaking up on her, shadowing her every move. She talks to my girls when she means for me to hear. Masungit siya.

Her silence toward me grows the memories. I could be stitching up Jun-Jun's ripped pantalon and suddenly I am twelve years old, asleep with my sisters and brother, then waking to the bombing of the sky and the crashing of windows and doors. I could be hiding under the bed from the scurry of little yellow men with silver bayonets invading our house.

The more I remember, the more I want to say it. But to whom? After all these years, Pepito would be so angry with me. Lying for almost fifty years. My children would look at me like I was what? Basura? And I cannot say it to the one person who knows, because she is the one who would be angriest of all.

So, one day I sneak away and visit this house they call Lolas' House and I look through the green gates and I see the women gathered in a circle, plates of sinigang and rice balancing on their laps. Some women are laughing, some whispering into each other's ears and still there are others dancing in the back, twirling one another to canned folk music coming from old speakers. This is who they are? I think. Like they have no care in the world. This is what it means? To stand up and cry your stories to the world, and then to sing and dance behind the green gates? I cannot decide if what I see is a new kind of freedom or if perhaps the rumors are true. Perhaps these women did not know war. Perhaps they are telling stories from their imagination. I cannot begin to see myself dancing with such joy.

Down the street, a motor-tricycle turns the corner, carrying two little old ladies like eggs in a basket. I better go, I think, before they see me. I better hide.

◊

Pepito wakes, but this morning instead of rising out of bed, he nestles his body close to mine. He kisses my belly.

"Old man, get up," I say, "You have work to do."

And that is when he pulls me to him, face to face, looks at me, he says, "Whatever it is, okay na."

I say nothing.

"Married forty-eight years is a long time, mahal. Di mo alam? Mahal na mahal kita." He brushes the hair out of my eyes and smiles. "I survived that war. I know many bad things happened to very good people."

I can feel myself trembling.

"Nothing would surprise me," he whispers.

Arms wrapped around me, breath on my body, my husband finds a way to tease the stories out of me.

◆

She calls me crazy. Her words fly out of her like angry monsoon winds ravaging these islands. There is no room for discussion, only crying. My sister has gone mad. Nawala siya sa sarili niya. Did I do this, I think. Was it the excitement in my voice? Or the way I told her about the second time I went to that Lolas' House and heard them talking about the war? Is it my fault?

I decide that I must do anything I can to calm her, so I start crying. I apologize. I tell her I will never bring it up again. I beg her to stop. But she is whirling around the room now, bumping into things, pointing her fingers at imaginary figures. All this time, she is telling them. All this time, I thought you were gone. I thought you had left me in peace, but here you are again.

What is it, the children want to know. What is wrong with Auntie? I don't know, I say. I tell them we must not upset her. Be quiet, I say. Be quiet, everyone.

◆

I never bring it up again, though I keep track of the old women, their coverage all over the news, traveling to and from Japan, standing at the courts and proclaiming every sordid detail of their capture, their imprisonment, the ravaging of their bodies.

At night, I dream it too. But in the dreams, I am setting the story free. I am releasing the images into the sky and I am offering them up to God and He takes them. The more I dream, the harder I sleep and the lighter I feel.

But Flora sits at the kitchen table each day, motionless. The cock comes into the kitchen and circles her, and she doesn't even flinch. Day and night, she holds a space in the corner of my hot kitchen. We talk to her but she doesn't answer. We feed her bowls of lugaw, but she barely tastes them.

◉

Today, I am standing at the stove, putting toyo and paminta into my sinigang when my son, the mechanic, slams the door and for the first time in a long time, Flora responds. She falls under the table. I think she may have slipped, but no, she is hiding. "Shh!" she says. "Shh! They will find us!"

I cannot talk her out from under the table. When I pull up the tablecloth, I see her crouched, her skinny arms wrapped tightly around her knees. Her eyes are shut tight and it looks as if she is holding her breath. She is willing herself invisible. I let her stay huddled under that table until late at night when everyone has gone to sleep. I reach my hand out to her. I wave. "It's okay, Flor," I say to her. "Umalis na sila. Wala na sila."

"No," she tells me. "Hide with me."

"No, Flor," I say again. "They are gone. The Americans have come, and they are gone."

And then she cocks her head. She listens. "Oo nga," she says. "Tahimik na."

Yes, the house is quiet. Everyone is gone. We are safe. I tug on her. I beg her to come out.

Flora reaches for my hand, and crawling out from under the table she embraces me and together, for the first time since the war, we cry.

When the Hibiscus Falls

I.

Maria Fe Punzalan Castro. It's about time, anak. Halika. You've lost weight. Take my hand. Bless, bless.

You smell like sun. Like wind has blown sand into your hair and dusted you with sky. A dirty child who needs a good wash. And ano ba ito? Those heavy bags under your eyes. Aren't you sleeping?

Call your sister. Don't be so stubborn. My cousin Mayari was like a sister. And I almost lost her. Paano?

That was the year all the gumamela fell. The gumamela. Goo-Mah-Mel-Ah. Sa English, hibiscus.

Yes. Hibiscus, full and beautiful in the morning, fallen by dusk.

That year, they fell so fast, hundreds, anak. All at once. Every morning we woke to a sea of red petals swirling at the edges of Mommy's garden, falling from blustery skies like snow.

Your great-auntie, Mayari, was twenty-two that year. That was the year she went lunatic. Crazy.

I followed her to Miami, tracked her down. I risked my life. Why?

II.

Child, that was the year of the Corona, when the cities fell silent and people holed up in their homes, slipping out to walk along the river, or sit on rocks near falling waters. The year we covered our faces from one another, hiding like bandits behind cloth masks, bandanas, and face shields. That was the year cars disappeared from U.S. freeways and the air was fresh once more. The year families turned inward, baked bibingka, flan, and Sans Rival butter cakes, when we ordered bamboo and red tissue paper and went back to using day-old rice for glue, making Christmas lanterns to hang in windows. Like my daddy used to make. It was that year. The year more than 350,267 souls rose like smoke into the night.

One night, Mayari took off. Left West Covina and hopped cheap flights from one coast to the other, meeting new people, having so-called adventures.

We got a call that she was in Miami. An uncle of a cousin who married into the family through a friend, a nurse at Jackson Memorial, said she was seen on television, dancing on tables, spewing toasts.

Nakú! It was a big deal. It was. No, she's nothing like me or you. She was no party girl! She was the eldest of my cousins. So well-behaved. A bookworm. No kidding. I was the one she used to scold, who got a little thrill from pocketing trinkets from the mall.

In fact, Mayari had been in PhD school, cataloging Philippine demigods—mga ahas, duwende, aswang, and multo—when the pandemic broke, when her college shut down and ordered everyone to go home. She was obsessed with the babaylan, upon writing her dissertation. You've heard of them, right? Spirit healers. Wise women and men. High priestesses. Blasphemous.

So anyway, we had all been trying to find her. Calling, texting, calling. We messaged her on Facebook—what? It was a social media platform. But nothing. No answer.

Once or twice, I heard she called our grandfather, Lolo Lalo. She never told him where she was. And he never asked. She liked talking to him, teasing him, checking up on him.

So, when I got this message that she was dancing-dancing on the beaches of Miami, that's where I went.

You should have seen me on the plane. I looked like a burglar. Black jeans, black shirt, and I wore a zipped sweatshirt with the hoodie up like this. Tapos, I put on goggles, and the mask and one of those shields the welders wear—you know the kind, that flip down on the face—but plastic. I didn't eat for almost twenty-four hours. Hindi rin ako umihi. Using public bathrooms in that time was so dangerous. I just held it.

This was before the sea rose up and swallowed the city. This was when the streets were lined in lighted palm trees and open-air cafés that smelled of fried garlic and Cuban coffee and salt from the ocean. If only you could have seen it.

III.

When I got to Miami, I went to South Beach and took my boots off, peeled my mask away. Inhaled the sea. Stood by myself, just watching the fall and rise of the waves. The sky was painted like one of Lolo Lalo's red-orange oils, smeared with streaks of yellow and little clumps of stained white clouds. The waters curled up to the shore in white foam. I was thinking how the ocean is so different here. How warm it was. Not like on the West Coast. Not like in the Philippines either. (Not that I would know, anak, because I have never been there.)

Anyway, I was walking when I heard a voice cutting across the tide, between the beating of waves.

In the beginning there was only sea and sky. No land. No mountain. No island.

There was a bird who needed rest. But there was nowhere to go. So that bird mocked the sea and sky and lit the two to war. Sky shot lightning down. Broke sea open, flung boulder. The fallen rocks piled back into the seas as mountains.

The bird found refuge on the newly formed islands.

Okay, okay, okay na. Maybe I couldn't hear what she was actually saying. But I could tell from the lilt in her voice. People had gathered around Mayari, listening. She whispered and drew them closer. Her words floated just above the waves.

The bodies held on to one another as she talked, hung their heads. Why, you ask?

Well, didn't I say that was the year the blossoms fell? So much pain that year. So many souls leaving their bodies without notice. Nobody wanted to think, not really. Nobody wanted to feel. Do you know what I mean?

I sauntered over to the group, masked so only my eyes were visible. I sat down behind a couple of kids.

Mayari's eyes were closed. Her hands folded between her knees. She spoke in sotto voce. Moonlight reflected off the sea.

After the islands formed, vegetation sprouted from the rocks. One day, still pissed off at the sea, the sky swirled like a typhoon across the islands and pulled at all the palms, the mango trees, broke the strong bamboo into pieces. In one of those shattered rods were the seeds of man and woman. And as time passed, that reed floated on the seven seas, the seeds blossomed, too big for that narrow reed.

Out of nowhere that trouble-making bird swept down upon the bamboo reed.

Peck! Peck! Peck! It attacked that stick. Peck! Peck! Peck!

She craned her neck left and right, her fingers clicking, her dimples creasing deeper into a wide smile.

And before you knew it, that damn bird cracked the bamboo wide open and boom! Man and Woman. Malakas and Maganda.

Strength. Beauty.

Humanity born.

Mayari opened her eyes and looked right at me. Her face went blank. Her hands fell to the sides of her body. She blinked. Then, taking a breath she regained her composure, and clapping, she jumped up. "Enough! Let's dance, people! Off your butts! Let's dance."

The moon shifted behind a river of clouds. I think it was a full moon. Maybe a harvest moon. The moon with the face of its goddess child. Mayari.

Well, no. I don't remember exactly, but it is true that Mayari was named after the Philippine moon goddess. Blasphemy. Right?

While the others danced to drums, she pranced over to me and hissed, "Do not kill my buzz, cuz."

"Come home," I answered.

"Leave me, Sol," she said as she swirled away in circles.

I followed her like a shadow. Me, calling to her, worrying about her unmasked face. Her friends, all stragglers on the beach, twenty-somethings living in a nearby youth hostel, paid no mind. I was just another one following Mayari.

"Your father has died," I called out, "Your mother is falling apart. Your brothers are stuck on their couches in front of a flat-screen TV. They need you."

The stars surrounded her like a halo. She reeled back and said, "Tell me something I don't know, Sol. You, go home!"

And then she ran down the shore of the Atlantic and the whole crowd followed her, a parade of indignant runaways, hands waving to the sky, heads bobbing to those goddamn drums.

IV.

Mayari may have been the eldest cousin. But I too was the eldest. I was the oldest child of Tito Primo and Tita Pita. My father was the senior uncle. I had a name too. Soledad Maria Punzalan. That gave me a little standing. I was the artist. The one who captured light. She, the quiet one. Cerebral. Rule follower.

Until now.

But you know, anak, no matter how difficult family is, family is. So, even as the hibiscus fell, and my lolo's and auntie's hearts were breaking, I fought for her.

I followed her and her band of friends home. I crossed myself and I prayed to Mama Mary, "Come with me."

Before entering, I donned my pandemic shield, gloves, and goggles. I stepped into the narrow hallways, tiptoeing around dusty corners. Heard them whispering. They who wore torn jeans, midriffs, and sundresses. They who slept on top of one another. Even though the unbathed watched me, I continued.

I found her sitting near a window, blowing smoke to the sky.

"Ate," I said, my voice cracking.

She took a drag from her cigarette, tilted her head and blew.

"What happened," I said. "This is not you."

She turned to me, stared me down. Exhaled that secondhand smoke and washed it all over me. "You look like an alien, cuz. What the fuck."

"Your mom is grieving, you know."

"My mom deserves it."

"Your mom—"

"Threw my dad out."

Why she twisted that story around, I don't know. Because the story goes, Uncle Pete was one of those essential workers, serving three-day shifts. He tended to the dying, washed their bodies, monitored their decline. He was the one who called after their loved ones were, you know, patay na. There was a lockdown and only guys like Uncle Pete were leaving the house.

Anyway, Tita Beng had a temper. Nothing was ever right. She didn't like him putting himself in so much danger. Coming home and sleeping in the attic for months. She didn't like not seeing her husband.

Auntie Beng hated that Mayari was getting her degree in ano— Philippine folklore and its effects on Fil Am culture. Ano ba yan, she used to ask. And why don't you study something practical and be a doctor, she'd say to Mayari. And Mayari would just smile and say, "I am going to be a doctor, Ma. Calm down."

One night, Uncle Pete came home so tired. He kicked off his thick tennis shoes and let them trail across the foyer, he left his jacket on a chair. His hat fell from his hands and landed on the bathroom floor. And Tita Beng took one look and lost it. She. Lost. It.

The fight was so loud their voices vibrated right out that house and into the neighborhood. She picked up his things and tossed them at him, hitting lamps as she went, knocking over wooden chairs, tripping over books. The boys jumped off that couch and ran up the stairs. No, not to protect their mother, no. Their father!

Uncle Pete hurled words at her while she threw down glass vases and plates that had been left out on the counter. "Why am I the only one cleaning around here?" she yelled.

He got so mad, he left and forgot to take his mask. His hand sanitizer was in his work jacket. The gloves had been scattered and lost in the fight. There he was out in the world, nothing to keep the germs from attacking him, walking off his anger. So mad.

He was gazing at the rising moon, the way light broke the darkness, when a beam of light swept around the corner, its horn sounding like a dying animal.

Yes, it hit him. A delivery truck. No, that didn't kill him. He was taken to the hospital, and that night the family began a text thread and we kept vigil over him, praying and sending blessings sa cell phone. Nobody could go to the hospital. Nobody could stop Corona either and when he lay there, all open wounded and vulnerable, that son of a bitch snuck into his room. Infected him. There he was, taking care of the infirmed, sanitizing every inch of himself before coming home and he gets hit by that truck and boom. Infected. Nakú!

Mayari didn't even stay for his online funeral. She split. She had had it with her mommy.

Now, at the youth hostel Mayari walked right past me, crushing her cigarette with the toe of her boot, a cloud of smoke wrapped around her, the nest of unbathed friends rolling about in a fog

V.

I went back to where I was staying—a condo up in North Miami, your great-great Tita Baby's winter getaway. Mayari could have gone there, but no, she chose that hostel. She'd rather be around strangers than her family. I had to figure out my strategy, how to get her to quiet down, look at me, listen.

The condo was on the 38th floor, and through thick hurricane-glass windows, I watched a sea of lights, wavering in the dark. The beaches were closed. The pools had been shut down. I couldn't breathe. I couldn't sit in that condo and do nothing. So, I walked the beaches, my rosary in hand, beseeching Mama Mary to come to our rescue. And you know what I heard? Nothing, anak. Just the waves hitting the shore. Just the errant horn blasting from the overpass, miles from the sea. I asked Mama Mary to visit Mayari, sit with her, knock some sense into her. I put my toes into the ocean and watched the tide wash over me. Nothing.

You know, once when we were younger, I threatened to run away. Eh—kasi I wanted to be an artist and they wanted me to join the family business, be a nurse. Or a doctor's wife. That was also one of the choices. Or I don't know what, but I wanted another life.

Look, I had said to Mayari over a triple chocolate caramel shake, I will die before I give my life away like that. Don't be so dramatic, she said. Get it together, she yelled at me. She thought I should just go to school and pretend to be a nurse. Take classes in figure drawing and painting and all of that instead. They won't know what you're doing and once they figure it out, too late, she said.

That cousin was gone. I didn't recognize this cousin.

I must have sat on that beach all night, just waiting for an answer, digging my heels into the wet sands, watching the moonlight roaming the seas.

VI.

Meanwhile, Mayari continued to party. Each night, she and her gang of dirty despots scattered all over the city, playing music in the parks, colliding with one another on stretches of white sand, running through empty alleys of Ocean Drive.

When one of the boys tested positive, they all stood in line at a clinic, waiting their turn. By then, she had lost her appetite and five pounds. She let the nurse stick that swab right up her nose.

"Okay," she yelled, throwing her arms up and walking out of the clinic. "I'm out."

To her adoring ring of fly-by-nights, she was invincible. But the truth was, she was feverish. Her voice cut in and out. She coughed into her sleeve every half hour or so. And she wanted her mommy. But it was too late. She had made her choice. She ignored the symptoms. She decided she was hungover and that was all.

Maybe it was the fatigue, but Mayari dreamed of Lolo Lalo. She saw him in glass panes and night skies. A wrinkled face, brown-skinned and framed in a halo of white hair, dodging in and out of her periphery. Finally, one night, Mayari broke down and called him.

"How are you, Lolo?" she asked. "You doing okay?"

The minute Mayari heard the old man's voice, her hands began to quiver. She nearly dropped the phone.

"Have you seen your cousin, Sol?" Lolo Lalo asked. "Are you two taking care of each other?"

"Sol's in town?" she said. "Where's she staying?"

Lolo knew she was lying, but he played along. Then he asked, "What's wrong, iha?"

"Nothing," she whispered.

But the truth was she had been having visions of her grandfather weeping. Surrounded by angels.

"You sure you're okay, Lolo?"

"Your mommy tends to me. I am fine," he said. "She misses you, anak."

"Whoops," Mayari said suddenly, "you're breaking up, Lolo. I gotta go."

VII.

That night, before the results came in, the stinky boys and girls went dancing. Mayari spun. She lifted her arms above her head and rotated her hips. She placed her hands on her thighs and she shook her ass.

She was spinning fast when her chest tightened, when the twinge inside turned into a sucker punch. Everything wrapped around her body—the smoke, the heat, the sound of all those voices. She gasped. Was breathless. Nakú, she collapsed, a bundle of bones, fallen under the glitter disco ball.

That nurse, the one who had initially called us, saw her come into the ER. Unconscious. High fever. Delirious. Calling out to her dead father.

"No," the nurse said, "don't come. They won't let you in. Basta, call and I will keep you abreast of her condition."

I drove back to the youth hostel, asked the wild-eyed friends, what happened?

"She just drank too much."

"She was hungry."

"Caught a cold," someone said.

"Hungover."

But the truth is, she had gone lunatic.

"A toast!" yelled the girl from Brazil.

"A toast!" called the boy from Minnesota.

And all the beautiful brown-skinned, long haired, just-turned-legal twenty-somethings raised their bottles. "To Mayari!"

VIII.

The nurse said she was in a coma. They put a tube in her. They isolated her and suddenly, her friends were all gone and the only ones circling about her were nurses and doctors suited up as if they were on the moon itself.

◦

During her coma, Mayari had visions. She went places. She saw her dead father.

Nothing like you'd expect. Not see-through. No wings. No shine. Just her dad. Uncle Pete, taking her by the hand, and walking her along death's corridor.

"Anak," he said, "it's not your time."

"It wasn't yours either," she mouthed off. "Why are you dead?"

And then she heard the angels, a choir of them hiss, "Susmariosep!" She looked up, but there was nothing but blue sky. She looked down and saw the soil beneath her bare feet. She listened to the rush of water.

Uncle Pete gestured with his head, come. He guided her to the mouth of a river that was wide and brown and quiet. There were barges made of thick bamboo roped together. On the barges were bins of rice. Statues of saints. Baskets woven of brightly stained hemp leaves. Each barge had one person standing at a corner, holding onto bamboo, guiding it down the river. They waved to them, called them each by name.

"Mayari! Mayari! Pete!"

"Pssst!"

"Mayari! Mayari! Pete!"

"Hoy!"

She ignored them. Whatever, she thought.

They stepped onto a bangka, rocking side to side as they made their way to opposite ends of the outrigger. The wings of the boat, thick bamboo poles on either side of the bangka, reached out like scaffolding.

"What the heck?" she said. "We die and we can't even get a yacht or even a speed boat?"

"You're not dead," Uncle Pete said, handing her an oar.

The two of them paddled upstream, against the flow of barges stacked with pineapples, coconuts, and a bounty of mangos.

She turned to her dad, who was whistling as he rowed with ease. An early evening moon lit his face. "Why are we going upstream?" she asked. "Clearly the party is that way!" She pointed to the barges passing them.

He hummed a ballad, one from the harana of his youth. It was mildly out of tune. Mayari held her breath. When some time had passed, she confessed, "I miss you, Dad."

"But I am always with you."

She made a face.

When he said, "How are your studies going?" What she heard was, "You still wasting your time?"

She wanted to tell him that now, especially now, you'd think he would get it. That documenting the lore from the Philippines was probably the only way Filipinos raised in the U.S. would ever know their culture, their stories, their histories. But when she looked at his face, so calm and unfettered, she said nothing. Instead, she let the fires lick her inside. Scrunched up her face into the ugliest of scowls. Where the fuck were they going?

Mayari paid no attention to the lush jungles on either side of the riverbanks. Scoffed at the small gathering of folk lining the waters and waving at them, calling out in Tagalog so deep she thought they were speaking gibberish.

"How rude," she told her father. "Why are they doing that?"

"Anak, they're greeting you."

She didn't recognize a single one of them. Not by the square shape of their bodies, nor the full cheeks on their faces. Not by the deep dimples that creased their countenances. Not by their coarse black hair with reddish streaks of brown. She could not see herself among them.

When Uncle Pete asked her how her mother was, Mayari heard, "Why do you break your mother's heart?"

"Why should you care?" was her answer. "She kicked you out and threw you right in front of a moving truck. She should rot."

Uncle Pete only clucked his tongue.

When he said, "What's wrong, iha?" she heard him saying, "What's wrong with you, girl? Wala kang galang. Nakakahiya."

"Who cares," she shouted at the sky. "Aren't you mad at Mom?" she asked. "She killed you."

"Your mom didn't kill me."

He did his best to explain how marriage worked, how they learned to deal with one another's ill temper. How you do not stop loving a person for making you mad. Sometimes you take a walk, calm yourself down, and then return. Except this time, the accident. "You must have patience. You must forgive."

Platitudes, she thought. Marriage is for suckers. Family is a construct.

He might have said, "And who do you think make up the Tagalog people? Your family, anak. The Punzalans." But he kept that to himself too.

The sky remained golden and the source of the light came from the mountaintop. Night was nowhere. The father and daughter pressed onward, and Mayari could not understand why it was so hard to paddle, why her breath was going shallow. "Where are we going?" she asked him. "Where are we?"

"Ito ang ilog natin," he said.

"What river?" she wanted to know. She didn't know we had our own river. She didn't even know our people were from the river. She looked up and down the banks, and floating there, between the bamboo barges, were red gumamela. Hundreds. No longer attached to their bushes, but free.

At the source of the river was a mountain lined in groves of coconut palms and banana plantations. Her father guided her up the slope.

"What the heck, Dad," she said. Her breathing was labored, and her legs were sore.

"Inay is waiting for you, anak," he said.

Mayari thought he meant his mother. She thought she was going to give her the old Catholic guilt. She prepared herself. Set her heart to stone. She locked her jaw. She took a breath and held it.

They arrived at nightfall, and the green jungle swayed. The leaves sang like waves in the sea. Below them was nothing but mountains. Against a night sky was a sprinkle of stars and the Moon.

Mayari gazed at the Moon's full belly.

"What are you doing here, anak?" the Moon asked.

"Good question," she answered. "What *am* I doing here?"

The Moon washed my cousin in light.

Mayari clenched her jaw. Set her anger in the curl of her fist. She resisted the Moon. And then it happened. From that ugly shell of Mayari's heart, sprouted the tiniest red bud, wound tight and hard. Yes, gumamela. The Moon sighed, and warmed Mayari. The bud blossomed. The flower filled the space of her heart, relaxed the palms of her hands.

"It is not your time. Stop this foolishness."

IX.

What? Oh hell no! She came out of that coma as difficult as ever. Cursing. First of all, she was embarrassed.

Auntie Beng and her sons had rented an RV and driven across America. Yes, may pandemic pa. But they had to get to Mayari and they couldn't fly. And they couldn't stop at hotels. And the bathrooms sa gas stations? Forget it.

That's not what embarrassed Mayari.

Auntie and the boys parked that thing not so far from the condo in North Miami. Each day, we sat in vigil, just outside the hospital, underneath the shade of several palm trees. We FaceTimed the Filipino American community of West Covina—all those beautiful loud aunties, the sullen uncles, the almost invisible teenagers—and we prayed the rosary. Out loud. Calling mysteries—Sorrowful, Joyful, Luminous, Glorious—pitiful mysteries, begging for mercy. For grace.

Pretty soon we had an audience. Health-care workers brought folding chairs and placed them ten feet away, mumbled Hail Marys and Our Fathers through surgical masks and face shields. We even had a priest on some days.

By then Mayari was awake, breathing oxygen through a mask. And every time we FaceTimed her and she saw the spectacle that was her family sitting on the hospital grounds like holy Bible thumpers, she cut out. Hung up on us, the aunties in West Covina, even her best twenty-something friends who had joined the chorus of the faithful.

The boy who tested positive, who sent them all to the clinic to be tested in the first place—that boy died—but Mayari survived. Her friends showed up each morning, in beachwear, bare-bellied, unwashed, and thoroughly devoted.

"She knows so many amazing stories about your people," they said to us.

"She's a goddess, you know," they told Auntie Beng.

Mayari's brothers stood guard around their mother.

Auntie Beng was all tears. She nodded to them in their wildly colored bandanas, yanking up on her own mask to suggest they pull theirs up a little higher. She leaned over to hug them, but her sons reached over, caught her from wrapping her arms around their filthy germ-ridden bodies.

"Let them stay," Auntie Beng said. "They love her too."

Mayari would not speak with us. "Tell them," she directed the nurse. "Tell them to go home."

I texted her. Said "Mahal kita" and "Can't wait to see you," but she never answered. I even tried reverse psychology: "Can you believe your mom?" It was too late. I waited too long. While she was in that coma, I prayed so hard, thinking maybe I should have handled it differently. Thank God she was coming out of it. Thank God she was angry enough to show us she was getting better, but I tell you, anak. My heart—ang sakit naman.

On the day the staff wheeled her out of the hospital and when she saw us tethered to golden balloons, applauding her, she rolled her eyes. Refused to get out of her chair. Crossed her arms and looked down at her chest.

Right. Most people come out of near-death experiences and they are changed. She was pissed. She was ready to start that war all over again.

But no one, not even Auntie Beng, scolded her. We rolled her out of that place, got her to the RV and the brothers lifted her— all three of them—and moved her into the back seat of that thing.

The plan was to cruise that house on wheels west, across the plains and the deserts and mountains. So red, white, and blue, no?

No. What happened was this—that was the year that the cities were set ablaze. The people, people like you and me, Black, Indigenous, people of color, people of the everyday, especially our Black brothers and sisters—and all those who really did believe what we used to call our constitutional rights—they all took to the streets. Protested cop brutality. When George Floyd was executed live for all to see, a White cop kneeling to no God, but there on top of George Floyd like that, squeezing the breath right out of him, when that happened, on camera—let me say—when that happened, the cities lit up. You couldn't make it through New York, or Chicago, or Boston, or Washington, D.C., without seeing smoke, without hearing voices rising into the air. The fight for justice filled the skies. It was that year. It was that moment. And when the Punzalans set the RV rolling up the highway ramp, we got stopped.

The highway in Miami shut down. The fire spread from city to city. Curfew set upon us as the sun went dark. There was danger first in that contagion Corona, and then in the way hatred and systematic killings of Black brothers and sisters set us all on fire. So, the motorhome that was as long as a city school bus pulled over to the side, waited while all the other cars scurried off the on ramp like ants on a hill.

We sat in that traffic for almost a day.

Mayari hissed and grunted. She held her face up to the window like she was traveling somewhere on her own. She didn't care that Tita Beng was wringing her hands, weeping.

"Why everyone so mad," asked one brother.

"We got all day," said another. "Black brothers dying like that is messed up."

"Yeah," said the third. "But what's that got to do with us? I wanna go home."

Mayari slowly rotated her body to face us, glancing at me first, waiting to see what I would do. She gave us all the side eye and that scared the shit out of all of us.

We got nowhere that week, nor the weeks after that. Tita Beng decided to rent a place in the suburbs of Miami, far from the ocean and deep into concrete yards where occasional palms shot out of sidewalks and clumped in crowded backyards. Not West Covina, but Westchester.

That nurse who was a friend of the family introduced me to your lolo Mati, a boy from the Caribbean. Miami became home.

Mayari stayed with her family until the congestion in her chest cleared, until she was able to stand up and walk on her own. And then she was gone. Stopped seeing any of us. She went back to school to finish that dissertation and get that degree out west. Didn't even go to her own mother's funeral years and years later. That Corona infected so many things and she let it.

X.

You'd think someone named after the moon goddess would know all about rising up among the mottled clouds. You'd think someone all about justice and decolonization would know how to hold up her people. She severed all her ties. And our hearts broke like eggs fried sunny-side up over a bed of garlic fried rice. It was awful.

High and fucking mighty, Mayari saw nothing of the beauty of our people—and by our people I don't mean just the Tagalog, I mean our family. I mean seriously, all you do is talk about where the ancestors come from and you can't see the people in your house? Can't love them with your goddamn PhD? One day we will all be the ancestors.

Mayari became a hotshot full professor. Whatever. Full of herself Professor. We used to hear about her from kids in the community who studied from her textbook, *The Filipino Inside You: Breaking from U.S. Assimilation.* Kids who said she was decolonizing their minds. Which is so good, you know? We need that. Kids need to know what it means to be Filipino American. We are Tagalog. But we are also Punzalan.

We watched from afar, even as she ran that center for Philippine folklore in the U.S. over there, sa Berkeley. We saw her posts on social media. But to us, she was always mean. Cold. Whatever blossom Moon Goddess planted in that girl died a long time ago. Shriveled up like an oak leaf in the dead of winter. She was an expert. One of those *if you can't do, teach* people.

And you know better than anyone, Maria Fe, you don't need to go to school to know where you come from. Know who you are. You don't need to be living in the Philippines to know you are Filipino. You can be American and still be Pinay.

XI.

It took a long time. Finally, when my oldest boy, your tito, died of a heart attack, she was standing at my backdoor, with tins of sweetcakes and a song in her voice. "Hey," she said, "that shit can't be easy."

Though her posture was stooped, though the frown lines were carved all along her mouth, I could see a little shine coming through. My body went weak. You know how that goes, when your heart stops for a moment, cracks in the center of your chest. I collapsed, taking her body into a long embrace, my face buried in her salt-and-pepper mane. The two of us sighed and wept. No words, anak. No words. You don't even realize how much a part of you is missing until it stands before you, holding out a tin of bibingka and puto, coconut shredded all over like that. You don't know how you were able to keep on going, to harden your heart, to dismiss the ache, until that moment when a voice, all twisted and foul with love, kisses you on the cheek and says, "I'm sorry."

Speaking of which—ano, Maria Fe? How is your mother? I hear her playing nocturnes late at night, each note sinking, dying. Minor chords like sighs. You should be patient, anak. She has lost someone too. You should listen to your mother, call your sister, be with your pamilya. It will help, anak.

How will you ever gain that weight back? How will you ever rest?

Me? Okay ako. The sun dapples the riverbanks. The breeze combs through leaves and feels like kiss, kiss. Lola sniffing skin. At night, I listen to the way the water washes stones, rushing downstream, trickling like a lullaby. I like the sound of tropical rains falling on palms, washing every sorrow away. And if I lie very still, I hear songs from neighboring villages, from distant cities. Makes me feel like dancing. Makes me hum along, little hymns to the moon, to the sun, to all the ancestors. Real nice. Some nights there is fiesta and all the family come.

I like it here. You would be pleased.

I will tell you now, so you can write it down.

XII.

I was born Soledad Maria Punzalan, American-born Pinay from West Covina, California. Raised Catholic, but a practicing ecumenical who also dabbled in Kashmir Shavism. I drank sodas growing up, ate pizza and snuck wine coolers out of the fridge when no one was looking. That was in high school. I loved driving. Kissing boys was one of my favorite pastimes.

In my twenties, our family resettled in Miami years before the sea swallowed her up. That was where my life as a painter came alive amid the music of my Cuban cousins, and the Brazilian lovers and the good Spanish of my Colombian friends. For me, this was really what it meant to be American. To be among these many cultures, iha. I met my love, my husband, my Mathias Manuel Castro, and fed my three children on mangos and bananas from our backyard. When the beaches fell into the open mouth of the sea, we had to relocate again, this time to a small plot of land in the mountains of Georgia. Still river people, we settled on the Toccoa River.

Mayari followed us to that mountain after my son, Mathias Junior, died. I was a widow by then. So my sister-cousin and I lived together in that cottage. She roamed the pages of her books, piled and set like mountains trailing across hardwood floors. I continued dreaming in colors, lost on the page in a much different way. Watercolors. Pastels. Pencils. Oils. Impressions, not realistic drawings. It was my go-to, especially when the pain was too much to bear. That is where I planted red hibiscus that mirrored my mother's garden in West Covina. And this is where I died, in that family cottage by the river, a three-bedroom cabin where you are now.

And even though Pilipinas was only a dream, my parents schooled me so I would never be too American. So I would remember who I am. And I taught my children, who have taught their children. Who have taught you.

I speak Tagalog because our ancestors were from the river, anak. I speak though I have never been, because we are Tagalog. All around you red blossoms have fallen along the banks and are swimming to the sea. Every night the moon graces the sky, and the sun warms us. Every day you rise, I am with you because family is family. Anak, I thought you'd know by now.

II

Foodie in the Philippines

Every time Clarissa closed her eyes, faces loomed in the dark, blooming and morphing. She didn't recognize them. Not the old men in turbans with their crooked noses. Not the old lady with a fat cigar in her mouth. The baby was not her toddler, Blake, but some infant bedecked in jewels. The man and woman in a suit and beaded dress, with blue skin and smiles wide as the sea, were strangers.

"What the hell!" she said, sitting up and throwing off the covers.

"Again?" Henry said. He rolled away from her and nestled his body deeper into the white linen sheets. "You're just anxious."

◆

Last night, a guide took them to some of Makati's five-star restaurants.

"We want to taste authentic Filipino," Clarissa told him. "We're doing research."

The man, slight and kind, with a perpetual pleasant look about him, drove them three hours from Ortigas to Makati. The passenger van crawled among a sea of red taillights dotting the wide roadways in a chaos of traffic. Some neighborhoods, with their high walls and elegantly painted gates, seemed okay to her. But then there were streets where shanties of corrugated roofs and cardboard walls crept along the edges of the road, a sharp contrast to the miles of mega malls lined along the superhighway, their buildings crowned with Godzillla-size billboard screens, lit bigger and gaudier than Times Square.

"Latin meals with an Asian twist," she had told Henry when she pitched the idea to him. "You'd be the chef and I'd run the business." Filipino cuisine had become a thing on the East and West coasts, but there was nothing in Miami. Clarissa had her eye on a spot on Brickell Avenue.

"And what about our food tours?" They had a business guiding tourists through Little Havana, South Beach, and the design district. Caminamos employed a dozen guides, in white tennis shoes and matching T-shirts, hiking through neighborhoods, speaking into headsets while carting portable speakers.

"That's our backup," she had said. "Come on, don't you want to try something new? Explore my ancestral kitchen?"

"Your ancestral kitchen?" Henry had slapped her bottom as she walked away. "You don't even know who's in your ancestral kitchen."

◆

Clarissa got up to check on Blake, sound asleep in his Pack 'N Play.

"You don't think firing the guide was over the top?" Henry asked.

"I told him we were doing research on Philippine cuisine. And where did he set us up?" She leaned over to sniff the boy's face, kiss his forehead.

"But it was good Italian, you gotta admit."

"And then the Thai restaurant? And then Indian after that?"

"You said Asian twist."

She threw a stuffed animal at him.

"It's our first night, relax!" He laughed. "There will be other nights."

"We don't need him. My cousin Perla and her husband said they'd show us around."

"That's good," Henry said. "You know them from before?"

She shook her head, leaned into their baby's crib. "Oh my God, Henry," she said, lifting a sippy cup from the child's bed.

"When is that? Tomorrow night?"

"Did you give him this?" She tossed the empty cup at him and he caught it with one hand.

"He was thirsty. Plus, he couldn't sleep, either."

"But we agreed. No sippy cups at bedtime. You're supposed to follow the rules."

Henry laughed then. "Rules?"

"You know what I mean."

❂

Her cousin Perla arrived at the Shangri-la Hotel in a black SUV. A driver stepped out and opened the door. Two little boys sat in the back seat.

"You can just put him there," Perla said. "Next to his pinsan. Boys, you kiss your cousin Blake."

"There's no car seat," Clarissa said.

"Just belt him in," Perla said. "He'll be fine."

Rudy, Perla's husband, sat next to the driver. He waved and said, "Don't worry, Junior is a good driver."

"He'll be okay," Henry said, guiding them into the car.

"But, honey," Clarissa said.

"You know he'll be fine," he whispered.

Blake smiled and reached for his cousins. Before she could say anything, the child squirmed out of her arms and into the seat between the boys. The cousins buckled him up. She relented.

The car smelled of leather and air freshener. The windows were tinted so that even though the sun lit everything outside and the traffic was crawling and loud, inside the SUV, it was dim and quiet.

She turned around to look at the row of little boys, her Blake light as whole milk, and happy. She watched him sitting next to his cousins. They were already high-fiving each other.

"He'll be okay," Henry whispered, tugging at her sleeve.

She nodded, looked out into the traffic, and saw the cars darting like cockroaches. When the SUV turned down an alley, a group of street kids in flip-flops and dirty T-shirts dashed to the vehicle. As they rolled by, the children made sad eyes. Held their paper cups to the window. And when they did not respond, tapped aggressively. Clarissa jumped. Checked the lock on the doors.

"No worry," Perla said. "Just kids."

Clarissa unbuckled her seat belt. "I'm sorry," she said. "Can't do it. Blake, buddy, come to Mama!" She pulled the boy free and sat him on her lap. He screamed and twisted in her arms.

"I'm sorry, buddy, but Mama wants you safe."

"You know that's less safe," Henry said.

She held Blake tighter, kissed him on the temple.

"So, you want to try some native food?" Perla asked her, over the crying toddler.

"That sounds good," Henry said. "You two are first cousins?"

"On Clarissa's mother's side," Perla said.

"Di ba," Rudy asked, "parang magkapatid sila? They have the same shape sa face."

"Rudy, ikaw naman. They don't speak Tagalog. I—English mo na." Perla turned to smile at them, her hair swinging as she moved, her face powdered and perfect. "Native food it is." Perla turned back to her husband and told him, "They want to open a Filipino restaurant in the States."

"You'll cook?" Rudy asked Clarissa.

"Not me," she answered. "Henry's the chef, I'm just the—"

"The boss," Henry said. "She's the boss."

"Sige," Perla said, "let's take them to Glorietta." She was talking to the driver. "Maybe we can catch the mass in the mall before we eat?"

"In the mall?" Henry asked.

Clarissa took a breath to speak, but Henry nudged.

"That would be awesome," Henry said. "We've never been to a mass in a mall. Have we, honey?"

And just like that, Clarissa found herself sitting on folding chairs in a concourse, flanked by high-end stores and designer boutiques.

The priest stood on a stage in the round, surrounded by Catholics. His words blasted throughout the shopping center, like a Kmart blue-light special.

The priest's voice reminded her of childhood afternoons—the fall and rise of his words. Clarissa and her siblings had lost their mother to breast cancer. It was her nanny who made them meals and got them to and from school while her dad worked long hours. The only time she saw her father was on Sundays, and those days were spent mostly being told to stop fighting, settle down, and pray.

Blake and the boys slipped off their folding chairs and crawled back and forth between the parents. Clarissa pulled on her boy's collar, hissing, "Blake, buddy, it's dirty down there!" Henry grabbed him up and walked him toward a toy store.

Clarissa closed her eyes, pretending to pray. And there they were again, the faces. The high cheekbones, the crow's feet around the eyes, the dimples on the old faces, hurling themselves at her from some unknown place. "Goddamn it," she whispered.

She opened her eyes then, focused on the priest's green robes, the broad strips of gold fabric running down the center of them. She couldn't understand his Tagalog, but she recognized the tone of his voice.

◆

Afterward, they dined at the five-star café on the second level. Her cousins ordered sticky rice cakes with fresh mango, fried fish, and bowls of stews soaked in coconut and soy sauce.

"You know," Perla told them, looking below where the next set of churchgoers gathered, "if you really want to eat authentic native, you should go to our lola and lolo's house."

"I didn't know your grandparents were still alive," Henry said to Clarissa.

"Oh, they're not!" Perla said. "Rudy, hand the rice to Clarissa."

"The servants are there," Rudy said. "Everyone else is here in the city." He was the kind of man who spoke with his mouth full and Clarissa could see everything. He held the dish up to her.

Clarissa put her hand up.

"You don't want rice?" Rudy made a face.

"I'm good, thanks."

Henry ate the pig's cheeks, the vegetables in shrimp paste, the pig intestines swimming in blood stew. She watched him open his mouth and taste. She knew by the way he tilted his head if the dish was a hit or not. She could stomach little of it. She had the chicken adobo. She had the wilted greens Perla called laing—smothered in coconut milk.

She fed Blake a spoonful of rice and chicken. His legs kicked as he bounced up and down. "You like that, buddy?"

"Aling Dora is the family cook," Perla said. "She can teach you everything!"

Clarissa winked at her husband. Family recipes. That could be a thing. He smiled.

"You're hardly eating," Perla said.

"It's jetlag. Not much appetite."

"She's having nightmares," Henry offered.

"What kind of nightmares?" Perla asked.

Clarissa shot him a look.

"You see faces, right?" Henry offered. "Old-time Filipinos and–"

"He exaggerates," Clarissa said.

"Wow," Perla said. "Do they talk to you?"

"No."

"Have you seen them before?"

"No."

Perla smiled. It was irritating. "Welcome home, cuz."

This was not home, Clarissa thought. How presumptuous. Home was Miami. Home was upstate New York. This was the opposite of home.

Henry reached for the dinuguan and spooned the last of it on his plate. "Man, this stuff is good. Blood stew, you said?"

"For an American, you're so game na game," Rudy said, patting Henry on the back.

Henry placed his hands on his belly and smiled wide. "I call it research."

●

They took a walking tour just for fun through the walled city of Intramuros, stepping along stone pathways, slipping into large Spanish-style cathedrals. They stood in front of the jail where the country's hero had been kept until he was led before a firing squad. Then they dined in bistros with white linen and fine lace, tasted meats sautéed in tomatoes, soy sauce, and garlic. Ate freshly baked bread puddings with coconut and sweet milk.

The tour guide was an actor, a magician with an arsenal of hats he donned and doffed as they moved through history and time. He gestured to either side of the street, walking backward, calling out great historical events. "This street," he said, "would have been packed with merchants, fruit stands, fish stands, even ladies washing rich families' garments."

Clarissa noticed women squatting before large rattan baskets, scrubbing laundry with their hands, their suds spilling onto the streets. They balanced on flat bare feet, knees bent, bottoms low to the ground, hems of their skirts drenched and filthy.

"They ironed cotton sheets and beautiful tablecloths by balancing on these old-time bongo boards for hours." The tour guide gestured to a flat board on top of a cylinder. "The contraptions were called prinsa de paa because the women used their feet to press fine linen."

At the corner, a woman in a full-length skirt, a cotton blouse with sleeves as wide as elephant's ears, balanced barefoot on a wooden board. Sandwiched between the wooden planks was a rolled-up piece of bedding. What struck Clarissa was the way the woman's daughters—maybe six and ten—also stood on the board, clinging to their mother's waist, balancing on the prinsa de paa too.

The woman was serious, her hair pulled off her forehead with a kerchief, her hands wrapped around a thick bamboo. Her face burnt from the sun. The children, solemn too, nestled their faces between the folds of her kamiseta. And even as Clarissa studied them, she felt as though she knew them.

Out on the cobblestone streets, they walked past so many people and it was the elders that caught her attention, Filipinos in old-world garments straight out of the Ilustrados of Spain, of nuns and priests in long dark robes, of vendors and their carts silently passing her, nodding to her.

Clarissa and Henry held onto Blake and the three of them were strolling down the street when the tour took a turn without them. Soon the family found themselves on a street with hardly a tourist in sight. A trio of stray dogs ran past them, and Blake broke free from his parents to chase them. The boy ran with his arms stretched before him, giggling. The dogs were mangy and odd-shaped mutts the color of sand.

"No, Blake!" Clarissa yelled. "Dirty!"

The dogs circled the boy, taunting him to catch their tails, to feed them scraps, to pet them. Blake jumped up and down, thrilled to make friends.

"No, Blake!"

"What's wrong now?" Henry asked.

"What if the dogs are rabid?"

"What dogs?" Henry walked away, stepping up to a cart and engaging the merchant there.

"Perla warned us about the street food," Clarissa called out as she hoisted Blake to her hip.

Henry ignored her. He paid the street vendor for a cup of sweet bean curd.

"What do you think?" Henry offered her a spoonful swimming in syrup. "That's tofu, right?"

Clarissa refused him. "If you get sick, that's your problem."

They walked through the market, past souvenir shops with trinkets made of coconut husks and shells, with fans that opened up and revealed the word "Intramuros" painted in black ink. Henry bought Blake a frog carving that croaked when you ran a piece of wood across its rugged back.

"All these people in costume, wandering like extras on a movie set. It must get so hot in that wardrobe."

"Where?"

She pointed at a group of girls sauntering by, their arms linked to one another like paper dolls. Their hair fell all the way down their backs. Their dusty skirts dragged behind them. Their blouses with lily-shaped sleeves hung loose on them, underneath stiff white shawls. Their feet were bare.

He glanced in their direction and shrugged. "What am I looking at?"

Clarissa turned him to her then. "All you see is food." She studied his face, his hazel eyes so round and beautiful. His face smooth from the morning's shave. She ran her palm along his jawline and kissed him. "You should pay more attention."

❀

Henry threatened to quit the project if she did not taste the food. She took a spoonful of every dish. Some foods she swallowed, but often she spat the food out into a napkin. She had cultivated a gluten-free American palate, munching carrots and celery sticks, drinking smoothies made of kale and green apples. The lack of fresh vegetables at the table left her hungry and constipated.

"Look, if you eat, you'll get regular again and if you're regular," Henry said, changing Blake's diaper, "you'll sleep."

"I can't sleep," she said. Her body was lost between time zones. She found herself groggy when the rest of the world was up, and wide awake when her family slept.

She paced the parquet floors of their hotel room, tugging at the curtains and looking out to the cityscape, as if she were waiting for something to happen. But she saw nothing, just a river of lights winding between buildings and the occasional rattle of a truck and its lights in the alleyway. Nothing felt right to her. She scratched at imaginary itches on her skin, at the bugs she was sure were crawling in their linen.

Sometimes the air was thick and humid as Miami, the nightlife in Makati brightly lit as South Beach, and this comforted her. The traffic was heavier and more chaotic, but not so different. And she was used to the change of temperature from the heat outside to the air-conditioned buildings.

But the dreaming? The other night, the faces rushing at her, came with a new thing. A soundtrack. The sound of primordial gongs echoing in minor notes against the syncopated heartbeat of tribal drums. No actual melodies but the rhythm of the drums stayed with her, those ethereal chimes dancing around them haunting her. The more taste-testing she did, the more vivid the faces. The louder the music. The more fatigued she felt.

Earlier that night, they sat in the lounge of the Shangri-La Hotel, drinking red wine and making chika-chika. Perla insisted their ancestors were coming to Clarissa in dreams, welcoming her home.

"Not possible. When you're dead, you're dead. Nowhere to go. Just dead."

"Oh cousin," Perla laughed, pouring them another glass of wine. "When we say 'Father, Son, and Holy Ghost,' we mean *ghost.*"

Perla took a drag from her cigarette and blew its smoke around them.

"Your mother never visited you from the other side?"

"No, has yours?"

"Always. You know our lola was a hilot."

She told Clarissa about their grandmother, who was a midwife and a healer known all over their province of Pampanga for her mystical powers. Lola Atanacia was the second daughter in a family of twelve. She was the beautiful one, according to Perla, and she was not supposed to inherit her father's gifts. It was supposed to be the other one, the elder, Lola Maria Elena, who was homelier, but kind and wise. She wanted to be a healer. Lola Atanacia was a flirt.

"So, they thought," Perla said, lighting another slim cigarette.

"Those things will kill you," Clarissa told her, waving the smoke away with her hand.

Perla tilted her lips and blew toward the table light. "Do you want to hear this or not?"

On the day their father died, the whole countryside went into mourning, and Maria Elena had not yet received a single lesson on how to be a healer. Could not intuit how to get home in the dark. Atanacia, on the other hand, was walking with a boy when three of her father's dogs came running down the dirt road, circling her, barking. When she ignored them, they jumped the boy, pulling him to the ground, ripping at his clothes, and gnawing at his legs. They say Atanacia bent down to help the boy and when she did, she moved the leg around and held her palms over the wound. She closed her eyes, and she could see her father, whispering to her. When she opened her eyes, the boy's leg was whole. There was no blood, though his pants were torn.

"So, you're saying her father transferred his powers to her?" Clarissa said.

Perla nodded.

"And that the dogs were in on it?"

"Yes."

Clarissa laughed. "Okay, cousin. If you say so."

The women ordered another bottle of red wine, toasted to their family.

"What's it like to be back home, cuz?" Perla asked.

"Home," Clarissa said. "I can't even get over this damn jetlag."

"You're one of us. A Lingat." Perla handed over keys. "Go to the country. Pay respects to the elders. You'll see."

Clarissa held the brass keys in the palm of her hand. They were worn and scratched. "I bet Aling Dora can teach Henry some family recipes, right?"

"And don't forget to make paalam when you go."

"What's that?" Clarissa asked.

Perla shook her head and laughed, blew smoke around her face and waved it up to the ceiling. "You are so American, cousin! Too much!"

◉

The driver picked them up at 4:00 a.m. To beat the traffic, they said. Junior wove the black SUV through Manila traffic. Next to him, Henry leaned against the passenger's window, eyes closed, head lolling back and forth. Clarissa was wide awake. She rocked Blake in her arms, swept the hair off his face and kissed his nose over and over again, occasionally leaning her ear to his mouth and listening to the sound of his breathing. Outside the window, the city lights fell away, and the sky lightened gradually, until they were rolling down the superhighway, rushing past rice fields. Manila streets reeked of garbage and diesel fuel. Everything about it was dirty. Maybe the fresh air would allow her to finally relax and sleep through a full night.

"What's making paalam?" Clarissa asked the driver.

"Actually, ma'am," the driver answered. "When you enter the compound, you make paalam to the spirits—you know, the bamboo dwarf and the other duwende. Greet them, ask permission to enter."

"Really?" Henry asked, smiling. "Why would we want to do that?"

"Out of respect, sir."

"So, you're superstitious too?" Clarissa said.

She leaned back then, closed her eyes. She took a deep breath and exhaled. There were no faces coming in the dark. Good, she thought. Henry's right, it's just stress. And as she fell asleep, the dreams began, images of old-time people walking dirt roads on the way home from the palengke, with big bushels of fruit and vegetables atop their heads and a cart carrying a pig's carcass being pushed through the crowds. She was relieved to see the green kangkong leaves in baskets as well as stalks of bok choy and green beans, and long slender pieces of purple eggplant.

◉

The Lingat ancestral compound was set in the middle of several hectares of wet rice paddies. In the distance, she saw a farmer in a cone-shaped hat, holding onto a plow led by a big brown kalabaw. It was a big house, like the one in the photo, hidden behind a high white wall where sampaguita flowers hung on delicate lattices.

Clarissa recognized the house from the one sepia-toned photo of the family she had seen, standing on the front porch. Her grandfather, a young Romero Lingat, the town mayor, wore a white suit with broad shoulders, a fat tie, and a fedora tipped to the side of his handsome face. Her grandmother, Atanacia, wore her dark hair pulled away from her face in beautiful curls that fell on either side of her shoulders.

That was the only image Clarissa had ever seen of her grandparents. She could see them now, the color of dried tobacco leaves, ageless and waiting for her to arrive.

A magnolia tree shaded the front yard, green branches hanging low. Chickens pecked at the dirt just to the side of the house. The SUV jiggled her awake.

"What's it feel like?" Henry asked her.

"What?" she asked as Junior pulled up the long driveway.

"To be here," Henry said. "To be home."

"Not you too," she said. She held Blake up to the window and waved his fat hand at the chickens in the yard. "What's that, buddy? A kitty?"

"Rooster!" the boy cried.

❧

The windows were as big as sliding doors, pushed open to let the breeze run through the sala and the dining room.

"This is amazing," Henry said. "Like stepping back in time." He ran his hands along a long narra wood table lined with ornate chairs carved and stained to match one another. "And look at these portraits!" At the entrance of the house were two giant paintings of Atanacia and Romero in their thirties, dressed in traditional Filipino formal attire, he in an eggshell-colored barong with elegant embroidery and she in a high-butterfly-sleeve dress, beaded with sequins and pearls.

"Your grandmother hated those portraits," Clarissa heard. "Too maarte for her."

Clarissa turned to see a small white-haired woman in a duster. "Hello," she said, reaching her hand out to the old woman.

The old woman waved her hand away. "Please, pu," she said, looking down at her feet.

"I'm Clarissa and this is my husband, Henry, and our son, Blake."

"Hey," said Henry, waving.

"Call me Aling Dora," said the old woman. "I'll be the one to show Sir around the kitchen."

"Aling Dora," Henry said, leaning over to hug the old woman. "Call me Henry."

"Yes, sir. Ma'am, your cousin Gema will be here to show you around the town. Maybe tomorrow."

"Perla says you are an excellent chef," Clarissa said.

"I'm just a country cook, pu," Aling Dora said. "Are you hungry?"

◆

They were shown to their bedroom for a late afternoon rest. It looked onto a view of rice paddies. The windows did not have glass, but translucent capiz shells. Light filtered into all areas of the space. Henry climbed onto the brass bed. It squeaked.

"Henry, your shoes!" Clarissa said.

"What about them?"

"Take them off, that's a white cotton spread!" She ran her fingers along the fine embroidery. "You'll soil everything!"

Henry laughed. He kicked his shoes off and pulled the boy onto the bed and watched Blake crawl among the pillows. They lay under the canopy of white, a mosquito net draped like curtains around them.

She nestled into the pillows, relaxed. It was nice to be in the country. She began drifting into sleep, the beating drums calling her, the chimes like sirens ringing softly. Blake curled up next to her, and Henry too wrapped his arms around them both.

A timid knock at the door summoned them to the dining room, where several dishes were laid out on porcelain plates. The sweet aroma of fresh cooked rice, fried garlic, soy sauce, and vinegar filled the air.

"Oh my God, does that smell good!" Henry said. "Are you hungry, buddy?" he said, placing Blake on a chair between them.

For the first time since they arrived, Clarissa felt a pang of hunger. She smiled at her husband as he looked up at Aling Dora.

"What have you done, Aling?"

Plates of sautéed meats, wilted greens, and bowls of crab stew were set on a dark wood table. Steam rose from a whole fish dressed in tomatoes, green onions, and little green limes. Deep-fried frog legs filled a silver plate. In the center of the table, on a fat green banana leaf, was a plate of sticky fried rice with peas, carrots, red peppers, and diced chicken.

"This is beautiful, Aling! What are these dishes?"

The old woman smiled, covering her toothless grin with her hand.

"Sir," she said, "allow me to serve you." She picked up one of the stews and held it for him as he dished some on his plate. "We have here aligui—what is this called in English—crab fat sautéed with garlic and lemon juice. And then over here," she said, picking up another colorful plate of fried meats with red and green peppers, "it is called sisig—to get it crispy like this, I boil it, and then grill it and fry it with lots of hot peppers and calamansi."

"Delicious," Henry said. "I like the texture and layers here. What is it, exactly?"

"Pig cheeks."

"I had pig cheeks in Manila."

"And the ears and snout."

"Oh my," Henry said, rubbing his palms together fast.

Clarissa refused the sisig. Same with the frog legs. But the fish she ate, and the morcon, and the wilted kangkong leaves with fresh tomato. For dessert, they ate mangos and drank tarragon tea.

She looked around the room, at the photos on the walls and the way the light fell through the room. In one of the sideboards were family photos, set in silver and capiz frames. That would be a nice touch for the restaurant, she thought. She wandered over to them, and she picked a photo up. Her grandparents were young here, and their children surrounded them. Which one was her mother? She would have been the youngest girl. But all the girls seemed about the same age, dressed in crisp white frocks, their hair cut into perfect little bobs. Which one are you, she asked her mother. Why don't I know you?

"Well, I'll say one thing," she told Henry. "I think these dishes are prettier than the ones we saw in the city."

"Aw honey," he said. "This is it. The bomb. I'm going to follow that little old woman around until I figure it all out. The bomb."

●

She woke to the cock crowing. She woke to crickets singing. She woke to a walis sweeping rhythmically across the yard. The sun had not yet come up. The husband's breath was deep, the boy slept and heard none of these things.

Clarissa stretched. Outside the moon was up, bright as a streetlight. She pushed the capiz windows open to let the night air in. An old woman was sweeping the front porch. Her small body moved to the rhythm of the walis brushing against the tile. From up here, her white halo of hair shone. God, thought Clarissa, why so early?

Back in bed, she watched Henry sleep. He was such a good man, always ready for the next adventure. She ran her finger around the curve of his ear, whispered, "Love you." He grunted. That was enough for her. This trip was easier on him than her. His body adjusted easily to the time change, and he didn't seem to mind trying all these exotic foods—crickets and frogs and duck eggs.

The woman swept the grounds, circling the compound, moving all the dirt around. The sound was comforting and lulled Clarissa back to sleep.

She dreamed of coffee, freshly ground. Dark. Brewing. She dreamed of bread pudding baked in condensed milk and coconut.

And then, she heard the sizzle of frying. Henry was still asleep, and the sky had lightened. The boy snored.

She made her way to the kitchen, where Aling Dora's kitchen was hot with plates of cooked food.

"Are you hungry, pu?" Aling asked her. "Maranup na ka?"

"Do you have coffee?" Clarissa asked her. "I smelled coffee."

Aling Dora poured hot water into a cup and offered it. Clarissa made a face. Noted the white creamy stuff on the surface of the cup.

"You try it," Aling said. "Three-in-one."

"What's that?"

"The packet has sugar, powdered milk, and kape—instant coffee, all in one."

She made another face.

"Areglado," Aling said again. "Try it. You can sit on the porch."

Clarissa tasted it. Sweet. Watery. Manufactured. She smiled at Aling, thanked her and took her cup out the door.

◦

Clarissa leaned over the wooden railing and tossed the coffee out into the bushes. When she turned around, she saw the old woman with the broom watching her

"I never liked that kape anyway," said the old woman. "I prefer the old-fashioned kind."

"Me too," Clarissa said.

The old woman stepped down onto the stone walkway. She swept.

"They told me you were coming," said the woman. "Nanu ka lagyu?"

"Clarissa, ma'am."

"No nickname?"

"No nickname. And you?"

"Lola Ashang, anak."

The woman brushed the stone walk. Clarissa watched her for a while. The broom was nothing more than a handful of palm midribs tied together with a string. She wore flip-flops and a long skirt and an oversized T-shirt. Her hair was pulled up off her brown neck and she moved as if she were a girl. Hush, hush, hush. Hush, hush, hush. Hush, hush, hush.

"You are learning about the family?" asked the old woman.

"We're doing research for a new restaurant," Clarissa told her. "My husband and I."

"And your son?"

"Blake? Well, we couldn't leave him in Miami."

"Wa. Right," said the old woman.

❋

Blake ran ahead of Clarissa, chasing after chicks in the yard. A wind swept through the trees and cooled her skin.

"Don't touch!" Clarissa yelled. "Birds are dirty!"

The boy squealed and the chicks scattered in all directions, clucking in wild distress.

"If you could just show me some of the history," Clarissa said. "Tell me some of the folklore. It'll be helpful."

Gema, home from college, was going to walk them around San Fernando.

"It's good you want to know about our family."

The sun was already high in the sky and it wasn't even ten in the morning. The rice fields had tiny green stalks peeking just above the waters, waving at them from the distance. A kalabaw was soaking in a nearby stream.

Clarissa pushed her sunglasses up her nose. "It's not for me," she said. "It's for the business."

When Gema didn't say anything, Clarissa rushed to add, "Our restaurant is going to serve authentic Filipino cuisine—well, fusion—but we don't want it to be just about the food. I want to simulate a cultural food tour. Maybe go from one Filipino kitchen to the next—where stories and families and culture make for delicious meals. It's the latest trend, you know?"

"You sound like a commercial," Gema said.

One of the hens turned around and chased after Blake. He laughed and ran, grabbing hold of Clarissa's legs.

"I don't mean to," Clarissa said. "It's just that's what it is. What's your major?"

"Political science," Gema said.

"I see."

"How's your Kapampangan?"

"I don't even speak Tagalog."

"Hmm," Gema said. "What's your favorite Filipino dish?"

"Oh, I don't know. Chicken adobo?"

"What'd you grow up eating?"

"Latin food, mostly."

"Well, then," Gema said, pushing the hair from her eyes and squinting at Clarissa, "I guess we'll start from the beginning."

Gema had them walking all over the countryside, under the boughs of banyan trees, moving along the river.

"Say tabi tabi po," Gema said. She was carrying the boy in her arms as he rested his head on her shoulder.

"Tabi tabi po," Blake whispered.

"That's it, tabi tabi po. 'Can we come through?'"

They walked the outskirts of rice fields on their way to town and Blake picked up his head. "Tabi tabi po!" he said, pointing in the direction of the fields as if he had seen an old friend.

"Good boy," Gema said.

He smiled at his mother, blew her a kiss. "Tabi tabi po!"

"Tabi tabi po!" Clarissa said back to him. "You like your auntie Gema, don't you?"

As they neared the town, Clarissa noted fruit stands lining the road, with boughs of lychee, bins of mangos, and bushels of green santol. She saw women bent over laundry, their clothing not in big rattan baskets but plastic tubs. Children in shorts and T-shirts with hand towels tucked into the back collars of their shirts ran in circles around their mothers. Their flip-flops slapped at their heels, kicking up dust.

And then, an image caught Clarissa's eye. The woman she had seen in Intramuros, the one balancing on the prinsa de paa, still in costume, hanging sheets on the limb of a tree. Her daughters held up the corners of the linen, their own skirts dragging behind them. She looked. Looked again, uncertain it was them.

Gema took them to the church where Clarissa's mother had been baptized. It was an old cathedral with life-size statues of Mary and Joseph guarding the entrance. A boy as big as Blake, nestled in their arms. An army of saints were stationed along the walls of the church, and at the altar, Jesus hung from the cross, bleeding. Stained-glass windows revealed brilliant blue skies, an emerald earth, rays of yellow, orange, and red coming from all the saints. Ornate wooden angels were carved into the pews, stained the color of country folks' skin. Two giant fans blew from the front of the church, reminding all of them how hot heaven could be.

"Tabi tabi po!" yelled Blake as he ran up to all the statues, touching their feet with his sticky fingers.

"Quiet, Blake," Clarissa whispered. "People are praying."

Old women in the pews turned to one another and murmured. A dove flew into the church, swooping right past Blake. "Tabi tabi po!" he yelled, waving his arms and running down the long aisle toward the altar. The bird lighted atop the crucifix. The old ladies watched the boy as Clarissa hurried after him, hissing, "Quiet, son! Stop it, now!"

Gema stood by the ladies, whispered something to them. Raising their cloth fans and waving the heat from their faces, they summoned Clarissa with big smiles.

"Anak neng Felly?" said one of the ladies.

"Malagu ya talaga!"

"Clarissa, are your ears burning?" Gema asked.

"Kalupa neng ima na," said the elder in a wheelchair.

Clarissa caught Blake, squeezed him tight even as he tried to get away.

"Hello," she said to the ladies.

"They think you look like Tita Felly," Gema told her.

"My mother?"

"They think you move like her. They knew her when she was a girl."

One of the old women made a sign of the cross. She waved and when Clarissa came near, the old woman grabbed her palm and looked at it. She traced her crooked finger along the lines of Clarissa's hand. She spoke her words like a prayer.

"What is she saying?" Clarissa asked.

The other women began talking at once, their voices rising to the rafters like birds.

"Wow," Gema said.

"What?" Clarissa asked her. "What are they saying?"

"You're a hilot like your mom, like your lola."

"A what?"

"A healer. It's your inheritance."

"I don't think so." Clarissa gently pulled her hand from the woman's grasp.

"I told them you came to find out where you come from."

Clarissa smiled at the ladies. Turning away from them, she walked down the aisle, dragging Blake out of the church.

●

Clarissa opened the door and saw the old woman sweeping the church steps. Bent over, she swept, her white hair around her head like a cloud. She shuffled her feet to the rhythm of the walis.

"Did they upset you, girl?" she asked.

Blake broke free from Clarissa and hugged the old woman's legs. "Apu," Lola Ashang cooed, smiling at him.

"People are just too—too—I don't know."

"Familiar?"

"Yeah. In your face, you know?"

"This is our way," the old woman said. "You'll get used to it. Won't ima, Blake?"

The boy laughed at the old woman, blew her a kiss, pulled her old hand to his forehead. Smiling, she said, "Bless, bless, bless."

Gema emerged from the church.

"I don't even know why you brought me here," Clarissa said, picking up the boy. "I told you I wanted a cultural tour of the area."

"Perla said you would be difficult," Gema said.

"What?"

Clarissa stomped down the church steps into the crowded streets, past markets with its shoppers and vendors, moving in the direction of the house. She had no idea where she was going. By now Blake was crying, his hands reaching back toward the church. "Tabi tabi po!" he cried. "Tabi tabi po!"

"Stop that nonsense now," she said.

◆

Clarissa hurried through the house, stinking of sun and sweat, limping from her leather sandals. The little boy cried and squirmed in her arms. She held on tighter, which made the boy scream louder. She hoisted him up, ignoring the lower ache in her back. "Shh, son, we're here now."

The afternoon light cut across the main sala and she could hear Henry in the kitchen with Aling Dora. They were singing. *Planting rice is never fun!* Oh my God, she thought. *Bent from morn to setting sun.*

"Mommy!" Blake cried. "Tabi tabi po!"

Cannot stand. Cannot sit. Cannot rest one little bit!

"Henry!" Clarissa yelled. "Come get the boy!" She carried him to the kitchen, ready to hand him off, when she saw the plates of frogs. Stuffed frogs.

"Sweethearts," Henry said, smiling. "Look what I've got for you today!"

She looked at the fat little bodies bloated with ground pork, tomatoes, onion, and garlic, breaded and fried to a beautiful golden brown. "What is that?" she demanded.

"Daddy!" Blake cried. She put the boy down and he went running to Henry.

The father picked him up and, smiling, said, "Can you say 'rice field frogs'?"

"No," said the boy.

"Betute tugak?"

"Bay-toot-to-guk," Blake said, wiping his eyes with the back of his fists.

"What's the matter, son? You tired?"

Aling Dora stood at the clay oven, wiping it down. The kitchen was warm from the heat of cooking. Clarissa ran her hands through her hair.

"Ugh. This will never fly in Miami."

"I don't know why not," Henry said. He smiled at her and she tried to smile back at him, but her lips trembled. "What's the matter, baby?"

She looked at the frogs, at the way their legs were bent as if ready to jump. "I don't know. Hello, Aling Dora," she called.

"Afternoon, ma'am."

The front door opened and closed. Gema was home.

Clarissa looked Henry in the eye, and she could feel the tears coming. "Can you watch Blake for a while?" she asked him. "I'll help clean up here."

He leaned in and kissed her. "Sure," he whispered. "I got him."

Clarissa cleared counters of dirty dishes, bringing them to the sink in the back. Once all were collected, she began to wash them. She liked the work. The water on her hands felt good. And even though the pots were filthy, she found it soothing to clean them, to breathe and focus on the scouring. The monotony of the task calmed her.

Clarissa seldom thought of her mom. Could barely remember her. This was the house Felly grew up in. The room they were staying in might have been hers. Except for her father who never talked about Felly, she knew no one who had known her mother. Much less said Clarissa looked like her. And what was with the palm reading? And what was with Gema? And why was she so emotional?

"Ma'am," Aling Dora said, "Aku na." She gave Clarissa a little push. "Paynawa na ka. Rest."

"No, Aling Dora," she said. "Let me help you. I can help."

The two of them stood by the sink, washing. The only sound was the rush and swirl of water, the clank of pots, and outside, the whistle of the wind.

"So, Aling Dora," Clarissa said. "How many work here besides you and Lola Ashang?"

"You saw Lola Ashang?" Aling Dora cast her a look.

"Yes," Clarissa answered as she cleaned every pot in the house. "Sweeping." She scrubbed all the dirty dishes. She dried them and put them in their place.

◦

That night she dreamed she was her mother, Felly, blue-skinned and dark-haired, walking along a lighted path. Behind her trailed three dogs, sniffing at the ground, barking at the skies. On either side of her, tall cogon grass moved to the wind. In the grass, Felly saw the small faces of tiny people, waving at her, nodding.

"Tabi tabi po!" she called to them.

In the trees above, the aswang perched themselves on slender limbs. They called to Felly, snapped their long tongues out to her in greeting. Use your powers for good, she thought. Enormous wings tucked under their arms, their hair shiny as silk, falling from the trees like the roots of banyan trees.

"Tabi tabi po!" she called to them.

In a nipa hut, a girl was writhing in pain on a mat on the floor. Her arms twisted and her hands pointed in unnatural directions. Her cries resounded all over the barangay. The child had fallen while climbing a coconut tree.

Felly had been summoned because her mother, Atanacia, was in another province, aiding in the birth of twins. Felly carried oils and herbs in her satchel. She also brought with her amulets, stones of brilliant colors, that might speed the healing along.

"Tabi tabi po!" Felly said to the house dwarves. She entered the room and saw her own blue hands moving toward the girl's limbs, manipulating her elbows, massaging the cartilage between the joints.

The girl screamed so loud Clarissa woke out of her dream, woke Henry too, and made the little boy cry. She rolled over and touched his face. She kissed her husband then, to wake her, to shake some sense into her, to bring her back to reality.

◊

Gema was taking them to the palengke. Clarissa focused on the bird-song in the trees, to the distant chimes of church bells. She walked a little faster than her natural gait and could hear her own breath.

"Tabi tabi po!" shouted Blake as he ran off the path and into the grass.

"Blake!" Gema called, chasing after him.

The movement of the cogon grass reminded Clarissa of last night. The dreams had grown more complicated and richer in detail. The faces no longer appeared to her, but the dreams were like little films. She took a deep breath and looked ahead.

"You know I made it home perfectly fine without you," she said to Gema, climbing back onto the road with the boy in her arms. "I could have gotten back to the town on my own."

"I promised Ate Perla that I would show you around," Gema said. "I will do it."

"I'm sure you will," said Clarissa, reaching over to pull a flower from the path.

"Those old ladies have known our family for a long long time and they didn't mean any harm."

"I know."

"Nakakahiya."

"What?" Clarissa asked her. "You know I don't speak Kapampangan."

"That was Tagalog."

"Whatever," Clarissa answered. "Well, thanks for taking the time."

The market wound around the church like a river. Vendors lined their stalls up shoulder to shoulder, crammed their goods—fake designer bags, T-shirts, and plastic toys—one on top of another. On the south side of the church, bins of rice, carts of freshly caught milkfish, and bushels of frogs and crickets lined the dirt streets. Green stalks of kangkong, pechay, and mustard greens caught Clarissa's eye. From the roof of the makeshift stalls, vendors hung green bananas and giant pods of jackfruit.

"But really," Clarissa said. "You could have warned me."

"Of what, how to behave in church?"

Clarissa stopped. "I never wanted to go to church." She picked up a small purple eggplant and rolled it back and forth in her hands while Gema counted pesos to pay for bags of boiled peanuts.

"You wanted a cultural tour. The church *is* our culture."

"Bullshit."

"You're so loud. So American." Gema handed the money to the vendor.

"I *am* American!" Clarissa yelled.

The old woman who had been waiting on the cousins stopped then. The wind died down. The traffic around the palengke quieted like waves rushing to the shore. And that was when Clarissa glanced down.

Where was Blake?

A woman carrying a package of fish bumped into Clarissa. The woman's skin smelled of sun and humidity. Clarissa stepped into the street, but the crowd around her was thick. All she saw was a mass of shoulders, the heads of black-haired people, and children running loose like strays.

"Blake?" she called.

Blake's cry rose above the market, sounded like the wail of a newborn in the middle of the night. The locals crowded around her. The air stank of unbathed bodies. She felt a hand on her arm and she pushed it away. Then someone tugged on her shirt sleeve and when she looked down, it was a beggar with his hand out.

"Mommy!" Blake called out. "Mommy! Mommy!"

Clarissa followed his cry, through the market, pushing past other shoppers, weaving around motor-tricycles and bamboo carts. Exhaust from jeepneys filled the air. Three stalls over, she found him, clinging to Lola Ashang's legs, hiccupping in the aftermath of tears. The old woman bent low and kissed the top of his head.

"Don't cry," she heard Lola tell him in Kapampangan. "Don't cry. Here comes Mommy na."

The sight of the two comforted Clarissa, the way the old woman's small body curled around the boy like an old banyan tree. "Thank you," she said. "Thank you!" The noise in the palengke was so loud, all the vendors calling to the shoppers, all the buyers bartering in their loudest voices. But for a moment, the sounds went dull and all she heard was Blake.

Clarissa kneeled, wiping the tears from the boy's face, pushing the curls from his sweaty head. She embraced him then, thanking Lola Ashang, even as she kissed the boy.

"I'm so glad he found you," she said.

"I am always here, anak," said Lola Ashang.

Blake buried his head in Clarissa's chest, gripping her shirt with his tiny fingers. Clarissa was so grateful. Maybe she would buy the old woman a sweet treat and sit with her for meryenda. Maybe she would ask Lola if she knew her mother. She hummed into her boy's ear, soothed him till he settled down. "How can I thank you?" she asked.

Clarissa felt a swelling inside of her. She wiped Blake's nose, kissed him on his dry cheek.

When she looked up to Lola Ashang there was no one there, only three stray dogs, the color of sand, running in circles, barking.

Hilot of Parañaque

Milagros wakes the next morning, hungry for him. Searching in all the places he might be, behind the house, praying under the guava tree, in the kitchen frying eggs, locked in the bathroom reading the newspaper. He is nowhere. She remembers now. He's driving Americans up the mountain. She breathes a sigh of relief.

She bathes in rainwater, washes the night from her skin. The children are still asleep. She combs the tangles from her hair. Dresses quickly and sits before Mama Mary, rosary in hand. It is Wednesday, the Glorious Mysteries, the day of the happy death. The prayers rise from her, a smoke of words swirling into the room beneath the sounds of roosters crowing and frying pans banging in the dark morning.

She closes her eyes and searches for the light, a little glimmer inside her. She nurtures it, feeds it silence, waits until she sees the faint violet shadow of it shifting, growing, moving. Today will be a good day. Her clients will come with their heartaches, with their broken arms and swollen glands, with their infected eyes and migraine headaches. She will place her hands on them. She will ask for mercy. She will invite Mama Mary to come with her, see them, ask her Son to heal them. It will be a good day.

Before she makes the sign of the cross, she looks into the glass beads of Mary's eyes, and says, "One more thing, Mama Mary. Ernesto. Watch over him. Bring him home safely."

Milagros has faith. She is obedient. She tends to her patients, holds her girls, waits. But he does not return.

●

Ernesto comes to her when the house is as dark as the new moon. Gently shaking her, he wakes her from a dream, tells her he is going away for good. Lost in all that night, she cannot see him. When the curtains blow, light shines on them. The smell of garbage in the alley rises. She makes out the shape of his face. She smiles then, puts her hand on his cheek.

"It's late," she tells him, "Undress na. Come to bed na."

"Milagros," he says again. "I am leaving. I am going."

She falls into her pillows, taking his hand with her. "That's not funny and it's late." He doesn't move.

"I've only come to say good-bye," he says. "I won't stay."

Something in his voice sounds different. She massages his hand and with her eyes still closed, she traces the lines in his palm. She counts the ticks and the scars where years of labor have marked him. His hands so rough, the veins pop up from under his brown skin.

When his head touches the pillow, he makes her look into his eyes. "Do you hear me," he says, "I'm not fooling. Aalis na ako."

●

She follows him for forty days. Begs him. Cries to him. Pulls at his hands. Kisses him—the lids of his eyes, his mouth, the Adam's apple she loves so well. She reasons with him.

"But our love, mahal."

"What about it?"

"And our girls."

"I will always be there for them—that won't stop."

They are in a bar near Clark Air Force Base. The lights flash red and blue and his body is hunched over a beer between sets. His drumsticks splay out like silverware waiting to be used. She swivels his stool and puts her arms around him.

"If this is what you'd rather do, play your music, sige, do it. I won't care. Just come home na," Milagros says. "Just come home."

She feels his body rise and sink as he releases a heavy sigh.

"Stop driving the foreigners," she says. "Go back to your music. We'll support you."

"You have to move on," he tells her. "You have to let go."

"But why," she says. "I don't understand."

●

The next time she finds him, he's sitting at the edge of a rice field, watching a farmer plow the fields. "What are you doing here?" she wants to know. "Why have you left the city?"

"I was born here," he says to her. "Dati, we used to have a house right here, before the fire."

"The girls want you home."

"You know, the house had no electricity back then."

"Brownouts?"

"I mean no electricity. I mean kandila lang."

He puffs on a long thin white cigarette, and she thinks it odd.

"When did you start smoking again?" Milagros asks.

"The city is no place for girls. You should follow the plan."

"Without you?"

"It'll be better there, easier for you. No brownouts. No country-side without electricity. No poor."

She looks around the land. Not far from the rice field, green kangkong peek up out of the water.

"Come home, mahal."

Finally, he holds her, the way he always has, wrapping his arms around her thin frame. He whispers in her ear and says he'll never stop loving her either. She buries her face in the crook of his neck and sniffs. His skin smells of soap. How could this be happening?

He slowly peels her off him—finger by finger, the hand in his back pocket, the other running through his thick black hair, then an arm—the right and the left—and even her legs, he has to untangle them from his own. He wipes her face with his old handkerchief. "Don't," he tells her. "Don't. Where is your dignity?"

●

At the house, her girls cry too. Think she has gone mad. You will understand, she thinks. When he comes home and we are all together again. When he is earning money for our passage to the States and I am a registered nurse, a healer. You girls will understand why I must follow him.

While she is texting him, the younger one puts her arms around Milagros's waist and rests her head on her chest.

"Inay," Lila whispers. "Inay, come back!"

Milagros taps out the words, letter by letter, absorbed in the beep-beep-beep of her message, struggles out of her daughter's embrace. Doesn't even bother to answer her.

Saan ka? she writes Ernesto. *I have been looking all over for you. Tell me, nasaan ka?*

●

One day, she sees him sitting in his van, along the wide avenues of Makati. He's leaning back into the seat with his eyes closed and his feet thrown up against the dashboard. She assumes he's waiting for his clients. So she raps on the window. He doesn't stir. She calls his name.

"Ernesto, mahal ko! Wake up," she yells. How is this happening?

A pulis officer places his hand on her shoulder. Asks her what she's doing.

"My husband," she tells him, "Something is wrong with him. He's not breathing. He's not answering."

"Ma'am," says the officer, "there's nobody there."

And when she looks into the van, she sees that he is missing.

●

That night, when the girls are sleeping, he comes to the house and they spin around the room—first in a breath, then a sigh, and then something like a storm.

"You see," she says. "You still love me."

"Of course," he says. "It isn't about that. I will always love you—but I have to go."

"Why?"

He looks at her and rolls his eyes. She knows why. He turns away from her. He traipses through the house, a pillowcase in hand, gathering his comb, a wallet, his St. Christopher's medallion. He cries too, bumping into the kitchen table, into freestanding lamps, footstools. He stumbles over the sleeping hen. She shakes her feathers and clucks at him. His breath is heavy and loud. He's touching everything with those hands—the metal blinds and the photos and fixtures in the wall. His footsteps thump and a tiny earthquake rattles the statues of Mary and Jesus. Knocks Joseph off the mantle.

"The girls," she says. "Shh!"

"It's better this way," he tells her.

And then she begins. A tear running down her face, followed by another. She lets them fall without wiping them away. She lets the tears wash over her. Look what you are doing to me. She stares at him, lets her nostrils flare, lets red veins invade her brown eyes. She pulls him into the girls' bedroom. "Look at your girls."

He leaves the room, calls out behind him.

"You have to move on."

Not without you, she thinks. Not unless you move on too.

And then he stops. Walks right up to her and he looks her in the eye. "Things have changed. I'm moving on."

○

Milagros walks down the long corridor, looking for her girls. The passageway is dark save the light from a window at the end of a hall. Bent over a bucket of soapy water, a girl scrubs concrete floors while church bells sing and sisters chant, "Hail Mary Full of Grace, pray for us."

Her hair is tied back into a loose low ponytail and strands of dark hair fall upon the child's face. Milagros hears herself breathing in the long, cavernous hall, she hears the hiccup that comes with too many tears. The child is barefoot, crawling on hands and knees, scouring the eternal dirty floor. And this is where Milagros stops. Holds her breath. Nearly runs to her girl, takes the rag out of her hands and washes the floors herself, but then, as she draws near, she sees it's not Lila after all, it's not Angel. It is Regina, the old maid living with the nuns. When Milagros gets to her, she sees the face, lined and worn. Stray gray hairs reach up out of her nest of black hair. She leans back on her heels, brushing the hair out of her eyes with a brown elbow.

"Good morning, ma'am," Regina says. "I'm sorry for your loss."

At dawn Milagros wakes her daughters lying in their shared bed, clutching at each other, the sheets strangling them. She pulls the girls apart.

"You better learn now. You can never love this much. You must learn to live independent of each other." They are crying, trying to reach out to her, to huddle their soft bodies around hers, but she shakes them off. "From now on," she tells them, "no more crying. Papang is gone."

She moves throughout the days now, without expression on her face. Without the touch of affection. Desire. She cleans her body thoroughly, tells herself he has gone on before her, instead of the other way around. She is the one who will earn the passage. Find the way.

When she visits the U.S. embassy to inquire, the line of Filipinos wraps around the city block and back again, leans on iron gates, moves at the pace of Manila traffic. Someone tells her, "If you have a parent already sa States, baka your wait is only six months. If not, forget it. A lifetime."

So, she thinks, a lifetime then. She has to find a way to bring the girls. His mother too.

One day an old Filipino from the United States sits on the stool before her, his shirt off, his belly hanging low. On his back are clumps of graying hair.

"Anak," he says, "my American doctors give me six months to live. What do they know?"

"Don't tell me you came home to die?"

"Hindi naman!" he says, shaking his head. "I came home to be healed. Can you do anything?"

He smiles at her then, winks at her too. A dimple creases its way along the side of the face. The teeth are big and white. So, in America, she thinks, the old save their teeth, grow them big, wash them whiter than the moon.

"I will try, sir." Milagros holds her hands up to his back and feels them being drawn in circles, low to his adrenal glands. She rubs ointment there. She says prayers in Tagalog. She sings.

He comes to her every day for two weeks in a row, stronger with each visit. Tells her stories about Chicago.

"Chicago?" she says. "My husband always wanted us to live in Chicago."

"And why didn't you?"

"He died."

"Come with me."

She laughs at the old flirt. "If only the lines at the embassy weren't so long," she says. "If only the wait for the visa was not years. I'll be older than you," she says, "when my turn comes along."

And this is how the old man comes to propose to her: She heals him. He flirts with her. She laughs at his audacity.

He says, "Come with me. Marry me."

Beyond the house, the cock crows above the noise of traffic. Diesel trucks bump and fart along the city skyline. "You are full of yourself, old man," she says.

She looks up at a photo of Ernesto and her, arm in arm, dancing at their wedding. "I could never do that again, you know. Marry."

"Come now," he says. "I am old. I am not stupid. I'm getting stronger with each visit. And we are friends. You don't have to love me, you know. You can be my hilot sa States. You can be my companion, di ba? Tapos, when you pass your boards, you can be an RN. Before you know it, the girls and your ina, and even that noisy hen, will be living in my big empty house in Chicago."

She takes the oils she has made, a mixture of coconut water, baby oil, and peppermint herbs and runs her hands around his bald head. The old man closes his eyes, says, "We can be friends. I will help you bring your family to Chicago. I will never ask you for anything more—my life is in your hands. I haven't felt this good in years. You are my hilot."

●

The thought of another man makes her want to throw up. As far as she's concerned, Ernesto is just on the other side of the screen, hearing everything. Sometimes late at night, when the house sleeps, she can hear him banging his drums, she feels his voice in the walls of the house, talking to her.

"You should do it," he says. "You should take this opportunity and go."

Since he has died, she has grown so angry. "Ito," she says, "first you die and now you push me into the arms of another man? Ano yan?"

She can hear him laughing. She can see the smirk on his face.

"These are difficult times," he tells her. "I am not here, mahal. I cannot touch you. Accept it na. Look out for the girls at pati kay Mommy."

"Crazy," she says, pulling the thin cotton sheet over her head. "Sira!"

"Move on, mahal."

"You want me to marry someone else?"

"What is your other plan? Even if you make the money for the passage, how will you get the visa?"

"You want me to use him like that?"

"He knows the story. He knows. Didn't you hear him? You make him happy. You heal him. That's enough."

All night she talks to the dead husband. She dreams he is in bed with her, that he is holding her and kissing her awake. They fight about the old man. They dream about other ways, but nothing seems as good as this.

"He will be good to you, I know."

"Sira!" she says into his ghost face. "Loko ka!"

But then she thinks of the girls, working as maids. Angel is a dalaga na, her little breasts burst from her too-tight T-shirts, her pants are too short. There are hips now. Milagros takes a breath, and before you know it, she tells herself, Lila too will be a young woman. Working as maids.

Then she sees Lola Ani, crying, bent before the giant pot of fish soup. She feels the heat of Ernesto's memory leaving her body. The voice goes faint. The hum in the walls dies. The drums go silent. He is gone, she cries, he is gone.

And suddenly it all makes sense, this passage to America, this gift of healing. She closes up the chambers of her heart. There is no more room for unruly emotions. She has daughters to raise.

When next the old man visits, Milagros changes out of her flip-flops, slips on a pair of sandals, and invites him to dine. She feeds him a hearty meal of fried fish, eggplant, and stewed kangkong. For dessert, a sweet cassava cake. That night, Milagros picks up her guitar, coaxes her daughters to sing, and the old man to dance.

Loud Girl

Karo rolled down the window, foot on the pedal, bass thumping on her radio. The sun slipped away in the west. Oranges, yellows, hot reds streaked her rearview mirror. Stacks of records, crates of books, and a heaping of clothing shifted in the backseat. Strapped in the passenger side, her electric typewriter gleamed in the setting sun.

The drive was only an hour long, the drive from the university to her parents' home, from autonomy so rare and delicious, to that *as long as you're-in-my-house* tyranny that had blighted her eighteen years.

She had gone to school thinking she would remake herself, shed those people from her hometown who pegged her a nerd. She would be outgoing and friends with whomever she pleased. She had tasted freedom and she loved it.

She paid little attention to the rolling highway, the green hills, the grazing cows, the billboards for outlet malls up ahead. Her sunglasses slipped down her nose as she peered over them and thought about her first year of college. Not the classes, nor the all-women's dorm, not the books in the stacks. But the boys. The parties.

Most weekends, Karo danced on the terrace at the Union, on the bar at Theta Mu Beta, or on a floating pier in the middle of the lake. She plied the jukebox with quarters. Sang at the top of her lungs with her girlfriends Sharon and Jen. That's how she met Kurt—spinning around, singing into a beer bottle, knocking right into him. In class the next day, he leaned over and said, "You and your girls sure can dance."

She said, "What do you care?"

Turned out he had green eyes. His hair was fine as corn silk. His family owned a dairy farm somewhere up north. He had worked up enough money to spend the summer riding trains and sleeping in youth hostels all over Europe. In two weeks the house was throwing a big party for him and a buddy. She had promised him to come.

She bounced in the car as if she were on stage dancing. Her foot pressed the pedal a little harder. The wheels spun faster.

When the cop car loomed in her rearview mirror, Karo felt her heart pound louder than the bass on her eight-track. Oh shit, she thought, pulling over. Shit, shit, shit—

The cop stepped to her window and motioned to her.

"Hey," she said, smiling.

"Miss, were you aware that you were going ninety miles an hour?"

"Oops . . ."

"Can I see your license and registration?"

She handed it over and as he walked to his patrol car, she began to worry. "Shit, shit, shit." This was not going to go over well at home.

●

Arturo held his VHS camera to one eye. He squinted into the viewfinder, at the blurry swirls. He fiddled with the lens, zooming wildly in and out until the picture became clear. The whole family lined up to greet their college girl. When Karo stepped out of the car, her mother, Lara, rushed to embrace their girl. His heart surged a little. Danny and Derick punched their sister in the arm. And the smallest of the children, Lia, roller-skated past Karo and yelled, "Home all summer, huh?"

●

For months—since Christmas break—Arturo had brooded in the sala. Did she lock the door to all her rooms—the bathroom, the dorm room, the passenger side of the car she drove? Back home she would have had chaperones. But here, in the U.S., everyone was so damn independent. The night before, he picked up the telephone. "Let's see how she's doing."

"She's busy," Lara said.

Karo took so long to answer, he worried something was the matter.

"Nothing, Dad," she said. "How are you?"

"When are you coming home?"

"Tomorrow, Dad," she answered, laughing. "Same answer as yesterday."

Hanging up, he shook his head. "Why did we let her go?"

His nightmares ran all night long—Karo running in the dark, a car spinning circles on the highway, a thief slipping his hand into her back pocket. Or the worst, some stranger touching her who knows where. He could not relax when she was away.

Years earlier when he himself had been a freshman, Arturo took a three-hour bus ride from Manila to the border of Pampanga, a province wide and green and wet with rice paddies. Once the bus let him off, he walked another two hours to get home. He hiked after dark, with only the moon and stars as his company. The city fell away, and the path was so silent, he thought he could hear his family, sitting in his mother's kitchen, waiting. Arturo was the first to attend school outside of their barrio.

At university, he saw things he'd never imagined. His heart broke in new ways and he thought that someday, when his own children would leave him, he would prepare them. Protect them.

Who knew it would be this hard? At least when she was home, and all the children were at the table, he knew she was safe.

"We raised her to be strong, mahal," Lara said. "Trust her."

"Oh," he said, taking a swig of his San Miguel beer, "Karo I trust."

On Friday, Karo's high school friends, JJ and Ella, picked her up in a red VW. They drove down to Lake Michigan and sat on the rocks. "What do you think he thinks I think?" she wanted to know. "I'm trying to be cool, but it's so hard when he looks at me like that."

The sky was clear. The moon was full and naked just over the horizon of the water. The sound of waves hitting rocks was calming. Karo looked at her watch, a red leather Timex her dad had given her last year at graduation. Nine p.m. She had missed her curfew.

"Has he kissed you?" JJ wanted to know.

"Not exactly."

"How many times have you gone out?" Ella asked.

"Mostly we go out in groups."

"Well, no wonder he hasn't kissed you," Ella said. "Go out with him alone."

The lake winds howled then, as if to underscore Ella's point. Karo pushed her hair out of her eyes. Thought about the last time Kurt had called her and made her promise to come to the party. He was so cute.

He was cooler than any boy in high school. He saw her in a way no other guy ever had. The boys around here were shy, too quiet to come to her. Well, that or she just wasn't tall enough. Blonde enough. Whatever. Enough.

"You better get me home," Karo said. "It's past midnight."

◆

Arturo waited for her in the family room. Copper light from street lamps dappled the ceiling with shadows the shape of palm leaves, reminded him of nights when he lay in his parents' house, listening to the river trickling outside his window. Seemed like every other day the sirens blasted from the town hall, and they were scrambling into a makeshift bunker, just behind the house. Gunfire rained from the sky and he imagined the bullets shattering dusty roads from their house to the town square. His father began each morning with prayer and afterward, he'd point to each of them. "Stay put," he warned them. "Stay home. No gallivanting."

When Karo's curfew came and went without a phone call, he waited up. To sit and pray and not to think what he was really thinking.

In the darkened room she walked past him like he wasn't there. He grabbed her by the arm.

"You're late."

"I'm home."

He shouted. Accused her of wildness. She didn't run from his words. She stood facing him. "Wala kang hiya!" he yelled like shame was something to wear like a badge. "Wala kang galang!"

He pulled an envelope out of his back pocket. He waved it in the air. "When were you going to tell us about this?"

"I can pay that!" Karo shouted.

"Kontrabida!" he called her.

Arturo watched Karo run out of the room, her clogs pounding on the hardwood floors, the small light of her leaving him in darkness. No respect. As if sending her off to college wasn't already too much. As if paying for her education, her car, her insurance wasn't enough to grant him some kind of answer. Talagang walang galang.

What other secrets was she keeping from him? What other trouble was she into? Back home, his father used to gather them at the table and lecture all night long. And they sat there quietly. Eyes down. Hands folded. Listening. Respectful.

He looked out the window, at the lights shining so bright on their quiet street. Upstairs, her steps landed like bad words. Loud. Angry. Rude. Until this year, all he saw was a child. A mouthy child. A smart and beautiful child. But then she went to college. The photos she sent home showed a girl who had leaned out. Curves revealed themselves. She wore blush on her cheeks, and powdery blue eye shadow. There were boys who looked like men. He detected hunger in their eyes.

Lara came into the family room, placed a hand on his shoulder. "Come to bed," she whispered in his ear.

"In a little while," he answered. Lara was too lenient with the kids. They always told her things. Secrets. Stories. "Why don't they talk to me?" he asked.

"They do," she said.

He felt a burning inside, like indigestion. Breathing hurt. "Hindi na bale," he said, shrugging. It's better this way. He never knew what to say to them anyway.

He turned on the television. The news flowed out like premonitions, cautionary tales.

⁍

The night gave way to a rainy morning and another set of rules were laid out before her. No phone calls. Grounded for the next month. Kitchen duty every night. No visitors.

Because Karo had gotten pulled over. Because Karo had broken her curfew. Because Karo had answered back.

She followed her mother's slim figure from room to room, wiping dust from furniture, vacuuming, washing. She swept the wide wooden planks in the family room, and begged for mercy. How could they expect her to come back to this?

"You know how your father gets," her mother said.

"But we were just talking!"

She pulled a toy from under the love seat and tossed it into a bin. If he had it his way, he would keep her locked up all summer long. "It isn't fair," she told her mother.

"You should have known better. And that speeding ticket."

"Mom, do something." She kissed her mom on the cheek and put her head on her shoulder.

"You're the oldest. Our first." Lara brushed Karo's hair out of her eyes.

"I know that."

"He's having a hard time letting go."

"Well, it's not fair."

Her mother said nothing. Silence filled the room and made her want to talk her way out of it. But she knew better.

✦

Arturo ran his fingers along her journal, tapped at the edges of the cover, contemplated what was in it. That morning, after breakfast, Karo left it sitting on a chair near the big bay window, its pages flipping back and forth under the current of the air conditioner. He didn't think anything of it until he sat down, the Sunday paper tucked under his arm. His eyes were drawn to her bubble penmanship, the way the letters sloped along the page in purple ink. He picked it up, buried it in the travel section, and took it with him to his office.

When Lara popped her head in and asked him if he wanted a snack, he nearly fell out of his easy chair. He gripped the journal in his hand.

"What are you doing, mahal?" Lara asked. "What is that?"

"Nothing," he answered. "Karo's notebook."

She sat down next to him, pulled the journal from him. "I'll give it to her."

"Wait." He held on.

"Oh, Arturo, no. You didn't."

"I did not," he answered. "But it could answer so many questions."

"About what?" Lara poked him in the shoulder. "What do you think, she's a spy?"

"You never know."

She shook her head then. She reminded him that things were different here. When they were children, parents played a stronger role, di ba, controlling every little thing. "Because of the war," she said. "But there is no war. She's okay."

He didn't agree. You didn't need a war to put a young woman in harm's way.

"You have to let the kids go," she said. "Make their own mistakes."

Karo was so much like him. Go, go, go. Never listening to her father. He handed his wife the journal and then he embraced her, sighing.

"Relax, mahal," Lara said. "Okay na."

He closed his eyes, and he could hear the children in the other rooms, calling to each other, laughing, playing rock and roll so loud the walls were vibrating.

●

While everyone slept, Karo picked up the phone from its cradle and called Kurt on the fraternity house phone. Some girl answered and there was music in the background.

"Is Kurt there?" she whispered.

"Who?" screamed the girl. She was drunk.

"Kurt."

"Kurt? Yeah. He's here."

The girl sat on the phone, singing "Paradise by the Dashboard Light" under her breath.

"Well, can you get him?" Karo asked.

"Depends. Who is this?"

"Forget it," she said.

●

Karo filed the charts alphabetically—Kunce, Lundy, Schneider, Zarn. She opened each folder and checked her father's handwriting— the lopsided letters chased across the white page, scrawled into a messy tangle of ink, and trailed off onto more unreadable pages. Occasionally, a blue-penned sketch of a kidney, a heart, or an elbow appeared on the center of the page. She looked for today's date: *6/10/80.*

"Excuse me, miss?"

Karo turned to see a small woman, wrinkles and cheeks caked in rouge. "Hello," she said, reaching for her pen. "Do you have an appointment with the doctor?"

"Yes, at 2. Evelyn Schaefer."

Karo ran her painted finger down a list of names. "There you are." She checked the woman's name off the list. "Please have a seat."

During the day, she helped at his office. She welcomed patients, brought them from the waiting room into examination rooms with the leather reclining beds and rolling sheets of paper. She made small talk and smiled. Sometimes she recited a line from a book she had read last semester—something Shakespeare, something William Carlos Williams.

Her father's patients were so old, soaked in heavy cologne. The women's faces were powdered and painted like polished china, their eyes blue and green and magnified behind thick lenses. She learned to love them. To listen to the conversations her father had with them behind the wooden doors, how he cajoled them to exercise or eat the right foods, how he listened to them tell him stories that had nothing to do with their health, but everything to do with how they felt.

The elders told her father how smart Karo was. "She takes after you," they'd tell him. She could tell it made him happy. She could tell by the way he talked to her in the car on the drive back home for lunch.

"You still want to major in journalism?"

"I was thinking about it." She put her sunglasses on.

"You could be the next Connie Chung," he said.

"Print journalism, Dad. Not television." People were always telling her she would be the next Connie Chung, a talking head with a helmet of black hair and skin the color of rice paper.

"Anyhow, you should think about cable television. They say it's going to be big." He turned his blinker on and took a right. "Mrs. Schaefer said you have grown up nicely."

"Thanks, Dad."

They slowed down at a four-way stop. He turned the music back up and flipped the radio from his classical music to her favorite rock station.

"Keep it up and I know you can do anything you want."

Deep Purple's guitar rang out from the speakers. "Smoke on the water," she sang under her breath.

"You really like this?" he asked her.

"It's got a good beat." She bobbed her head to the rhythm. "Speaking of dancing, there's a really important party at school this weekend."

"Karo—" His voice rose.

"And you know Kurt is leaving for the whole summer and I promised."

"Who is this Kurt?"

She could tell where this was going.

◆

Inside their bedroom, a symphony floated out from two gigantic speakers. Arturo and Lara read the evening newspaper. She skimmed through the various sections of the *Journal,* moving swiftly to grocery store coupons. He read the same headline over and over again. He stared at the newsprint, at a grainy photo of the mayor waving at a crowd. He sighed. He grunted.

"What's wrong," Lara asked him in Tagalog.

"Wala."

She put the paper down and looked at him. "Something."

"She keeps asking."

"He's just a boy she has a crush on."

He knew what boys were capable of. He understood that when a young girl is before you and alcohol . . . Well, he understood.

"She's a child."

He rustled the paper loudly, shook it so hard the corner tore away from his hand.

◆

Karo got a love note in a plain white envelope. Kurt's handwriting was blue and small as a line of ants. He told her he missed her. He described the sunset over the lake. He wanted to take her for a canoe ride. Called her beautiful. She *had* to go.

The moody sky lit the living room in hues of blue. Karo hunched over the keys of their piano. Her body moved to a dark and dramatic sonata. She loved the minor chords, the way they wept with sadness. Living at home felt like prison. Too many expectations. Too many rules. She wanted to be back at school, free to be her own person. She might be at a coffee shop tonight. She might be at a bar. Or maybe at choir practice. Her own person. Not their daughter.

"Iha," her father called from another room. "Play Scott Joplin. Something happy."

"But Dad . . ." she said. "Not feeling it."

"And turn the light on. Why are you playing in the dark?"

"Because I'm living in the dark ages," she said.

"Oh, come on," he roared. Her father turned the light on. Everything looked yellow. His voice rose above the music. He was singing to Chopin. He was making up words. She tried not to smile. She wanted him to know she was mad. His lyrics were mostly "pum pada pum. Pum pum de dumb."

"Dad," she moaned.

"Okay, now play 'The Entertainer,'" he said, smiling. "Like a good girl, play."

She relented. With a heavy hand she played. He nodded and said, "Now you're cooking with gas."

⬤

Arturo found a letter folded into three parts and tucked into the international section of his newspaper. A hand-drawn heart on the seal of the envelope in red marker. Inside, he found Karo's proposal—reasons why she *had* to go. Karo had drawn a savvy list of pros and cons, one he could admire for its creativity, but not one he could condone.

When he was a teenager, he, like Karo, was cavalier. Stubborn. Just the thought of it made the veins in his temples throb, his head swirl with the kind of pain that only meant a migraine was imminent. He would not have it. "Karo!" he yelled, walking from room to room, his voice transcending the noise of the television, the war cries of the boys, and the music someone was blaring.

When he found her, she was eating lunch.

"What is this?" he asked her, waving the envelope in the air.

"Dad, my friend is leaving for the summer. I want to say good-bye."

"In my day, the girl would never chase the boy."

"I'm not chasing him. He invited me. It's a despedida."

She offered not only to pay for the ticket, but to wash the car and get all the tires checked. She said she'd work overtime in the office. For free. The whole thing made his blood boil.

"It's not about the money."

Every time she asked him, he could feel his blood pressure go up and he threatened to lengthen the punishment.

Arturo watched her shoulders roll forward, watched the way her torso collapsed around her heart. She stirred a bowl of soup, the spoon going round and round the bowl. The boys talked over one another, their arms gesturing. Rice and chicken spilled from the corners of their mouths.

"Don't talk with your mouth full," he said.

Karo sighed. Her ponytail had fallen limp down her back. Kawawa naman, he thought. He knew he should let her go, but he could not. Maybe one of those friends could go with her—the tall red-haired girl and the little fat one, Ella. But where would they stay? And it wouldn't be safe to drive back in the middle of the night. No, he told himself, no. Two years ago, he read about a group of college students driving back from a concert in Chicago. They were not drunk, but the driver who plowed into them was.

●

She was not going to stop asking. She was going. She schemed. She debated. She begged. He would not hear of it and so she wept. Threw herself down on the floor, clutching floor pillows and throw blankets, wailing to the music of Carole King. Her life was lost. She would die a virgin. A never-been-kissed Pinay. A nerd.

●

Arturo went golfing on Saturday. Packed his clubs after polishing each one. Reminded Lara that if there was a medical emergency, the patient should page him. He and his kumpare were notorious on the public golf courses, a band of brothers, laughing at each hole, encouraging each other's swing, chasing errant golf balls into the weeds. It was his moment to forget about troubles. It was a time when nothing could snuff their mirth, not even the players behind them egging them to move on, to be quiet, to respect the game.

Soon after the second hole, his pager went off. He pulled the thing from the clip on his belt and saw the number. "One moment," he told his pare. "You go on." He made his way to the front office and threw a quarter into the pay phone.

"Is everything okay?" he asked.

"Yes, Dad," she said. "I just wanted to know if you'd give me permission to go."

"Iha, I told you."

"But, Dad."

"Be good and maybe next time." He hung up.

After the fourth page, he stopped calling back. The more he ignored her the more she paged, beeping and beeping him.

"Sino ba yan?" asked Rolly.

"Anak ko," he answered. "Sorry, guys. Nakakahiya."

He was embarrassed, true, but there was something about the way Karo persisted. At least, he thought, I know she'll fight for what she wants.

They chased their golf balls up and down the green hills, a thing they wouldn't think of doing back home. Their voices rose into the sky as they exchanged horror stories about raising kids in America, the way it tested their patience, made them so angry. Made them realize how much they loved their kids.

By the end of the day, Arturo felt so bad for the girl, he stopped at the local ice cream shop and picked up three pints of the kids' favorite custard—chocolate mint, chocolate chip, and butter pecan.

◆

That night, after the house grew quiet, Karo rose and wiggled into her bell-bottom jeans. She put on a loose top and curled her hair with fat electric rollers. She lined her eyes with a smoky blue liner. She glossed her lips with Sweet Watermelon Frost. Makeup did little to hide the puffy eyes from all her crying. She put her sunglasses on. It was a look. Then she snuck out of the house. So there, she thought. See if I care.

The moon lighted the whole sky, hung low to the earth. She drove with windows down, cranking her eight-track all the way. The car vibrated in beats as she headed west on 94. She shuddered uneasily. "Calm down," she whispered to herself. "Breathe." But it was no use. Instead of imagining Kurt, she saw her dad. He'd ground her for life. Her mother would not defend her. She imagined iron bars on all the windows. She wiped tears away with the back of her hand.

An hour later, she pulled into the parking lot of the Theta Mu Beta house. Music blasted from the house windows. The lights from a disco ball fluttered across the walls. She took a Kleenex out and blew her nose. She wondered if everyone back home was sleeping. If her parents were collapsed in an embrace. If her sister was dreaming of unicorns, her brothers snoring. "You see," she said to the rearview mirror, "you won't even miss me." She sniffled and wondered if Kurt would care that she was a mess. She heard her mother's voice. "If he really likes you, he'll understand." She took another deep breath. Okay, she told herself, opening the door.

●

The house reeked of beer. Her sandals stuck to the wood as she wove her way through the dance floor. All the furniture had been pulled out and stacked on the porch and there were sweaty bodies everywhere. A punk rock version of "Money" blasted across the room, the electric bam-bam so deep, she felt it in her chest. A cluster of girls sang, fists up in the air, bodies jumping to the beat. "That's what I want!"

One of Kurt's frat brothers was dancing by himself in a corner. He too wore sunglasses. "Jack," she shouted, as she neared him. "Jack, have you seen Kurt?" He pointed to the balcony.

"Check the pier."

She stood on the balcony, where a swarm of people danced. Below her the pier stretched like a long narrow catwalk. She squinted, trying to make out the bodies. Some of the girls and guys had leapt into the lake and were floating on a giant raft. Others sat with their feet dangling at the edge of the water. She could not see him, could not tell if he was down there.

"Looking for Kurt?" Tori asked. She had her arms wrapped around a drunk boy. "I saw him head down there."

Karo nodded and made her way down the rocky slope, holding onto the railing, stepping casually down each step. The pier was painted white and it was wet and slippery under her feet. She called his name as she walked. As she slipped and slid down the center of the pier she realized that everyone was paired up.

"Kurt?" she called again.

And there he was, in the water with some blonde, their bodies tangled like seaweed, their lips locked. She could see even with her sunglasses on, she could see in the way his hair shined under that big fat moon. And just to make sure, she said it again, "Kurt?"

◆

Arturo got up in the middle of the night to get a glass of water. Crickets warbled from beneath the floorboards as he walked through the house. He was still thinking of Karo, how broken she looked, how sad. He walked past her bedroom and opened the door. He leaned in and when he saw the bed was empty he searched the house, counting to himself, calming himself. He should have known she'd sneak out. Always something with that girl.

He looked out the window. The car was gone. He sat in his recliner and waited for her, telling himself she'd be fine. There was an ache inside him, like a block of bad gas. Like a heart attack. So he breathed deep and said a prayer.

"Who is this Kurt?" he said aloud.

"That's the boy Karo likes," came the answer.

He looked up and his youngest, Lia, was standing in the kitchen doorway, dressed in mismatched socks, a football jersey, and shorts. In her hands were two big bowls of ice cream.

"What are you doing up?" he asked her.

"I figured you might need company," Lia said. "Karo can be pretty mean."

His heart melted then, at the sight of his daughter, this small figure lit by the lamps in the kitchen, with a voice like the angel of God.

"Want one?" Lia asked, offering him a bowl. "It's mint chocolate chip."

·

On the way to the Philippine Independence Day picnic, Karo sat in the middle seat, crammed between Derick and Daniel. Lia had crawled to the back of the station wagon and was singing to the radio.

"Why are you wearing sunglasses?" Derick asked her. "There's no sun out."

"Why are you such a jerk?" she answered.

"Are you lovesick?" Daniel asked.

"Shut up," Karo said.

And then her father. "What's all that noise back there?"

"Karo's boyfriend called her this morning," Derick said.

"He's not my boyfriend."

"He's your lover boy."

"Shut up."

"Your dream come true!"

"Boys," her mother warned.

"Leave her alone. She didn't even talk to him," Lia said. "She told me to tell him she wasn't home."

Karo watched the rearview mirror, the way her father's eyes filled the frame, the way the arch of his brow raised just a little bit. She knew she was in for it. "That's enough," her father said. "We're going to a picnic, and you are all going to get along. You hear me? You are going to have fun."

❡

Under the shade of a gazebo, Arturo sat with the men, crouched around picnic tables, playing poker. They talked over one another. They puffed on slim cigarettes, blowing smoke into the air, sipping everything from cold Coca-Cola to cool beers and whiskeys on ice, at ease after a long week. On the other side of the clearing, the women were rolling mah-jongg tiles, building marble walls, calling PONG and CHOW and ESCALERA with an occasional PUNYETA in the mix.

Leaving home was not easy. Back home he swam in a school of fish and they all understood the currents, the colors of the sea, the tide's rhythmic push and pull. But here, in the Midwest of the United States, this so-called heartland was constantly testing him, his patience, his trust in God. Sometimes even the nurses at the hospital questioned his decisions. Here, he worked day and night to feed and protect his family, and even his children acted like he was their enemy. But in this park, on this Philippine Independence Day, surrounded by his kumpare and kumare, the festive noise calmed him, made him feel there was a chance of inculcating their children with a piece of home.

Children ran around, squirting each other with water guns, tossing balloons in the air, and screaming. In the corner of the park, an adult band played old Carpenter songs, Philippine folk songs, and the ever-popular "Feelings." Food was displayed at every table, and instead of hot dogs and burgers there were pots of rice, chicken adobo, and egg rolls. There were huge aluminum pans of roasted pig next to paper plates of cakes and cookies and giant bins of cut-up watermelon. Styrofoam cups of Coke and orange soda dotted the array of food like stars. Lia and Derick had just finished performing the tinikling.

Every now and then, Arturo surveyed the park, eyeing the children and Lara. His heart collapsed a little when he saw Karo stooped, crumpled like a piece of old newsprint. He didn't know what had happened the night before. At least she returned whole. But this? What to do? Kawawa naman, he thought.

◖

Karo and Ella kept cool under the shade of a giant Philippine flag. They looked out at the picnic like they were sitting at the lake, watching the tide roll in.

"You look like shit," Ella said.

Karo pushed her sunglasses up her nose.

"What happened last night?"

Karo's dad motioned her to join him. "Dance with your daddy," he called.

She shook her head. From behind her shades he looked like a cartoon figure, arms akimbo, shoulders rising to the beat. He bent his knees and stuck his butt out.

"He's so embarrassing," she whispered to Ella. "Why can't he be like your dad?"

"My dad?" Ella said laughing. "You have no idea."

◖

For the Philippine Independence Day program, the picnic tables had been arranged like seats in an amphitheater, and at the edge of the grass was the band and the microphone. The aunties and uncles sitting on lawn chairs and tabletops clapped for the emcee who had announced Arturo, a pillar of the community, a native of Pampanga, the local historian of all things Filipino.

Karo heard her father's voice stretching across the park green.

He was talking about their independence from Spain. "Many other countries have also occupied the Philippines—the Japanese during World War II, the U.S. for fifty years after that. Some country is always claiming us, and the Filipino fights for independence every day. For me, it was the second world war."

Karo looked up, watching reluctantly. Her father held the microphone in his hands, pacing as he talked. He listed dates, battles, atrocities. Someone's beeper went off. Arturo gestured with his hands. Even in this new country he had learned to be watchful.

A toddler ran across the grass before him, his older sister chasing after him, their mother calling out, "Halika!"

The clouds revealed the sun and for a moment, he was lost in all that light. He shared his personal experience. How during the war, they had nothing. How all around them the bombs were dropping. How children went without school for years. How the people were left traumatized.

And then, Karo saw the heads turning to one another, slowly, like a quiet wave stretching out to sea. The bodies were fidgeting. The interest waning. There was a hum rising among them. Karo felt a heat in her belly, small and persistent. Two women stood up, walked right past Arturo as if he were not speaking. They stood at the tables, grazing on rice and egg rolls, picking at cut pieces of watermelon, grabbing a cup of ice for Coca-Cola.

"These days of commemoration are important," Arturo said.

And even though whispers rose like smoke, he continued.

Karo watched people standing up one at a time. The listeners dwindled right before her father. Now her own heart was hurting. Sit down, you assholes, she thought. Shut up.

One day, he said, he and his younger brothers and sisters snuck out of the house and wandered to the town square. There was a Japanese vendor, an old-timer. His sisters wanted ice cream, but the boys wanted to play basketball. He gave the sisters pesos to get them out of his hair. He dribbled the ball and shot. "Go, I said, and come right back." But they didn't come back. When he went in search of the sisters, the cart and the vendor were gone. The sisters were nowhere.

Ella leaned on her hands, placed one foot on the ground. Karo grabbed onto her. "Shh," she said. "He's not done."

Behind her dad the drummer tripped into the cymbals. Her father jumped toward the speakers and feedback reverberated in the park.

◆

Afterward, Karo wound her way through the tables, stepping over children who were sitting on the ground. The band had struck up another song. "Muskrat Love."

"Dad!" she called.

But all she saw were the backs of people's heads. She could hear his voice rising above the din of the picnic.

When she got to him, he motioned her to dance. She let him drag her to the middle of the grass, closer to the band. They did a slow waltz to "Superstar."

"I never knew you lost your sisters in the war. You should have told us."

"Sure I have. Lots of times."

She pictured him at the dinner table, in the car, seated in the family room in the dark, lecturing her. Hmph, she thought, he probably has.

Karo put her head on her dad's shoulder.

Arturo hummed along to "Superstar." He kissed her on the crown of her head. Karo took a deep breath and let the tears roll.

"You know you're grounded, right?"

"I figured."

She leaned on her dad. She was tired of fighting.

Holy Thursday

Nora massaged Lola E's forearm, ran her thumb through the thick of the old lady's yellow skin. The wrinkles were fine. A constellation of freckles—little moons and stars and planets—dipped and turned around the bend of the elbow. Lola E closed her eyes.

"I used to take care of my lola-lola in just the same way, you know," Lola Epang said. "I had strong little hands like yours." The old woman mewed like an alley cat. "When you get old, every little thing hurts, nini."

Nora pressed down but not too hard. She imagined Lola E was her grandmother. The child's skin had been sun-kissed and washed in the sea almost every day. Her dark fingers moved fast, kneading Lola E's arm over and over. "Ganito, po?"

"Perfect, nini. I love you best."

●

Nora's parents were the caretakers of the Mayor's house, a mansion that stood at the top of their little fishing village. Just below the three-story house, the sea. The Mayor's children were grown and living in America so the only people in the house were Nora and her little brothers, Washington and Edison, her parents, the Mayor, his wife—the former Miss Metro Manila 1968—and the Mayor's mother, Lola Epang.

Nora was too little to cook, but she was quick and ran errands for her mother, went fishing with her father, and after school, she was always allowed to go into Lola Epang's bedroom to sit in air conditioning and watch the telenovelas from Korea.

"Look at her throwing herself at him," Lola E said, pointing to the pouty white-faced lawyer. "She should have more dignity."

The whole thing was dubbed in Tagalog. The voices of Filipino actors and actresses sang over the stoic faces of the Korean characters. Overacting, Nora thought.

"Pero, La, tingnan mo—gwapo yan," Nora's ina said. Auring bathed Lola E from a basin of warm water, starting right at the top of the old woman's forehead and washing down the nape of her neck, gently rubbing at the bony shoulders and the sunken dib-dib just under her duster. "They call him Romeo."

"Ikaw naman, Auring," Lola E said. "Smart women don't need men like that, no matter how handsome."

The sun was high and the room was hot, even with the rattling window air con. Nora looked up at her mother. The washcloth swabbed at the nub just below Lola E's ankle. Nora craned her neck just a little when she got to the other leg, infected where the toes used to be.

Downstairs the door creaked open and Mrs. Mayor was singing, "Hello! Hello!" She plodded up the stairs and called, "Bring my tsinelas, Nora!"

One time, Cher, the town tsismoso, the most beautiful man Nora had ever seen, told her Mrs. Mayor was a distant cousin of Imelda Marcos. She had moved out of the provinces to attend university in Manila. But instead of a degree, Mrs. Mayor brought home a tiara, a silver crown studded with diamonds and pearls, standing at least six inches on top of her perfectly coiffed beehive.

"Real diamonds?" Nora had asked.

"What do you think? She was so gorgeous," Cher had said. "Every week the wealthiest and most gwapo bachelors courted her. She ignored all of them."

"Until Mr. Mayor," Nora whispered.

"Yes," Cher agreed. "Until Mr. Mayor, Prince Charming himself."

All the society pages tracked Miss Metro Manila 1968 from party to party, snapping photos, popping flashbulbs, shouting questions befitting the most famous of stars. The queen was known for her smile, for the way she tilted her head and looked right at the camera.

She was not happy when she had to return to the province. There were no occasions to wear false eyelashes, to dress in sequin ball gowns, or to be seen at all. And worst of all, no one noticed her because her mother-in-law, Epang, was more beautiful. And kind. She was the actual queen of their fishing village.

●

Lola E closed her eyes. She rolled her body away from the door and pulled the covers up to her neck.

"Nora!" called Mrs. Mayor. "Where are my tsinelas?"

Mrs. Mayor stumbled right into the room, talking quick like a commercial interrupting the telenovela. She turned the screen off, turned the air con off, pulled the curtains shut. "Wasting electricity."

Mrs. Mayor's belly sagged just underneath her pillowy breasts. She still swept her hair into a beehive, hung earrings like old Christmas ornaments. Orange lipstick bled from the outline of her mouth, and on her cheeks were patches of red blush. Nora saw a clown, not a beauty queen.

"Ma'am, it's too hot," said Nora's mother. "Kawawa naman si Lola."

"So, draw the drapes and turn off all these appliances and when the sun goes down it will be cool." She peered over Lola E's shoulder, pulling the sheet taut as if she cared.

Lola E winked at Nora, put her finger to her lips.

"Mama, you sleeping? Let me see, Auring, what are you doing?" Mrs. Mayor looked where the foot had been amputated, at the wound still bleeding in quiet little streams. "Put the wet towel on it."

"But ma'am, the doktora said to keep it dry . . ."

"Doktora, doktora. What does she know? Let's keep the wound moist and see how God will fix it. Nora, my slippers, anak. How many times must I ask?"

Nora ran from the room and across the wood floors, in search of Mrs. Mayor's bamboo slippers.

❖

When the sun began to slip down into the sea, the Mayor entered the house and an orange glow spilled all over, painting the dark furniture and its ornate carvings—the day bed with its pillows, the two narra wood thrones before a giant wall of ancestors. Throughout the top floor, the wide-open windows invited the evening light, the branches from the trees and the wind.

Nora set the dining room table, counting the silverware in her hands, but now and then, she'd watch the Mayor standing at Lola E's door, watching his mother sleep. He remained there until the sunlight set. He stood like he was standing at the beautiful stained-glass window in the corner of their church in town, studying the lines and colors, the shape of Mama Mary and her arms, holding up her son, the only One, lying dead in her arms.

After a while he called out to his mother.

"Ma, kumusta ka?"

His shoulders drooped and his voice was small. She probably didn't hear him. Her hearing was not so good.

"Ma! Gising ka na ba? It's me, Sonny boy. How was your day?"

If she doesn't answer you, she is sleeping, Nora thought. She only pretends with Mrs. Mayor. You, she loves.

❖

At night, curled next to her brothers on a cot just outside the kitchen, Nora dreamed of aswang creeping out from under the beds of the house, feeding on the blood of Mrs. Mayor. With eyes that glowed Jell-O green, Mrs. Mayor schemed with all the witches, found ways to make Lola E's life miserable. Nora hated her. Nora wished her dead.

Once, when she lay awake, worrying about the fate of Lola Epang, Nora heard the Mayor and his wife talking. Mrs. Mayor was using her singsong voice, her words like cricket chirps echoing in the dark. She was telling him of a movie premiere in Manila, that she had read all the socialites from her time would be there.

"Imagine, mahal," she said. "Dressing up. White gloves all the way to here, satin dress for me and barong Tagalog for you! We could be the handsomest couple on the red carpet!"

Mr. Mayor laughed, and Mrs. Mayor clucked her tongue. "Why are you laughing?"

"You're dreaming."

"We could go for a week. Maybe two? See our old friends. Be sophisticated again."

"Mama is not well. We're not leaving her."

That was when Nora first heard the witch say awful things about Lola E. How her mother-in-law had ruined her life, holding them captive in this little fishing town. "So crude," she said. "So boring." How the old woman, even at her death bed, garnered more attention than her, Maria Esperanza Gonzalez, Miss Metro Manila 1968, reigning wife of the Mayor.

●

Nora invited the moon to come in, to wash the house in its ethereal light and cleanse it from all evil. She asked the angels to hover over Lola E. "She is old," Nora said. "She can't fight for herself, and Mrs. Mayor is an aswang."

When she woke, her mother was holding her and wiping the tears from Nora's eyes. Edison and Washington growled like wild pigs to slaughter. Moonlight was everywhere.

"Dream lang, anak," her mother said. "Wake up. Okay ka. Dream lang."

She couldn't distinguish day from night. She couldn't tell if her mother's arms were real. It took her a while to feel the kisses on her forehead. "Ina," she told her mother now. "We have to help Lola E."

"Shhh, anak. We help her every day."

Nora's wailing bounced against the walls. She was lost and the only one who saw what was happening.

"What is happening," asked Edison.

"Aswang," answered Washington. "Mumu."

"Stop it, boys," their mother said. "Walang ghosts. Nightmare lang."

◦

Nora and her brothers were just climbing out of the motorboat when the Americana stepped out of the van. The children ran up the hill to see her long legs, her thin white arms, and a pair of sunglasses sitting so big on her tiny nose, Nora figured she had to be a movie star.

"She's so big, naman," said Washington. "She's a man?"

"No, stupid," Nora told him. "She's American. Americans are gigantic from all the vegetables they eat. I hear she eats no meat. Gulay lang."

Americana wore no makeup save a little bit of lip balm. Her blouse, made of gauze with sleeves wide as wings, blew in the wind. Her hair hung loose around her face and down her back. Color, brown with hints of red. Her linen pants were fitted in such a way that they accentuated her thin legs and drew attention to the feet. To the platform sandals that made her ten feet tall. To the toenails painted like little red cherries. The sun sailed down on her as she surveyed the village street, one hand shielding her eyes, the other tucked into her pocket. A superhero.

"Who is she?" asked Edison.

"Pinsan ni Mayor," said Washington.

"Daughter of Lola Letty," Nora said. Edison's small brown face stared at her blankly, "You remember, she was the lola from Chicago, the one who married the man from Davao?"

"Oh, she's pretty too," Washington said. "Chinese eyes. Remember her visit last year?"

"Aha," said Nora. She thought about that Americana, who was much smaller than this Americana, but light-skinned like her, elegant, and old. "She is the daughter of that one."

Americana lifted shopping bags and other supot out of the back of the Mayor's van. The children watched her, their feet still sandy and wet from the dagat. Over their shoulders rested three fish they had caught.

"Will she stay long," asked Edison.

"Will she swim with us?"

"Better than that," Nora whispered. "She will save Lola E."

"From what," Washington laughed. "The mumu?"

Nora handed the fish to her brothers. "Take these to Ina," she ordered them. "I'm going to help." When the Mayor saw Nora running from behind the truck, he waved her over.

"Help Ate bring her bags up," he said. "Be careful not to fall."

The Americana squatted to meet Nora eye to eye. "So beautiful," she said. "And look at this little sundress! So sweet. Ano ang pangalan mo?"

Her words were broken up, like shells that had been crushed and scattered in the sand. "Eleanora, po," Nora answered. "After Mrs. Roosevelt."

"Wow," said Americana. "Such a name!" She put her hand out to Nora. "Sige, Eleanora, take me to Auntie Josefa."

"Si Lola Epang?"

"The one and only," Americana said, smiling.

"Take her, but don't wake Lola E up, Nora," said the Mayor.

❦

Americana barreled into the room with her arms out, calling, "Auntie, it's me!" Then, to Nora's surprise, Americana crawled into the bed and kissed her tita's face. "Auntie," whispered the Americana, "it's me, your namesake, your Josie, it's me." She pulled Lola E's hair off the forehead and kissed there too. The old woman's face was at rest like she was in a deep sleep and maybe dreaming.

But even this did not stop Americana. And when the old woman opened her eyes and saw Americana's face shining over her like a full moon, the old woman cracked a smile. A smile! She took Americana's face into her hands and pulled her to her and kissed her back. And then she snapped her head back and said, "Ha!" She pinched the Americana's arm.

"Auntie!"

Lola E made a face, pouted, pinched Americana again. "Didn't I tell you?"

"I tried! There's no one!"

"Didn't you promise me?" Lola E pulled away and then to Nora she said, "I told her to settle down. She says, 'Oo, po.' And then she comes back. Wala pang asawa. You are not a batang dalaga anymore, Josie. Sana you get married na!"

"I am not an old maid either," laughed Americana. "Auntie," she said, running her hands up and down the old lola, kissing her hands and laughing. "No one marries in the States."

"Listen to this kulit talk," Lola Epang said to Nora. "Ang kulit naman." She pinched Americana's arm. "You speak in Tagalog. You're out of practice," she told Americana.

The old woman was right, Nora thought. Americana's Tagalog was a little mixed up, her words came out backward, turned inside out like laundry hung to dry.

"Oo, po," said the niece, "sige. Tatagalog ko na."

Americana leaned over the bed and from her supot she revealed a handful of chocolates covered in shiny gold tinsel. "Your favorite," Americana said, unwrapping a piece. Lola E winked at her then and opened her mouth and stuck her tongue out. Americana fed Lola the piece of chocolate.

Lola Epang smiled big and wide, her false teeth sparkling in the afternoon light. "I love you best, my girl. I love you best."

"Po," Nora said, "Lola E is not supposed to eat sugar."

"Silly girl," Americana said, placing a chocolate in Nora's hand. "Now and then. It's not going to kill her."

The cocoa melted in Nora's mouth and filled her up with sweetness, but all she could taste was bitter. She loves me best, Nora thought. She loves me.

Auring fixed Lola Epang a tray of lugaw, broth so transparent there seemed to be no trace of rice, of fish, of ginger or kamatis. She placed a tasa of calmansi juice and a saucer of pills on the tray. She finished off the tray with a miniature flower vase. The breeze floated in from an open window. The sound of the children's Holy Week parade could be heard in the distance.

Americana was looking over Ina's shoulders. "Wow. That's a lot of medication. Does she need all that?"

"For the pain, po. For the infection in the foot."

"And those pink ones?"

"For the diabetes."

"And those white ones?"

"High blood, po."

"Once a day?"

"Three times, po."

Outside, the children drew closer. A big bass drum and horns and little bells. Holy Thursday, school was getting out. The whole town was getting ready for the Last Supper. In the middle of the parade, twelve disciples, and a man to play Jesus.

Americana turned to the open back door, high above the street, and waved at the parade. "Are those your boys?" she asked Ina. Washington and Edison were in a kazoo band, waving their arms to the sky, jumping up high as if to leap to the window.

Ina called to them and when the two were not looking, Mrs. Mayor came to the kitchen and took the tray to Lola Epang.

Nora followed the Mayor's wife, as she always did. She studied Mrs. Mayor's crooked back, the way it snaked up her shirt and turned in circles back down her spine. She stood in the hallway, just far enough away to see Mrs. Mayor placing the tray down on Lola E's dressing table, swiping the saucer of medicine and tossing the pills into her purse.

"Come on, Mama, wake up!" said Mrs. Mayor. "Let me subu you this lugaw." She placed a tissue under Lola E's chin, and carefully, she spooned the soup up to the old woman's lips. Lola E refused to open her mouth.

"Please, Mama, you need your strength." She pried the old woman's lips open and shoved the spoon in fast. Lola Epang spat the food out, spewed rice all over Mrs. Mayor's silk white dress.

"Auring!" called Mrs. Mayor. "There's been an accident!"

◉

After siesta, Americana slipped back into Lola Epang's room and the two of them made tsismis, spinning stories of all the aunts and uncles, of all the lola and lolo and all the cousins they called family. The television sat cold, the telenovelas silenced. Nora watched from a porch window, just across from Lola Epang's bedroom. What about Romeo, thought Nora. Doesn't she want to know? Americana was always touching Lola. Always bending down to kiss her hand. She was a tease. All afternoon their voices rose up and down, teetering like the cicadas in the trees.

In the next few days, Nora watched Americana from the shadows. When she wasn't in Lola E's kuwarto, kissing up to her and making Nora feel all kinds of anger toward her, Americana wandered the house, examining family portraits, reading ancient books with their falling-apart pages, looking over their shoulders as they cooked, or cleaned, or prepared the next house chore, all the while asking questions. Like a detective, Nora thought. Or a spy.

At sundown, the Mayor stood at the door, watching as he always did. Silent.

Mrs. Mayor called his name from downstairs, and he ignored her. She snuck up behind him then, and wrapped her arms around him, whispered. He scratched his ear, wriggled free from her. Hardly noticed when Mrs. Mayor stomped away, cursing him, calling him a mama's boy. He didn't answer. Instead, he watched Americana and his mother, lying like mother and child, sleeping. His breath rose and fell like wind before a typhoon. From where Nora sat, she saw that he was crying.

◉

When the priest arrived that night to put his cool hand on Lola E's head, to bless her and pray with her, to give her a taste of the Host, Americana sat on a chair, holding Lola's hand. Mrs. Mayor closed her eyes, chanted Our Father, Hail Mary, and Glory Be louder than the priest. Her voice carried high above the clatter of the children bouncing basketballs on the streets, rattled through the house like a lost set of marbles. Everyone closed their eyes.

Nora took the chance to sneak into Mrs. Mayor's bedroom, to slink into her closet. Beaded dresses with butterfly sleeves, embroidered in colorful pineapple threads, hung all around the closet like heavy curtains. On the floor a cityscape of sandals, pumps, and delicate slippers were stacked in see-through containers. Mrs. Mayor's purses were piled high above a chest of drawers. The former beauty queen had arranged beautiful hand mirrors, silver brushes, and pearl-studded combs on a vanity made of the darkest narra wood.

Nora was careful not to touch anything. She let her eyes scan the objects. She was in search of one thing: Mrs. Mayor's everyday purse. That little clutch, embroidered with abaca flowers, held the evidence she needed to show Americana.

And then there, sitting on a shelf of handbags, the purse! She crawled her way up on a step ladder, reaching up and falling just short. Then she heard, "Nora! Where's the meryenda?" Mrs. Mayor on the warpath. As if they were all starving.

●

Sitting on the balcony, Mrs. Mayor entertained the priest and the Americana. Nora served them miniature rice cakes with sweet orange soda, and pretended she wasn't listening. She could see Lola E in her bedroom, head back and stirring, pain welling up and releasing from her in little moans.

"I don't know what to do," said Mrs. Mayor. "It's good that you come every day. My husband's heart breaks every time he enters this house. We are grieving already."

"Her heart seems strong," the priest said. "Her faith too. What do the doctors say?"

Americana agreed. "I spent all day with her today. She seemed fine."

Mrs. Mayor shook her head. "Malapit na," she whispered, leaning over her dessert plate. "You can see. Death is near."

Not true, thinks Nora. Not true. You mean old witch. You aswang. Not true.

◉

Because it was Holy Thursday, the whole town stayed awake, making preparations for Good Friday. Nora and the Americana walked through the village where the houses were on hills and the streets wound in lazy loops.

"I bet you take good care of Auntie," Americana said, brushing her hair behind her ear.

"Opo," Nora answered.

"Auntie says you watch telenovelas with her," Americana said, winking.

"Every day." Nora smiled to herself.

"Wish I could too," Americana said.

The women in the church had already begun singing and the voices called to them. All night they would sing to Jesus, the Lord. Keep Him company as they washed His full-size body, lying in the glass casket. He was made of the same stuff as dolls, but large with wounds in the hands, feet, and side. Tonight was the night of His suffering and all the town's women would sing to him. Wait with Him, for death was near. Tonight, the moon was nearly full.

They arrived just as they were pulling the Lord out of the glass casket, pulling him by His bloody feet. The church smelled of rosewater and each of the dozen women were busy washing the legs and the arms and the torso, swabbing each wound with the holiest water. They dressed Him in a purple garment. They zipped His pants and buttoned up the coat. If He weren't dead already, He'd die of heat, thought Nora. The oldest manang, Charing, brought the special Christ wig out of its box—blond, long and full of ringlets— and placed it carefully on His head. She kissed Jesus's cheek.

Nora sat in a pew next to Americana, watching her head bowed and swaying, watching her breath move in and out of her chest. The shoulders caved downward. She placed her brown hand on Americana's back. She patted her. She rubbed her smooth arm. Americana sighed. Nora saw the tears coming down. She closed her eyes and said a prayer. If I tell you, she wondered, would you save her?

Nora thought about it all night long, through the prayers of the town women, through the dawn when the two walked back to the house, followed by stray kittens and errant chickens. She would sneak her into Mrs. Mayor's bedroom. She would direct the tall Americana to pull the purse from the top shelf, to pop the clutch open. A thousand pink, blue, and yellow pills would rain from the purse. They would exchange a look. She knew Americana would do something.

They took the slow walk home, winding up and down the road. Americana was so tall she could reach up and pull the blossoms from the trees. "I'll bring some to Auntie," she said, smiling.

"Opo," Nora said. She wanted to say something more but didn't know how.

"Hey," Americana said, touching Nora by the sleeve, "Does my kuya ever visit Auntie?"

"Every day po," Nora said. "When he comes home from the office."

"I mean, does he come into the bedroom, sit with her?"

"Sa tingin ko, hindi niya kaya po."

"He can't?" Americana kept on walking. The sun was coming up, and all around them was birdsong, cricket chirps, and roosters ringing in the day. Wind swirled through the trees and rustled the leaves. "How sad."

○

At the house, Nora took Americana's hand and led her up the stairs. Voices drifted through the halls. Sunlight streaked across the banisters. The voices were strong.

"Get out," they heard Lola Epang say. "Get out."

And there the Mayor's wife stood over Lola Epang's bed, gripping the old woman's legs.

The drapes were drawn tightly, but the sun insisted and pushed through the curtains, illuminating everything.

Hot Mommies

Augustina looked through the viewfinder at shadows breaking up the flat set. In the center of the frame, a 1950s kitchen table sat with ten retro chairs artfully placed around it. A dappling of light danced from the window where the boys had rigged a branch.

She hit the light meter once more. Pop. Pop. Pop. The whole room flashed. "Adjust the fill," she told her assistant. "Then we're ready."

The make-up artist dusted the girls in powder and the stylists teased their hair. Wardrobe yanked at their boobs, pinned their clothing tight to their bodies. "Enough!" Augustina called again. "Let's shoot this."

She placed them like mannequins across the set—holding a birthday cake, waving a cigarette, mixing a pitcher of lemonade. She set them at the counter, on a stool, or standing at the sink. One sat cross-legged on the floor. She posed the women around the kitchen as if they were ornaments, not mothers. Ten of them. All hot. All White. All polished like apples.

"Do you want the wind machine?" asked the art director.

Augustina turned. "What for?"

"I don't know." He moved his arms in the air like he was conjuring up a reason. "To give the shot some movement?"

The models sat under the hot lights, perfectly frozen, their eyes wide as the glass eyes of porcelain dolls, their faces blank as paper.

Little beads of sweat were forming on the face of the 1980s mom. She was in khaki pants, white Keds, and a white button-down shirt. Her hair drooped a little in the front. Augustina bent down to snap a picture, but before she could say anything at all, hair and makeup were all over the hot mom.

◆

Augustina heard them before she saw them. Three sets of platforms marched across the studio loft. There was giggling. And then the voices she had grown accustomed to hearing in her own kitchen.

"Oh my God!"

"This is awesome!"

"Right? I told you!"

"Ginger, your sister is dope!"

"I want hair and makeup."

From beyond the clients' chairs, the teenagers tramped onto set.

"Ginger!" Augustina hissed as she ran to meet them.

"Hey, Ate Augs," Ginger called.

"Hey," said Trisha.

"Hey," called the little one, Sissy.

"You girls ought to be in school," Augustina whispered.

"We're on lunch." Ginger leaned in to give a kiss on the cheek.

The friends wrapped their arms around Augustina, each one reaching to kiss her on the cheek too.

"Yeah, all-day lunch!" Sissy said.

"Are you girls drunk?" Augustina sniffed their breath. She was new at this mommy thing.

"No!" Ginger yelled. "I wanted to show them your set."

"Hell, yeah," Trisha said. She was the tall one. "This is so cool."

Augustina waved the set production assistant over. "Feed them something from craft service," she said. "Set them up. Keep 'em quiet."

She waved a finger at Ginger. "Later. We'll deal with this later. Sit. Be quiet. And you can stay. Otherwise, Patti, kick them out."

Walking back to set, her phone dinged. It was Juan Ignacio, texting from the Philippines. *Wish you were here. The farmers are giving Arroyo hell. Love you.*

She answered with a heart emoji. What she wouldn't give to be shooting a political protest instead of a fashion shoot today. *Hey,* she texted back. *You think Arroyo is a hot mommy?*

No, he answered. *I'll tell you who is, though . . .*

Augustina looked through the lens of her thirty-five millimeter camera. The models had relaxed. They slouched. They looked down and away. They buried their heads in their hands. They leaned back, as if napping. She shot a slew of photos and then called, "Makeup!"

●

When Augustina had returned from abroad, the only room available was their bedroom. She dumped her suitcases next to their queen-size bed and lived out of her luggage for the next three months. She found her mother's favorite teacup on the side table along with a half-done crossword puzzle. On the margins of the *Chicago Tribune* her mother had spelled out a few words—*pirouette, esquire, laborer.* Daddy's vinyl records were stacked like a deck of cards next to the window. His slippers, scuffed and threadbare, sat under the kitchen table. A laundry basket full of clean white T-shirts and socks waited by the dresser.

She considered stripping the bed for new linen but thought better of it. She had not talked to them in six months. She had not written them like she intended to. Her postcards from around the world were tucked along the vanity mirror. Her photos had been torn from magazines and taped to the door.

In the corner of the room, rosaries and plastic flowers adorned a doll-size version of Mama Mary. Every night since her arrival, Augustina set her jewelry at the Virgin's feet in exchange for one of her mother's rosaries. Every night she prayed.

At sixteen, she had fought with them daily, but after she left home, she understood them better. She thought about motherhood and was glad for the two of them. She would never have been able to do it alone. Salamat, po, she whispered like a mantra. Salamat, po. For everything.

"Rise above them," she once texted Ginger. "It doesn't seem like it, but they're looking out for you. I promise."

"Right," Ginger wrote her back. "Didn't they send you away?"

Ginger was at war with them then. Challenged them. Augustina heard it from both sides.

"She makes you look like a saint," her mother emailed. "Maybe even a martyr."

❦

The road was wet, the trees in mid-bloom. All that pollen filled her head, made her foggy. Augustina took the girls for pizza, then dropped them at their respective homes.

"You ought to know better," she told Ginger.

They drove up Clark Street, past the lighted windows of noodle shops, antique stores, and little neighborhood libraries. Red and yellow lights blinked.

"You know," Augustina said, "it's okay to cry."

"You don't."

She did, though. Augustina grieved—driving to the studio, showering in the bathroom, touching up digital photos in the dark. She wept. She found herself looking for her parents in the family room, knocking on the bathroom door, culling through their mail. If Ginger walked in on her, she'd sniffle like it was allergies.

"It's not natural, Ginger."

"Look, they were always on me, watching me." Ginger put her hands up in the air. "Protecting me."

"They were our parents. Show them respect." Augustina leaned over and pinched her.

"Ow!" Ginger screamed. "I thought you were the cool one."

"No cutting classes. No staying out late. No drinking. And hey, no drugs."

"Oh, great. Now you sound like them. Who made you my mom?"

Ginger flipped on the radio. Augustina turned the knob down low, threw the girl a look. Put her hand up when Ginger tried to answer her.

●

Augustina came onto the project after they had cast the women, after the initial meetings on concept and budget. Just shoot it, she told herself. Hold your nose, look away, and shoot.

It's just one shoot, Juan Ignacio texted her.

Would you do it?

If it was the only work, yes.

Three months ago, she was a photojournalist in Asia. She loved her beat—social unrest, politics, the visibility of women in power. She placed the photos in major magazines—*Time, Newsweek,* and *National Geographic.*

Now this.

The hot mommies were glamourous silhouettes. The kitchen was sterile.

Augustina's mother worked in an office for thirty years, answering phones and taking down messages. She took the el train to work and got home just in time to cook the rice. Sauté onions and garlic. Stew the meat. Her mom was glamorous. Wore sunglasses like a starlet on the outside and shed her makeup and heels when she got home. Kept the house immaculate. Her mom raised her and then Ginger too. Two girls, seventeen years apart. A supermom. But isn't that what real moms did? Lead a double life?

She picked up her phone and texted Andrew.

We need to reshoot.

What? You mean there's nothing?

Nothing. The files are messed up. She was lying.

Not a single image?

Nope. Sorry.

She scrolled through the photos and then she came to the ones where the girls were relaxed and waiting. The soccer mom had a mischievous grin. The flapper mom tilted her head bored. The 1960s mom knelt next to the yoga mom and filed her nails. The hippie mom reached around the 1950s mom and whispered in her ear.

Augustina took her sketch pad out and drew long sloppy lines across the oversized pages. She was thinking of darkness and light. She was thinking of shapes. Shadows. Something honest.

She would reshoot the Hot Mommies spread and they would love it.

●

Augustina climbed the platform at the stop, her steps slow and deliberate. She was thinking about the meeting with the agency. How she would have to bring them around. She stood among traders, lawyers, and high-end shopkeepers. A Chicago breeze sailed through and blew the hair off her forehead. It was cool and sharp and woke her up.

Earlier that morning she had fought with Ginger to get out of bed. That child, she thought. That little monster. She had gone into the room that once was her bedroom, and underneath a pile of quilts, she found Ginger, snoozing away.

"I don't want to get up," she said.

"You cannot miss another day. I have a meeting at the agency and then an appointment to see your principal later."

"What for?" Ginger moaned. She pulled the sheets back over her head and tunneled her way deeper under the blankets.

"As if you don't know. Didn't I say no cutting classes? No drinking, no drugs? Didn't I say behave?"

"Morning voice!" Ginger grumbled, her words muffled and sleepy. "Shhh!"

Across the platform, a group of teenagers huddled, shoulders up by their ears, cigarettes poised on the fat of their painted lips. Sunglasses big as saucers on each face. They looked like hoodlums. Just washed, newly awakened hoodlums.

Augustina could not imagine what her parents had gone through. Was I that bad? she thought. Maybe she should have come back with them. Helped them. They were so much older than Ginger, from another country and old-fashioned. Augustina had stayed away too long. And what was she to do now? No matter what she said, the girl ignored her. Charmed her way right out of detention. Augustina was not cut out for this.

The train came barreling down the tracks, slid into the station, and stopped with a jolt. The yuppies stepped aside, let the people off the train—men in work boots and women in heavy coats and scarves. She knew where they were going. To clean houses, she thought. To fix pipes and lights. To do things people getting on the train will never do.

All through the ride, she tried to focus on the meeting, but her mind wandered back to those hoodlums. They were cute, she thought, all puffed up like they were going to do some damage. Through the train windows, Chicago's back porches, alleys, and mismatched buildings glided past her. The train rounded the corner. Sun rays filled the car with so much light. She heard a woman behind her taking a call.

"Does he have a fever? Should I come get him?"

When Augustina turned her head, a blonde in a navy suit smiled at her, said, "My kid. What are you going to do?"

Augustina nodded, took her cell phone out and shot photos of the car, all the people sitting there, rocking back and forth. People of all sizes stacked up against each other, snug and fit, ready to whisper into one another's ear. Shadows darted in and out of the car. Hoodlums. An old woman hung on the arm of a middle-aged man. She had a face of beautiful wrinkles, her coat worn, but clean. Augustina grabbed shots out the window. The streets. School buses full of kids. Traffic. That sun.

◆

At Monty, Schmidt, and Franklin, Augustina told the creatives all the images had come up distorted, the frames were eaten up and the photos were unusable.

"How is that possible?" asked the boss.

"A virus," she answered.

"So we need to rebook everything?"

"No," she said. "And let me tell you why." She waved at Andrew, who put slides up from her portfolio—portraits of women in doorways, in kitchens and bus stops. The women's faces were relaxed. They were brown, yellow, and black. Their lips fell half open. Their clothing was their own. In Manila, she had shot a series of faces of women marching in the streets. "The women you cast were not mothers."

"But that was the concept," said the creative with cat's-eye glasses. "Hot mommies."

"Yeah," said the one wearing a thin necktie. "They were hot."

"Do you want twenty-something high-fashion out-of-touch models?" she asked them. "Or do you want moms?"

"We want hot moms."

Augustina nodded at Andrew. "Could you move to the next image, Andrew?" She waited. "When you hired me, you got Augustina Cruz—not just my brand, but my photos." She waved at the screen.

Shots of people on the el train flashed before them. The blonde on her cell phone, her brows furrowed and lips pursed. An old woman and her son, haloed in morning light. A young woman with a baby wrapped tight in her arms. The sunshine across the train drew shadows on the people's faces, shaped them in delicate ways, made way for the thoughts running through their minds.

"The files are gone from the last shoot, but we have the opportunity to do this the Augustina Cruz way. I can do it for half the budget. I will use natural light and you'll see hot mommies. I promise you. Hot mommies."

Everyone turned to the boss, a woman in a wool pencil skirt and silk blouse. She lifted a cup of tea with two hands. "Real mothers," she said. "There's an idea."

◊

Holy Angels High School, set just behind the cathedral, had not changed since Augustina's days there. Well, she thought, except the metal detectors, and the cops at the entrance. Except for that, the yellow brick building with its wide linoleum floors and its rusted green lockers looked exactly the same.

Sitting in the waiting room felt familiar. She looked up at the clock, at its old white face and its thin second hand running swiftly round and round. Augustina could hear talking, that same deep voice reciting lectures to some unfortunate senior. Oh God, Augustina thought. I hope she's forgotten me.

The door opened. A mouse of a girl, covered in acne, ran out. And then a voice. "Is she waiting?"

"Yes, Mother," answered the secretary.

"Well? Send her in."

Augustina scratched at the rash on her arm. I can't believe I'm nervous, she thought.

Mother Maureen had not aged. Her broad shoulders sat square as a marble bust. A face with a wide forehead and long thin nose bore no wrinkles. Her habit was pressed and perfect. She wore the same glasses she had sixteen years ago. When Mother saw Augustina, she did something unusual. She smiled.

"Mother," Augustina said, taking her hand.

"I was sorry to hear about your parents, Augustina. It must have been awful for the two of you."

"Yes. Still can't believe it, actually."

Mother Maureen threw a manila folder on the desk. Papers slid out. "I wish this was a social call." She pointed at the folder. "Go on, take a look."

Augustina pulled the papers to her. There it was, a calendar of sins. Every missed class. Every brazen remark. Every nicotine and drug offense. The handwriting loping in perfect lines across the pages, each letter, each loop, each line a charge of misbehavior. "Ginger doesn't want to be here," Mother said.

"At Holy Angels?"

"Just before your parents' accident she and her little circle of friends had been arrested."

"Smoking weed?"

"Selling it. This new form. As oil."

"Oil?"

"And drinking with boys. Getting high in the parking lot."

"In the parking lot? You mean behind the church?"

"Perhaps you can find a way to reach her."

"And if she doesn't listen?"

"She should have been expelled long ago. But we were waiting for you. You know, with the loss of her guardians and all."

"Well, here I am." Augustina felt queasy, but she looked the nun in the eye.

"She's a lot like you."

"I'll handle it."

The old Mother smiled, looked away. "Good. We'll give her another chance."

She offered a three-day leave to get their family back in order. "Take her," Mother advised. "Spend time with her, mother her."

Three days to get their act together and if not, Ginger would be expelled.

◊

After Ricardo and Mona sent sixteen-year-old Augustina to the Philippines, she disowned them. She was not wild. She was not bad. She just wanted to be heard. But in their old-world ways, the child was to be silent, respectful. Non-thinking. A child should be grateful. When trouble arose, they sent her off.

A year later, they came to her, but she refused them. They stayed for a month and she pretended like they weren't there. Not even when her heart fluttered upon seeing them. Not even when her mother ran her hands through Augustina's hair. Not even when they cradled Ginger for the first time, Ginger who was too small to know the difference. Nor when they held the baby up to Augustina to say good-bye. She ignored them. How dare they. They came and went. They took the baby. Fine. She stayed.

She might have been pissed off forever had Papa not had that heart attack. She might have stayed in the Philippines. But when she got that call, she flew back. She traveled through the night and stood at the foot of his hospital bed, followed every single tube that went from his body to some machine, examined the dark circles under his eyes, giant bruises as if he'd been beaten up. And that's when she saw him as he truly was. A man. He was just a man.

Augustina's mother held his hand. The baby, a toddler now, slept on Mama's torso, breathing with her as if they were one. Mama didn't see Augustina walk in, but when she saw her, her tears burst anew.

◆

She worked at home, culling through photos and planning the reshoot as she waited for the girl to come home. She wanted to go scouting for mothers. Take a Polaroid camera out and snap a zillion photos of potential mothers. She planned to go for a mix of women, cross-generational, from the wide expanse of Chicagoland. She pulled up a map on her laptop, and her eye went to the time. Six p.m. Ginger should have been home by now.

How's it going? Juan Ignacio texted.

Working at home. Waiting for Ginger. She's late as usual.

You hanging in there?

Barely. Miss you

It was dinnertime. She decided to continue working, to trust the girl.

But then it wasn't dinnertime anymore. It was closer to nine, and Augustina had not stopped staring at the map on her computer, had not bothered to make a meal for herself or Ginger. And then the doorbell.

"Did you forget your keys?" she called as she looked through the peephole. The face loomed large and distorted. The hair was curly and wild. The man had not shaved and there was dark stubble around his jawline. The lips were set in a pout. She knew that mouth!

"Juan Ignacio!"

She let him into the house, filthy from travel, bags falling off his shoulders. He reached for her but she held her arm up. "What are you doing here?"

"You look awful," he said, putting his arms around her, and she let him. "Have you slept at all?"

And there it was, the support she needed, wrapping around her, holding her up, breathing into her neck. She broke down and wept and this made him pull her tighter into him. She tried to stop, but only cried out louder.

"You have no idea," she told him.

"Where is she?"

"Who knows?" She pulled her phone out and texted Ginger for the tenth time that night. "She's making me nuts." She sneezed and wiped her nose with her sleeve.

"Aw, baby," he said, smiling. "Let me help."

She smiled a sad smile. "I have to do this alone."

He kissed her. "No, you don't."

"Yes, I do." She kissed him back. "Aren't you on assignment?"

"I'm off for a week."

She had met him when they kept showing up at the same political events in the Philippines. At first they didn't speak. They'd see each other and nod. They'd stand next to one another, cameras poised to the eye, breathing.

"Ginger's impossible. And this shooting for clients with 'creatives' is a fucking joke."

"You gonna tell her?"

He brushed the hair from her eye and kissed her cheek.

"I don't know," she sighed. "We'll see."

Arms around one another, they danced their way to the bedroom where they made out like teenagers, tasting one another, sighing like they might die. And through it all, she wept, her breathing deep and sad.

They fell asleep, legs tangled, arms gripping tight around one another. The weight of him helped her sleep. And when her phone rang, she sat up as if waking from a nightmare.

●

Augustina and Juan Ignacio hurried into the ER, hair disheveled, clothes rumpled. The doctors were looking for her parents. The rules would not allow them to go in.

"But I am next of kin," Augustina told the nurse. "Isn't that the phrase, 'next of kin'?"

Juan Ignacio leaned into the desk and whispered, though Augustina could still hear him. "Come on, their parents passed away recently."

"I'm her guardian now," Augustina said. "It's me!"

The nurse tapped on her computer screen and waited. Her plastic glasses slipped down the slope of her nose. "The rules around minors are pretty strict," she whispered back. "I'm doing the best that I can."

"She must be freaking out," Augustina said. She handed the nurse her passport. "I've been abroad until recently. Come on. I'm her sister."

The nurse stood up, handed them a piece of paper.

"Third curtain on the left," she said. "Oh, and the police were here."

"The police?" Augustina asked. "Are they still here?"

The woman raised her brow. Shrugged. "See for yourself. Over there."

∮

Ginger leaned back on the examination table, her jeans torn and her face all patched up with gauze. She was talking fast as the doctor stitched up her left knee. When she saw Augustina, she smiled.

"Ate Augs, you made it! And who is this cutie? Here three months and she's already got a hottie!"

"Are you okay?" Augustina asked her. "Is she okay?"

"A few bruises," said the doctor. "I've sewn up a small wound just above her eye and this," she gestured to the knee. "We've done X-rays and she's clear."

"I went for a ride with the girls." Ginger leaned over and hugged her sister, kissed her on the cheek. "Doc, this is my big sis, she look like me?"

"And," the doctor said, "she's high."

Juan Ignacio stood on the other side of the table. "She looks just like you, babe."

"'Babe'?" Ginger said. "That's interesting."

"Can you tell me what happened?" Augustina asked.

"A tree," Ginger said.

"A tree?"

"A tree jumped right up and out of nowhere. Stopped us dead." She giggled.

"And the other girls?" Augustina asked.

"They're all right. Bumps and bruises," the doctor said.

"Who was driving? Trisha?"

"Maybe Trisha? Maybe Sissy? I can't remember."

Juan Ignacio whispered in Augustina's ear, "Ask her about the police."

"What did you tell the police?" Augustina asked.

"Nothing."

"What do you mean, nothing?" Augustina's voice was getting louder. Juan Ignacio rubbed her shoulder. "Can you believe this?" she asked him.

"It's not so bad," he answered.

Augustina threw him a look.

"I like him!" Ginger said, pointing to Juan Ignacio.

◦

Ginger propped herself up on the couch, flipping channels. The sound blasted through the house and kept her from answering Augustina who was standing over her, lecturing.

"You could have been killed!" Augustina grabbed the remote and muted the sound.

Ginger reached. Augustina held it over her head, high enough to keep her from taking it.

"But I wasn't."

"You've got to shape up."

"Shut up."

"Do not tell me to shut up." She sat down on the coffee table and stared the girl down.

"Or what? You going to ground me? Kick me out? You are not my mother!"

Augustina sighed.

Juan Ignacio came out of the bedroom. "Ginger," he began.

"I got this, Juan Ignacio," Augustina shouted. When he didn't move, she pointed at the bedroom door. "Please, I got this."

She waited for him to exit the living room before she began to punch her thighs, yelling. "This has got to stop!"

"You have no idea what it's like—oh, no, maybe you do, Ate Augs." She pointed to the furniture, to the walls, to the large wooden spoon and fork mounted on the wall. "This is hell! And you're not helping!"

"I am helping! You won't let me!"

"You're not listening!"

That was when Augustina slapped Ginger, her hand rearing back, her slender fingers cupping around the child's beautiful face.

The two of them sat for a long moment, gazing at one another, breathing hard, and when Augustina thought she could no longer stand it, Ginger leaned into her and cried.

⊕

At night Augustina knelt at the feet of Mama Mary and fingered her mother's rosary. The stones were the color of summer flowers—hot pinks and oranges, purples and blues—miniature marbles, smooth and cool to the touch. Only three months, and the child was making her lose her mind. Chanting Hail Marys over and over like a secret calmed her. Took the burden from her for just a few minutes.

She had encouraged Juan Ignacio to take an assignment in Thailand. Ginger's knee was healing fast. The agency wanted to know what the holdup was. Mother's Day was right around the corner and they needed her photos. She was going to have to find counseling for Ginger, maybe for the two of them. And there was the matter of the accident.

Augustina stared at Mama Mary's painted toenails, at her holy feet planted on a colorful globe and the serpent sliding around her ankles. This is not the way it was supposed to end up, she thought. What she wanted to do was take the next plane out. Pretend none of this mattered. What she wanted to do was shoot pictures of the world, things that were really happening, not made up, not assimilated. She was not supposed to be the mom.

She had not meant to hit Ginger. Her own parents never laid a hand on her. Where had that come from? Should she apologize? Uneasiness washed over her, the same kind of nausea she felt when she cut her parents off.

She placed her mother's favorite grapes at the feet of the Virgin. She lined the empty ashtray with her father's filtered cigarettes and matches too. She put fresh flowers on the windowsill. She lit a candle for each of them, for Ginger, for herself, and for Juan Ignacio. She begged her parents to guide her out of this mess. "Please," she whispered in between a Hail Mary and a Glory Be. "Please help me through this. For everything I ever did to you, I'm sorry."

They came that night, slipping between her dreams, whispering their own prayers to her. Wishing her well. Blessing her with their hands on her heart, on her forehead, at the bottom of her feet. They told her she was ready. It was time. This was hers and she could do it. They fell deep into the very bottom of her heart and sang to the rhythm they found there, serenading her with an old Filipino love song. You can do this, they told her, you can do this.

◦

Augustina and Ginger sat in the Holy Angels parking lot, waiting for people to come out of mass. They were in their mother's Honda Civic, a car from the late 1990s. Augustina handed her sister a Polaroid camera.

"Now, you know what to do?"

"Shoot and point. Put their names on the bottom of the photo. And their phone numbers. Use this black marker. Make no promises. We only want to know if they are willing."

"It's point and shoot," Augustina said. "Point then shoot."

Ginger rolled her eyes. "Whatever. Tell me again why I'm doing this?"

"We're looking for mothers."

"What kind of mothers?"

"All kinds."

"What was wrong with the models from the other day? They were hot."

"Exactly. We're looking for mothers."

"Who says mothers can't be hot?" Ginger wanted to know. "If you were a mom you'd be a hot mom."

"That's not the point."

"How will I know if she's a mom?"

"You have to guess. Tell her that we're scouting for moms and tell them it's for *Outer Loop*." She held the camera up and shot a photo of Ginger. The film popped out of the camera's mouth, like a receipt in an ATM teller. "What do you think a mother looks like?"

"I don't know. A prison guard?" She yanked the photo from Augustina. "My turn. Look like a mom."

Augustina held her breath, stared into the camera, pursed her lips and squinted. "We have to find a way to make this work, Ginger. You and me. I'm here for you."

Ginger pulled the film from the camera. "That's what they all say," she said, shaking the two Polaroid prints.

The images appeared like ghosts coming out of a fog. Ginger blew on them. Augustina could not believe what she was seeing. Their faces—each line, each curve, each hit of light and the look on their faces. At first she couldn't tell which photo belonged to her. They had tilted their heads the same exact way. They were making the same scornful little face. They had her father's stern expression. Ginger scrawled their names onto the bottom of each photo.

"Stop your gallibanting, ha?" Their dad's favorite command.

The two of them broke into laughter.

The church bells rang, and the sisters stepped out of the car. Ginger leaned on two steel gray crutches and hung the camera around her neck. She hobbled her way toward the crowd, chatting up some of her friends' moms. Augustina took a moment to watch her, to follow. Charming Ginger might grow up to be a politician, she thought.

That day they traveled all over Chicago—first the church, then a Polish diner in old Wicker Park where women still wore beehive hairdos, a Chinese market up on Clark and Ashland, a gym with workout moms, and then a Trader Joe's in the heart of Lincoln Park. They stopped young moms with kids swaddled across their torsos, and old ladies with blue hair pushing grocery carts and guided by younger versions of themselves. They snapped photos of mom-and-kid runners along Lake Shore path. They even went to a gallery somewhere near the Loop. The women were the women of Chicago—some Black, some White, a few Asians, and a bunch of Latinas.

At a shelter, they had to convince the front desk to let them talk to any of the women.

"Why here?" Ginger asked.

"There are mothers here," Augustina told her.

"Yeah, but do you really think anyone's going to want to have their picture taken?"

"You never know."

Only one woman at the shelter allowed them to shoot her. She was middle aged and tall. Augustina could see that she had once been a beauty. Her name was Stella. "If I get the part," she said, "I want to be the star."

"You got it, Stella," Ginger told her. "You'll be the hottest mom of all."

"That's right," Stella said. "I will."

They got back into the car and slipped onto the expressway. The sun was going down and a light rain began to kiss the windshield of their mother's Honda.

"I'm hungry," Ginger said.

"After Old Orchard Mall," Augustina said, "let's go to a Walmart."

"We're not done?"

"Got a lot of catching up to do," Augustina told her. "Your little accident threw me off production in a big way."

The car shifted with a strong wind, pulled away from the road just a little bit. Augustina held her breath. "I hate driving in the rain."

"So did Mom and Dad," Ginger said. "Whenever it rained they made me drive."

"Oh really?"

"Except that night. I was mad at them and I didn't want to go to another community party. God, I hate those things."

The tires whirled on the wet pavement.

"We got into a fight—again. But this time I won."

Augustina thought about throwing her two cents in. Thought better of it. Waited.

"So they took off all huffy and self-righteous. But it was raining out. And icy. And I was pissed at them so I decided to stay at Sissy's for the night and not tell them. Let them worry, I thought." Ginger turned away.

Augustina put her hand on Ginger, but the girl shrugged her away. She could practically hear Mama and Papa egging her on. Tell her, they said, hold her. Say, it's not your fault. But all she did was glance at the girl, noted the way her hair fell straight down her back like a piece of night sky, the way her narrow shoulders sat square on her frame, the slow rise and fall of them. Ginger wiped her face with the sleeve of her army jacket.

"Sorry I slapped you," Augustina said.

"Forget about it," Ginger answered. "I was being a brat."

In the distance, the trees' fingerlike branches pointed in all directions, calling to the night.

"Your project is weird," Ginger said after a while. "You should have just shot those models. You should let me be one of them."

"They weren't real moms," Augustina said. "It was all wrong."

Ginger turned back toward Augustina, who looked to the road ahead of them, holding two hands on the wheel and weaving with the wind. "This is okay too," Ginger said.

"What?"

"You. Here. Finally."

❦

On the day of the shoot, Augustina made Ginger the mom wrangler. She took her stack of Polaroids and threw them down one at a time like cards in a poker game. "Wardrobe knows how to dress them—not high fashion, not chic, but clean and simple. If a mom doesn't feel comfortable in the clothes they give her, wardrobe knows to change them."

She went down the list—ten women—Amelia the baker, Juanita the nurse, Joan the lawyer, Malaya the dancer, Stella the waitress, Kim the maid, Ondra the retired principal, Lucy the basketball coach, and Shayna the stay-at-home mom. "Don't forget that Ondra is elderly, so you don't want her on her feet too long," Augustina said, waving her photo.

"And who else is wrangling them besides me and what is that?" Ginger asked.

"Just you," Augustina answered.

"Just me?"

"Make sure hair and makeup can find them when they want them. Same with wardrobe. Let me know once they're ready and I'll tell you when to bring them out."

"Just me?"

"Why not?" Augustina smiled.

❦

The shot was on the elevated platform at Armitage. There was an empty car with its doors slid wide open. Augustina called the mothers out one by one, and Ginger placed them on their mark, holding them by the hand or guiding them by the waist. The women sat at the windows of the car, or they leaned on chrome poles and stood in the aisle. Some of the mothers were placed outside of the car. Every woman was asked to face the camera, a wide-angle lens set as far back as the ticket booth, just by the stairwell.

Next to the moms, Augustina positioned their children—babies, high school kids, and grown men and women. Each mother put a hand or an arm on her child.

"Hot mommies," Ginger whispered in her ear.

Augustina nodded, her eye on the lens. "Thank you," she answered. "Good job, little Cruz."

When magic hour came, a soft breeze brushed through the train stop, the not quite setting sun lit each woman's face with a magnificent glow. The hems of their skirts fluttered. Augustina put her hand up to halt hair and makeup from swooping in. Stella, the woman from the shelter, stood in the center of the frame in jeans and a gauzy peasant blouse, her hair falling past her shoulders, her grown daughters flanking her. The sky was streaked with orange and red flares.

In the distance below, the storefronts of Lincoln Park rose up like ocean waves. Augustina leaned into her lens, surveying the shot, the way the bodies rolled across the frame like music, the way the women populated the train station. She took a breath and waited and when the time was right, she shot.

III

Deflowering the Sampaguita

First Holy Communion

First. Like never before. Like when you know everyone is doing it. Teenage girls sitting at the back of the bus among boys; older cousins with flip-teased dos and padded bras; the babysitter reeking of nicotine and cheap eau de toilette; most beautiful auntie who flies from Russia to China to Norway to you; Mommy, sleek and steady, smart and calm; and even your very old and shaky lola. They are doing it. Every week. Every Sunday. Some even every day. And up until now, on this, the first weekend in May, you have always been too young. Too innocent. Too irresponsible.

The priest has told you and an entire classroom of girls just like you: when you have matured. When you are able to understand and appreciate, you will have your turn. A chance. An opportunity to receive the body. To hold the body. To feel its texture on the tip of the tongue where you will hold Him. You will bond with Him. The first time is always the most special, Father tells you.

Until today, you were not part of the club. You watched the older women float down the aisle, arms held up in prayer, eyes lowered. For years, you have imagined yourself in line with them. Cloaked in white. Until today, you were not worthy. At last, it's your turn.

For the last month, you have spent your Sunday mornings preparing yourself. Locked up in the safety of your bathroom, you practiced walking down the narrow aisle—you lined your toes up and marched down the skinny row of tiles between the tub and the sink and toilet. Hands folded, eyes lowered, you walked right up to the edge of the full-length mirror. Stared yourself down, brown eye to brown eye. Studied the dark flecks in the center of your pupil. Looked for the light. The mystery. The glow you knew you'd possess once you received. "Body of Christ," you imagined Father saying.

"Amen," you answered. You stuck out your tongue, pressed it to the cold, hard reflection in the glass, closed your eyes the way you'd seen Tita Peachy close her eyes—lashes fluttering—and you imagined holiness coursing through your body. Your soul, light and winged, soared to places you had never known. Took you up to heaven and back, to the outer limits of the universe, maybe as far away as Jupiter. You left your body and, for a moment, you were one with God. You communed with Him and the saints and all the angels, tangible cherubs amid white gauze, luminous skies, and the clouds.

You know today you will know this. This is what you've been told. Here is how we come to learn of Jesus, our Savior. Here is what they tell us. First Holy Communion. Like the first time you are with the man you love—but they don't say that part. Even though they dress you up in white lace and pearls and satin and white veils. The nuns, the fathers, even your older brothers and sisters will tell you—First Holy Communion is just like that.

As girls, we are taught "The Way." Given all the tools. In our quest to be true, to have faith, to love, we seek love. Love of God and love of family and love, true love.

How You Learn About It

Slumber party. Sometime during fifth grade—the Barczaks' basement. You don't even know what they told you. Who knows? All those seedy details cloaked in giggles and whispers:

"Uh-huh."

"No way."

"Gross."

What you remember is the damp smell of cement. The gray bricks, steel poles cold as ice in the bottom of a McDonald's soda. What you see is the pitch of midnight and ten-year-olds clustered together like caterpillars wrapped tightly in their sleeping bag cocoons. That's when you first heard about it. And it was as true then as it is now. Yuck. Gross. No way my momma and daddy would ever do that. Why? It sounded so disgusting. And then the thought of it, awkward and misshapen—of the two of them doing *that*. No way.

What for? To make a baby. To make you and Danny and Tony. Unbelievable.

No talk that night of love and desire. No connections between wanting, needing, giving. No understanding of the body and how it can be this gift like springtime in February, or recess all day long, or chocolate for breakfast, lunch, *and* dinner. It was something grown-ups did to make a baby. You imagined they closed their eyes when they did it. You imagined they turned their faces away in embarrassment—like when someone has farted and you pretend not to notice.

Shouldn't someone have explained sex to you? Told you, this is what happens, here is what to expect, here is what to do. Shouldn't you have been trained for this?

Of course, the one you kiss is the one who teaches you. Together, you explore, experiment, nudge your way around a lip, and slip the tongue just so, across a row of teeth, smooth and white as a necklace of shiny pearls. Together you learn when to swallow, when to breathe, when to open your eyes. Together, you learn about dancing your body around his, how to slide an arm, a leg, a finger just so. You learn to alter breath, to whisper. You learn about timing, how it is everything. It is when you experiment that you learn the difference between love, lust, and the thing they share—desire.

But who tells you what it means? How come when the breathing falls and rises and falls, your hands want to move around? A kiss becomes a fondle, the fondle initiates the undressing. The hook unhooked makes zippers slide, buttons snap. Why is it when he rolls his hips over yours, dances his way into you, teasing you like this, you ache? Something blossoms wild, petals open petal on petal. You can hardly stand it and you don't know why. And what about that moment—you know the one—the no-turning-back moment where it doesn't matter if you love him or know him? What do you do then? What happens that moment you let go?

And what has that to do with love? When one body slides over another, and he slips part of him into you, and you find yourself floating to some distant planet—is that love? Does it have anything at all to do with companionship or friendship—and why is it more fun with some than others and is it about making babies after all?

Your mother should tell you. But your mother is silent. Babies are a gift from God, she says. She and your father love each other. They had to fuck each other to make you.

So what's a girl to do? What's she to think? How's she to find a life partner, without guidance?

Figure out sex on your own. Search and practice and watch. You may never make the connections. You may even come to think there are no ties between love, lust, and baby making.

Silence

With silence comes disapproval. What is not spoken is not happening. Not to men and women, not to married couples, and never to single women. And don't even dare think a boy and girl would ever—not even when no one's watching, not even when their parents have discreetly left the lesson out of all their never-ending lectures.

They taught you how to speak, how to listen, how to behave in every circumstance imaginable—to all your lola and lolo, to the uncles and aunties you are not related to, to your teachers, priests, nuns, and even to the strangers in the grocery store. You know how to make mano, offer anyone in a five-mile radius of your house something to drink, something to eat, a place to take a nap. Even now you hear your Tito Boy invite the plumber in. Say, "Wanna eat? Want rice? How 'bout a beer?" You know how to behave at baptisms, weddings, and even you, at five or six, have been briefed on the etiquette of funeral masses. You have been taught to respect people and their feelings, to be giving—so what's this? Why hasn't anyone told you how to act around a boy?

When the two of you are sitting so close that you feel him breathing; when the tiny wind that soars from the words he whispers spirals through you like some kind of strange monsoon. Suddenly you feel faint, your body melting like mozzarella on pepperoni and black olives—and what you want and how you act and what you say conflict with everything Father, Son, and Holy Ghost have not said. Your body has taken a turn—and from the way your family acts, you believe it might be for the worst.

At night, you shift the shade from your lamp; cast a giant shadow of your body across the wall of your teenage bedroom. You lift your arms up and with your eyes you trace your body—outline your breasts, tiny shells cupped and perfect. Circle the space where you imagine a heart. Slide your fingers down the length of you, in and out where the hips, not yet planted, but hopeful and anxious, will someday be. Brush the soft hairs, growing, silky like milkweed, hiding what? Covering whom? Protecting some buried treasure, or is it a curse? Is something wrong with your body? Why is it you like him so and still, you don't know how to say it and how to act when the heat of his body affects your skin, your muscles, you, like this.

Once your mother stood up high against the windowpane of the living room and watched you sitting on a tree stump, hand in hand with the boy next door. When he leaned into you, put his arm around you, she pounded on the glass. She shook her head at you. Later she forbade you to see him, speak to him. Hung the phone up on him when he called. Your father took to ignoring him, looked right through him when he stood on the threshold of the door, referred to him as "that guy." They never told you why.

What your mother didn't know is that while you sat there with him, listening to your transistor radio blurt, "All you need is love," a storm whirled inside your belly. A host of discrepancies inhabited your body like demons taking possession of your soul. You wanted to kiss him. You didn't. You liked him, but you knew you shouldn't. You wanted nothing more than to lie with him, naked, wrapped only in his embrace. You felt guilty thinking this was not a dirty image at all—it was beautiful. You didn't know why. And before your mother knocked on that glass, you were pushing him away from you, slapping him for touching you. Today because he did, tomorrow because he wouldn't.

Years later, you and your college boyfriend fall asleep on the couch, watching *The Way We Were.* Your parents, coming home from a Saturday night of poker and mah-jongg, suspect there must be something amiss when they enter a dark house.

BOOM. Your father's voice calls your name, your mother bangs the den door wide open, and streaks of light reveal their silhouettes, large, luminous, and angry. Their bodies merge, one gigantic torso. There are two heads. Arms flail in the night like giant bird wings swooping down on the two of you. "How could you do this to us?" your mother cries. "How could you?"

How could you do what? They never tell you. They never bring it up again. After your boyfriend leaves, the only thing your daddy says is, "Behave."

Here, the silence, unbearable, tense, and fraught with disapproval, leaves you confused. So you stop watching old movies. Refrain from references to Robert Redford and Barbra Streisand. You stop holding your boyfriend's hand in public. Pull away from him when your mother calls you. Move out of his embrace at the very mention of your family. Stop speaking altogether. Behave.

Say prayers instead. Read books. Go to theaters where it is impossible to fall asleep. Years later, avoid those questions, the ones aunties and uncles throw at you. "So when are you going to get married?" and "Do you have a boyfriend yet?" Keep your love life to yourself. Like them, remain silent. Pretend your silence is tantamount to abstinence, virginity, and holiness.

Deflowering the Sampaguita

With a group of your best Pinay friends, and their boyfriends, pile into a van and take over a local dance club. Dance less than a breath apart.

Crowd the floor like a cluster of red grapes, threaded together by a single vine. You have colored your mouth burgundy, teased your hair, and decorated your neck, your ears, your skinny brown arms with gold and copper bangles. You have stretched a cotton shirt, scoop necked and slightly swollen at the breast, around your body. Your pants hang low, slide across your hips, just about reveal your belly. You and your friends are fragrant, sweet, ripe. You draw your boyfriend close. He hovers above you. Gazes into your eyes. Runs his strong hands along your waist, torso, thigh. Dance holding hands. Move together. To the beat. Closer and closer. Close your eyes and he wraps his arms around you. Taken.

It is as though you move to that tribal gong. Your hips and legs move and sway, knees bend and pose, like a mountain princess crossing the river—head up, eye to eye. The drumming brings you closer; the bells chiming in the distance dispel reality. It is the kulintang, dense rhythmic drumming. And even though you were never a mountain princess, even though you never took a folk-dance lesson in your life, the pressure of the heels, down on the linoleum floor; the way you hold your back up straight, tall, and proud; the way you cast your spell, hypnotic and full as the golden moon; the way you float right out of consciousness is something that comes easily, part of your blood, indeed, part of your human condition.

Amid the confusion of what to say, to think, to feel, you lose yourself someplace in the middle of a kiss. Feel stars bursting, oceans washing up against your hips, water welling and brimming just below your pelvis, and before you can swim your way back to your senses, he is deep inside you. "This way," you whisper. Become part of this wave, this delightful tumult. Know nothing, only that you hope this feeling never stops. This is right. This is natural. This is your intuitive self, honest and true.

In the aftermath, chaos begins. Picture your mother and father, sitting in a pew before God and all the heavens. Think, better to die than ever let them know. Better to keep things a secret. Wonder how something this beautiful can be that wicked? Are you going to hell?

The very first time, when you knew little of love, when hormones controlled the sky and moon, he slipped in and out and in and out of you and you thought, *So?* He came and you said to yourself, "Is that all?"

And still, you couldn't help yourself, you opened up. Again and again. For years, you switched boys, lovers, men. You learned about give and take and generosity. You went surfing, riding a wave high, wild, free, and dangerous. Instead of "Is that all," you thought, "Please, let's don't ever stop." You learned the difference between fucking and making love. You preferred the latter and saved your body for men you loved. You liked it best when making love was also a good fuck. The act became a gift you shared with lovers.

And when a baby grows, you confess. Are sent away. You have a baby. You do one of two things: You give her away, like a door prize on Philippine Independence Day, or you bring her home and she becomes your baby sister. Your baby is not your baby. Your mommy no longer looks at you as if she were your mommy. Your daddy stops speaking. Be grateful, they tell you; you are lucky this is all.

The other Pinay from your First Holy Communion didn't get this far. Never got to see her babies. Sleeping was easier for her, dying was less disgraceful than bearing a child. There was no stopping the chaos in her body, no one to talk to, and there the fight died. And who could blame her? All that confusion bottled up inside, all that and a child to boot.

Or maybe you are one of the many who marry after all. Three months pregnant, twenty years young, loving your high school sweetheart. Nobody knows, just you and your boyfriend, your parents and his. No one tells. You bear your child, you bear many, and nobody is wiser. Not a word spoken. When your daughter and son grow, when their bodies change and their voices drift away from childhood, you begin the practice of silent disapproval; you continue the cycle. You insist on impossible chastity.

You live your life like a spy. Secret Agent 99, complete with a double life. Another you. The doctor daughter, the lawyer daughter, the wife daughter, the well-behaved daughter. You cook, you serve, you lead the family prayers. And when you leave your parents, you slow your walk. You sway. Smile. Whisper. Charmer you, you seduce knowingly. Walk into your cousin's office and kiss her boss on top of his head. Do it because you are young. Do it because you know this and a thousand other traditionally unacceptable gestures are things you and only you can get away with. When your ate tells you to cut it out, and, "Don't go kissing my boss on the crest of his balding head," say, "But he's so delicious." Your mother, who knows you better than you think, who secretly knows what it's like to be this young, this beautiful, this powerful, says, "You've got to learn to control yourself, iha, even if he is delicious."

Sex stimulates you like a drug, empowers you in new ways. Teaches you about walking around slinky and smooth, as if in constant dance. Teaches you that men want to do your bidding when you smile just so or look away just when. Sex and being sexy charms you. You can't help it. And when you try, when you let your two selves battle right and wrong, marry love and lust, there is nothing but turmoil. Your lover wonders why he can never do anything right. "You are a walking contradiction," he tells you.

Because there is family. Think. What if they found out? This prospect haunts you like ghosts in an old hotel. Pops up when you least expect, in the breath you take just after you've been together. Think if on top of defiling your body, you make a baby too. Run away, first choice. Suicide, second. No, suicide, first, run away after failed suicide. You would rather die. You would rather float away in a stream, clear and cold. Take me far away, you think, where Mom and Dad will never see me. Never be embarrassed because of me. Ultimately, you worry their worry is what others will say.

Wild and free, little white star with fragrant petals, you're left clinging to the vine that is the family. Face up to the sun, stretching out, reaching, but never breaking free, you are tangled in two worlds—wanting and not wanting. Speaking and silent at once. Filipina girl, American born and of two cultures, Western like MTV, tropical as the sampaguita, you are left alone to figure out the rest. Because no one dares to tell you that when he leans over for that first kiss, sinking into you long and slow, it is your First Holy Communion all over again. Spirit floating high in the sky and then, for an instant, for one breath, you are one.

Fighting Filipina

When the virus first hit and the nation went into lockdown, Mahal fled from Miami back to Milwaukee, face bound in double surgical masks. Every inch of her body was covered. She wore jeans and hiking boots, a navy hoodie covered her jet-black hair, and on her hands she wore fitted latex gloves.

No one would have recognized her, and still, when she got off the plane to make her connecting flight, people saw her coming and snaked around her, looked away from her. At first, she thought it was in her head, but then one college kid, no taller than her own five foot two inches, raced past her, shouldering a heavy duffel bag, and spat, "Fucking Chink." Mahal put her head down, took the blow like a soldier. Walked as if she didn't know the "fucking Chink" he was referring to.

On the connecting flight, an old couple sitting across the aisle asked to be moved. Their request stirred a commotion, with rows of people rising, bags being moved closer to the front. And then the seats all around Mahal were empty.

None of this should have been new to her.

●

When Mahal got to Lola Faustina's, she stripped down to her underwear in the mud room and ran through the house. Her grandmother trailed after her, waving her bony arms, in search of an embrace.

"Wait!" Mahal yelled, locking herself in the bathroom.

She ran scalding water, steamed up the whole bathroom, and let the needles of the spray hit her. Washed the travel off her skin. She felt so dirty. Germy. The mere threat of the virus attacked Mahal there in her gut, ate at her brain.

❀

One year later, she's back at school, scrolling through her phone, standing in the commons, waiting to pick up her dinner—a paper bag meal of chips, an Italian sub, and a dry chocolate chip cookie. She scrolls through the images, past loaves of freshly baked sourdough breads, past co-ed selfies masked like bandits, past digital memes for Black Lives Matters. She pauses on a video of a sixty-year-old tita in New York. The lady walks toward an ATM entrance, passersby on either side of her, when a Black man shoots around the corner and shoves her into traffic.

The tita's body takes flight backward. She slams into a parked car, slips down the hood of a blue Civic, falls onto asphalt.

Mahal bursts into tears. Calls Lola. Asks her, "Are you okay?"

"Are you crying?" Lola asks.

"No," she answers. "The mango trees are blooming everywhere. Allergies."

❀

The next time it happens, Mahal is in her dorm room, on Zoom for a remote history class. Her camera is off and the teacher drones into her mic, her voice fading in and out, her words garbled with intermittent Wi-Fi. Mahal turns back to her phone, scrolls and scrolls and pauses on the video of an old Chinese grandma in San Francisco, holding court in an open market, shouting in Chinese at the cameras. Her eyes are swollen black and blue, the bridge of her nose as fat as her finger. Her black cropped hair, spiked with shocks of white, is in disarray. She doesn't seem to care that none of the reporters understand her. She doesn't care that tears are streaming down her face or that her voice is cracking, her chest hiccupping. She holds a two-by-four in her hand.

A White man had attacked her on the square. In response, she grabbed a piece of wood and hit him back. Over and over. The video cuts to a wide shot, a security camera, from across the street. The people are small as ants on Mahal's screen, but she can see the old grandma thrusting the wood at the man, beating him as he attacks her.

Mahal doesn't feel it coming. Her body suddenly contorts, spasms. She yanks the wastebasket to her side.

The professor is calling her to turn on her camera. The Chinese grandma continues shouting and her voice fills the small dorm room. A call to action. A warning.

◦

Mahal cannot sleep. Whenever she tries, shutting the blinds in her dorm, playing white noise, or running a small fan in the room, a little tremor in her stomach persists, keeps her awake. She cannot shake this image of her lola, her superhero, cornered in the alley behind the shop, beating back White men in running suits. She video chats Lola first thing in the morning, then at lunch, and then shortly after six, every day.

"You okay, Lola?" Mahal asks. She studies her grandmother's face on the computer screen, how brown and wrinkle-less, how shaped the eyebrows, how severe the pout.

"Why you keep asking?"

Mahal holds up her cell phone where the Chinese grandma's image has been paused. Lola waves her away, frowns her whole face at her—the brows, the mouth, the nose, all collapsing in a singular act of disapproval.

Mahal shakes her head. "This shit is real, Lola."

Lola looks away from the screen, shaking her head.

"I'm serious, Lola."

And suddenly the screen goes dark. The video call ends. Mahal wonders how her grandmother could be so old and wise and stupid all at once.

❦

Orange couches line the floor's common area, arranged like a formal living room. A giant flat-screen television hangs across an empty wall, projecting images of K-pop boy bands. The girls from her floor scatter throughout the room, propped up on lounge chairs and giant bean bags. Thick hurricane-glass windows shield the girls from a wild wind whipping through palm trees. Mahal carries two big bowls of popcorn.

"Anyone seen Trudy?" she asks a group of girls piled up like throw pillows. She hands them the popcorn and a stack of plastic cups. She dips a red cup into the bowl and scoops herself a serving.

"Not since Sunday," says Avery.

"I think she's been moved to the hotel," says Liza.

"Dang Wuhan flu," Samantha says.

"Coronavirus," Mahal corrects her.

"Why you gotta be so racist?" Avery says, poking Samantha.

"Xenophobic," Liza answers, stuffing popcorn into her mouth.

"Okay," Mahal says, walking away. "Could you all spread out? Six feet apart. Don't want you to go missing too."

The freshmen pull away from one another, even as one calls out, "We're masked up!"

Mahal nods, waves. She takes the stairs down eleven flights.

❦

The lobby is as spacious as an art museum. The floors, spotless white marble, shine under fluorescent lights. A group of masked freshmen walk past her, call to her. At the front desk, she signs in, relieves Kendall.

"You ready, girl?" Kendall asks. "These residents are restless."

"I think Trudy's been sent to isolation."

Kendall holds up an arm. Mahal sighs, raises hers, and they touch elbow to elbow. "Give you a hug if I could."

Above, the residents buzz like bees, but down here, Mahal can hear the breeze knocking branches, palm leaves brushing one against the other like a soft broom swirling on wood floors. Around two in the morning, the elevator dings and two unmasked freshmen trip and stumble out the silver sliding doors. They walk and swerve, arms swinging by their sides, half singing their words.

"Oh!" says the blond boy, pulling on his mask and pointing at Mahal. "Wuhan flu over there!"

The other, a Black boy, swaggers toward the front desk. He turns the brim of his cap from front to back, lifts the bandana around his neck to his face. Teeters before her like a modern-day bandit.

"Don't get too close, bro!" says the first boy, throwing an arm out in her direction.

Mahal braces herself. Holds her breath. Then.

"What floor you boys on?" she calls out, texting Darnell and Candice to come.

"We on this floor."

"What floor you on, China girl?"

"First of all, don't call me 'China girl.' Second of all, you know you're not to drink on campus. And you can't be walking all over the building without your masks on. I am writing you up." From down the hall she can hear the squeak of Darnell's sneakers. When she sees the two come round the corner, she nods to them and gets up.

"Boys!" yells Darnell. "Are you inebriated?"

"Can you write them up?" Mahal says.

◦

In a bathroom stall, she pulls off her surgical mask, exhaling long and low. She's feeling waves of nausea rolling through her. Squats, head down on her knees, and lets the tears fall. She times herself. Five minutes.

She thinks of Lola Faustina sitting in her recliner, kicking back before late-night TV, asleep. She's safe, Mahal tells herself. She's home. Nothing's got her.

But then the boys, younger versions of those middle-aged assholes running through the streets, beating elders. The tremor in her stomach has moved to her leg. Her heel taps at the floor. Jiggles her leg. Tears come so fast she cannot catch her breath.

After five minutes, she blows her nose on the cheap industrial toilet paper, takes a breath, and makes her way out of the stall.

It's not like she's never heard that crap before. Chinese, Vietnamese, Japanese. But this? The virus runs people's hate to the surface like a fever and even though she knows not to take it personally, the incident leaves her breath stuck.

When she thinks about it, Mahal doesn't see that old Chinese grandma waving a two-by-four in her hand, taking down that White dude. She sees her lola—small, feisty, and loud. The guy has his hands up by his face. Cussing at her. Her lola talks him down in straight-up Tagalog, hurls punyeta and gago and letse at him. Swats him with her hairbrush. This image should calm Mahal, but the whole thing seems too real. She picks up her phone and the numbers light up. Three a.m. Too late to call Lola.

●

Last summer was rough. Lola pretended nothing was different. She had a habit of walking out of the house without the mask. She insisted on going to the lumpia shop on the bus and tending to the store.

"Lola," Mahal scolded, "do you want to get sick?"

"Fake news!" Lola said. Still, whenever Mahal caught the old woman, Lola rooted around in her pockets and pulled a crumpled mask out and attached it to her ears, her complaints muffled and lost.

One night, after protesting downtown, Mahal stepped into the kitchen covered in grime and sweat. She yanked her mask off her face and threw her sign down on the floor. At the sink she ran the water cold and cupped her hand under its flow. Drank.

"What's this?" Lola asked. "'Fighting Filipina stands with Black Lives Matter.' Ano ba yan?"

"You see what it is, Lola. My protest sign." Mahal dried her face with the back of her sleeve.

"Laging fighting, fighting," Lola said. "Why can't you just be content, iha?"

"If we don't stand up, who will?"

"Not your business," Lola warned her. "Why put yourself in danger? They're shooting rubber bullets, anak! You didn't even know the guy."

But she did know the guy. She knew the police. She knew the situation. When she saw that news, watched that cop on his neck like that, Mahal could not stop crying. She imagined her friend Troy under the weight of that man's knee. She saw Candice. She saw Darnell. It could have been *anyone*. "Lola," Mahal had pleaded, "don't you see? Breonna Taylor, Trayvon Martin, Eric Garner, Tamir Rice, Sandra Bland, Michael Brown—"

"Nakú, anak," Lola said, holding up her hand. "Hindi ka itim."

"You don't have to be Black to care, Lola. You can be an ally. Come on. Lolo would understand."

She felt bad arguing with her grandmother. Mahal knew she was being disrespectful, but she couldn't be silent either. She *had* to do something. Plus, she wasn't sure, but she thought she might have heard a tinge of racism in Lola's voice, in the way she said, "Hindi ka itim," like that should matter.

●

On her day off, Mahal drives to the beach near the lighthouse and sits near the water. It is just after a milky sunrise. She watches fog dissipate from the sea to meet the rain. The drops are soft and almost nonexistent. She thinks about the old Chinese lola's tears falling constantly like rain.

"That old woman could have gotten herself killed," Lola Faustina said on the night it happened.

"You sure you wouldn't have done the same thing?" Mahal had asked her.

"I wouldn't be walking around in a pandemic, not out where anyone can get you."

Lola was full of shit. She was probably going to the grocery store, pulling her metal cart behind her, walking into the Pick and Save, choosing her own vegetables and fruit, tapping at meat. Touching everything in sight.

Out here, Mahal knows there is nothing she can do about anything. Not about Black Lives Matter, not about the virus, not about those racist assholes beating up on poor Asian lolas and lolos. Not about her own lola sneaking out into the city to run her errands. So out here, she lets her worries rise like morning fog. Just for a moment. She takes a breath.

If she could, Mahal would quit school and babysit Lola for the rest of her life. She'd army up and send guardian angels to all the Asian American elders—all the aunties and uncles, all the lola and lolo. She'd take all the dead who had been accused of Wuhan flu and anoint them super angels, saints.

Mahal takes another slow breath in, closes her eyes, fills her lungs with sea air.

The waves calm her, until she hears a noise. A pelican skims the ocean surface, dives beak first right before her, wrestles a big old silver fish out of the sea.

◦

Class pops up online and Mahal's history professor and classmates populate the Zoom call like squares on a game show. It is a course called "Rebellion History." Each year, all the hippies-turned-professors teach this collaborative seminar, talk war and politics and protest. At the end of the course, faculty come together and perform on a stage somewhere on campus—as if they were rock stars. Mahal has been trying to get into this course and it's taken her three tries.

Goddamn Zoom, she thinks. If only they were in person. She sighs, waiting for the professor to turn her camera on. So far, the course has disappointed her. The teacher has turned all these historic moments into theories laced with academic jargon. She feels no people power. Mahal mutes herself and plays music while she waits.

When her grandfather was a student in the Philippines, he marched his campus, protesting martial law, fighting against the corruption of Marcos and all his rich, pomade-greased cronies. Her lolo went to jail for his beliefs. She grew up hearing those stories. Waited all her life to be in the position to raise her fist, but now, it's all online.

The course has gone through the Civil Rights movement, the Gay Liberation and the Feminist movements, and all of it sounded so far away and distant. Hours have been spent dissecting the drug, sex, and rock-and-roll culture of Woodstock. She has waded through footage of hairy White men and women protesting the Vietnam War. Mahal thought the studies on the different counterculture movements would inspire her. She thought they would give her a way of understanding the moment they are in now, but somehow, the course drags on as if they are enumerating great battles of the Civil War, or the Boston Tea Party.

When the professor unmutes her mic, shows up like a flare of white light on the screen, she talks for nearly seventy-five minutes. Her voice is a tide, soft and blurred, lapping the shore. Her words, bleached with theoretical rhetoric, wash over Mahal. Her mind floats far from the lecture.

When the teacher asks Benton a question about the New Left movement and receives no answer, she leans into the mic and calls to Benton, "Are you there, Benton? Turn on your camera. Benton, are you there?"

Mahal types in the chat, "Professor, are we ever going to study Larry Itliong and Cesar Chavez?"

No response.

"The 1960s Delano Grape Strike?"

Nothing.

"Filipino American icon?"

The online silence reverberates in feedback as the professor's voice calls out to Benton, "Stay after, Benton!" and "Your papers are due at midnight!" And before she can say anything at all, Mahal sees a flurry of squares flying off the computer, disappearing like distant stars. Her question hangs like a fingernail moon on the flat wide screen.

◊

"How's school?" Lola asks. Her head sinks at the bottom of the screen so all Mahal sees is her grandmother's brown forehead and the cap of her white hair.

"Frustrating," Mahal answers. "How's the shop?"

"Good," Lola answers. "If only I had customers ulit."

"Aha!" Mahal says, half smiling, half ready to scold her. "So you've been to the shop!"

"Anak, what's the crime of checking on my building? That's our insurance. That's how we pay for your school."

"But you can't get there unless you take the bus, Lola."

"Oo nga, that's right. I take the bus."

"If Lolo were here—"

"If your lolo were here, he'd say even now, like this, America is still beautiful."

◊

The next day, at her RA meeting, Mahal sits with Kendall, Darnell, Candice, and Jen, planning a building-wide program. Their team leader is a professor from Women Studies. Soft spoken, with a face that always looks a little worried, Karen offers them a dinner of tacos and yellow rice. Very bland, Mahal thinks.

"We should do something about the Black Lives Matter movement," Darnell says.

"Or," Candice says, "what about something around the coronavirus?"

"Maybe we could do something with the counseling center," Kendall says. "It's trippy when the residents go missing."

"Well," Karen says, "they're not really going missing. They're being quarantined."

"Yeah, but why don't they tell us that?" Mahal says. "Far as I know, they're going missing."

"It seems that way," Karen says, her eyebrows rising in concern. "But the law protects their privacy."

"Even if we're supposed to be responsible for them?" Mahal says. "That's fucked up."

Every Tuesday since they returned, the RA meetings are on the patio, just off the man-made lake, just under a circle of palm trees. A breeze makes the moments tolerable, but the heat Mahal feels is rising. She is unable to hold still.

The days pile up and one microaggression after another gets pushed to the bottom of her gut. She has lost her sense of direction. Were these people her friends? Was this school looking out for her?

"We should do something about this rise of anti-Asian violence."

"A Black Lives Matter event would have a bigger impact."

"There are also residents who are being affected by this anti-Asian violence."

"We could do something around the riots."

"They're not riots," Mahal shouts. She clenches her fists. She sucks air through her teeth, looking right at Darnell. "I read your write-up from the other night, the one about the boys? Why is it that even though I told you what happened all you wrote down was that they were drunk?"

"Well, yeah, they were drunk."

"They were calling out racial slurs, Darnell."

"I didn't hear it." He throws a fist into an open palm.

"I told you. That should have been enough."

"Then you shoulda written them up."

"Uh, kids," Karen says, patting Mahal's back, "maybe this isn't the time."

"Don't touch me." Mahal pulls away.

And then all the unspoken histories erupt from her—the Chinese Exclusion Act, the Japanese internment camps, Monkey Go Home slurs, the Delano Grape Strike, the WWII Filipino Veterano, all the Asian American elders slain on the streets because of a virus, a fever, an infection of hate.

Karen's lips wobble and the tears form.

"You have got to be kidding," Mahal shouts, standing. She nearly loses her balance. Her heart thumps heavy and fast.

Kendall reaches for her arm, but Mahal waves her away.

"Mahal," calls Candice, but it's too late.

Mahal paces the patio. Her arms sweep through the space, cleanse the air. She enunciates each vowel in case they think she is not speaking English. "What the fuck? Of all the people in the world, I thought you guys would get it!"

Darnell stares at his shoelaces, his body slumps forward as Mahal storms past him. Above them, Mahal catches a glimpse of the Chinese grandma looming in the sky, her face bigger than all that blue, eyes scrunched up, worry lines streaking in contrails across the sky. Her voice rising and falling, calling to Mahal. Mahal who is silent no more, who breathes with the lungs of a warrior, rising to meet the moment, arms up, fists held up, ready to fight.

The Kiss

Prudence Mercado watched the dark clouds approaching. From her penthouse garden, high above the Atlantic Ocean, she could smell the rain. Directly overhead, the sky was cloudless. Blue. But she could see the storm drifting east, the rain falling in dark sheets across the horizon.

"Should we go inside?" asked her nurse.

"Not yet," she answered. Prudence pulled her sweater tight around her torso. The breeze made her feel kissed by the sea. "Benita will be here soon enough. We can go in then."

Prudence placed two hands on her walker. The nurse moved toward her, but Pru waved her away. "Ako na!"

"Let me help."

"I said I can do it!" She waved the nurse away. She shifted her weight and pulled herself up. She released a deep breath. "Let me walk na!"

Prudence surveyed the roof garden as she wound her away around eureka palms, gardenia bushes, and banana plants. Her garden in the sky. Around the bend were gumamela, red and orange and hot pink blossoms, splayed open like the skirts of whirling dervishes. She reached down to pluck a flower, examined the petals and, turning to the penthouse railing, tossed the offering to the sea.

All around the high rise, the ocean hissed. The city, built on steel beams and concrete stilts, reminded Prudence of the archival photos she had seen of nipa huts perched on bamboo stilts and hovering over monsoon-swollen rice paddies. Her lolo-lolo's barangay rowed boats down a river of streets, passing tables, chairs, and dressers set adrift during month-long storms. That must have been something. That time long ago when people were cast and organized by the color of skin, by the faith practiced, by the money gathered, held onto, and spent. When men and women were unequal. When people raised a fist to the sky, proclaimed their heritage. Those times.

That was the time before the Story Revolution.

"Ate Prudence," said the nurse, "your niece is home."

"Lola Tita Pru!" Benita called from the sliding glass door. "A storm is coming. Come inside."

Prudence leaned on the railing and watched the sea crashing at the rocks below. "Not for a while," she answered.

"I brought your trophy," Benita said, making her way around the garden path. She held the golden blossom up.

Prudence said, "You keep it."

Benita reached her Lola Tita Prudence and leaned toward her to kiss her hello.

"Oh, so now you are giving kisses!"

"Lola Auntie!"

"How could you? After everything Rosario has done for you? Nakú. Nakakahiya."

Long ago, the country, a nation of digital natives, swiping, posting, tweeting culture and opinion, perpetuated social injustice by ignoring all others' stories. Pru and her sister-activists organized a national rebellion. It took several generations to rewrite the stories of that nation they called home. At 103, Prudence was among the last of the living Story Revolutionaries.

Last night, Benita climbed the steps of the Jackie Gleason Theater to accept Pru's lifetime achievement award. Rosario Trinidad, Pru's former student and an academic scholar of the time, narrated the origin of the Story Revolution.

When the moment came to deliver the award, Rosario handed the trophy to Benita and planted a kiss on her cheek.

A kiss!

The audience gasped. The house lights flashed. Assistants in gender-neutral formal wear whisked Rosario off that stage before it went dark. When the lights came back up, Benita had disappeared.

Public kisses had been taboo for years. No touching. No hand-shaking, no hugging. No jabbing for jokes. No kisses.

"How could I what, Lola Auntie? She kissed me! And on public television! What was I to do?"

"She's like an older sister to you!"

"Then she should have known."

Prudence explored her niece's face, how the eyebrows bunched up into one long line, how the mouth puckered. The scowl was too familiar. She reminded Pru of her own mother. So strong and defiant. Benita's hair was thrown into a messy ponytail and strands fell all around her face. Pru did not know what to do. She could not understand the lack of loyalty.

"You canceled her."

"I did not cancel her. Her actions canceled her."

"And when you saw her the week before, at dinner. Did she kiss you then?"

"And I kissed her, but that was different. That was private."

"Where is your dignity?"

●

Instead of celebrating Prudence Mercado's revolutionary work, online journals posted Rosario's kiss. They played the moment over and over, slowing it down. Rolled that video. Rosario standing tall as she delivers her speech and then her body curving into a giant question mark, her lips pulling off to the side, smooching Benita's cheek. Just barely.

Hashtag R. Trinidad Breaks Social Code. #StolenKiss #WasIt Appropriate?

People returned Rosario's books to stores unread. Sales dropped. Professors denounced her work on NPR. Commentators over-analyzed the kiss.

Rosario went into hiding. And Benita? She posted the video and canceled Rosario too.

Prudence pulled on the threads of her sweater. She turned away from Benita and breathed in the sea air. In the distance, thunder boomed. The breeze on the roof had turned cool. The clouds were moving closer.

"Your ate Rosario is bringing dinner," she said, turning her walker away from her great-grandniece and moving toward the wall-size glass doors. "You'll stay."

§

Benita's parents drowned when she was only ten. Both sets of grandparents had disowned them for taking part in Lola Tita Pru's revolution, so Lola Tita Pru took her in. Raised her.

The moon was a tiny coin of light. Benita watched the rivulets of rain running down the glass walls. The penthouse greenery, a replica of Miami gardens before the sinking, blurred. Palm trees leaned like dancers back bending, their leaves spread out like slender arms reaching for the patio dirt. The wind whistled.

Lola Auntie's revolution was so old, it had become an institution. Benita and her generation no longer believed that people were reading stories. No longer hungered to speak their histories. No longer integrated politics into their art. It was time to move on. Live in the moment. Because of the revolution, there was equality in all things. Benita's murals were abstract colors, shapes connected to no message, no lesson, no past.

She agreed to be the one to accept the award because she was a descendant of Lola Auntie, a student of the presenter, a catalyst for the future.

A gust of wind whipped the plants into a frenzy and the rain-drops fell in sheets across the windowpane.

Benita fiddled with the remote and turned the volume up. The beats of the music reverberated in the room, challenged the storm outside, silenced the thoughts rising from within. Lola Tita Pru meant well, but her ways were old. Her tools, outdated. Her relevance—well.

The kiss was quick. Familiar. The kind they exchanged every week at Sunday dinner. Benita almost didn't react. She was stand-ing on that stage, lights blinding her. Ate Rosario was going on and on when Benita spaced out for a moment. Thought about the after-party for just one second. And then there was Ate Rosario mov-ing in, so close everything went out of focus. The kiss smacked the air, not her cheek, but all the same, it was a kiss. And the lights went dark.

When she realized what had happened, the sweat came on her, a kind of raining from the inside out. "Oh shit," she said, "oh shit, oh shit, oh shit!" What just happened?

Benita ran down the steps, the golden flower in her hand. She sprinted down the aisle and out the doors.

"Benita!" called her auntie. "Do you want us to go deaf?" The old woman rolled in on her wheelchair. Her voice soared above the storm. "Turn that music down."

Ate Rosario entered through the doorway, her posture slumped, her steps uneven. She handed the nurse two giant shopping bags of food.

"Your ate Rosario has brought us dinner."

Ate Rosario approached Benita. Just the sight of her brought tears to Benita. "I'm sorry," Ate Rosario said.

"I'm sorry too," Benita answered.

"Are you really?" Prudence asked.

"Of course I am." Benita placed her arms around Rosario. "I am sorry, Ate."

"Then you will say it publicly?" Prudence asked. "You will re-instate your mentor, then?"

"I can't."

"Wala kang kahihiyan."

◦

Rosario kept her head down, pushing vegetables and rice around in the broth. The sound of spoons and forks clicking on china accentuated the thunder outside.

"Remember when tinola had chicken?" Prudence asked.

"We used to make it with pork," Rosario said. "That was in Iowa."

"Gross." Benita's face scrunched up. "Carnivores. Planet killers."

Prudence wiped her mouth with her napkin. She moved the pechay and ginger around with the curve of her spoon, asked Rosario, "How are you?"

"I'm okay."

"Good. Don't let it get to you," Prudence said. "Your work is solid. This will pass and you'll be stronger for it."

"Right," Rosario said, sighing. "I know."

Rosario thought about all the work she had done, all the stories she had told and the ones she still wanted to write. She let worry move through her. Could she lose tenure?

"What possessed you to kiss her on stage?"

"I got swept up in the moment," Rosario said. "And she looked so much like you when you were young. So beautiful."

"That's offensive, Ate," Benita chimed in. "We don't call people beautiful. Remember?"

"But—"

"I think she looks like my mother," Prudence said. "She was beautiful."

Rosario studied under Prudence at the university shortly before the Story Revolution. She worked as her teaching assistant, a quiet young woman from Iowa. Her grandparents had been part of the third-wave movement of Filipino immigrants to the U.S., medical professionals who left the Philippines during the Great Brain Drain. She had been raised in the middle of nowhere.

"Nothing but corn," her mother used to say.

"Go back to where you came from," her father's patients used to say.

Her classmates were children of pig farmers. She was a casualty of their jokes.

"Ching-chang-chong," they used to say, tugging at the corners of their eyes.

"I'm not Chinese."

At recess, she used to climb the oak at the corner of the schoolyard and sit on a limb, reading books. She loved the one about the girl rebel who was a pest, who walked with her arms akimbo and got into everyone's business. That girl was her hero. But in those days, all the girls in those books were the same. Not pig farmers' daughters, but blondes, blue-eyed, pale-skinned.

In college, Rosario found Prudence's novel about teenage Filipinas living on the West Coast in the 1980s. When one of the protagonists was admonished for swimming all day ("You'll get too dark," said the mother), Rosario teared up.

Of course, that was in a time when people still claimed their nationalities. Filipina, Chinese, Korean, Jamaican, Nigerian, and Dominican. Can't do that anymore either, Rosario thought. Too divisive.

"We've come so far," she said.

"Too far," Prudence muttered.

"And here you were—Professor Prudence Mercado, the last living Story Revolutionary, receiving a lifetime achievement for the advancement of human rights." Rosario's voice cracked. "I was overcome with emotion."

"Public spaces are no place to have feelings," Prudence said.

"If she says that's what she felt, it's what she felt," Benita chimed in. "She's allowed her feelings."

"Is that so," Prudence asked. "That's why you abandoned her."

"She had no choice," Rosario answered. "She has to protect herself."

"You're defending her?" Prudence asked.

"She's a public figure too," Rosario said. "A rising artist."

◆

Shards of lightning illuminated everything. Thick gray clouds blanketed the stars. Boom! The thunder. Boom! The thunder.

Inside, the women's voices rivaled the storm. All clamoring at once. All losing their practice—to listen, to reflect, to wait to respond. To respect one another. The building lost power and the room went dark. Silent. The tempest swept across the ocean and hit the windows.

Benita's phone blew up too. One flash after another. She pushed it to the side.

"Lola Auntie," she said.

"Don't 'Lola Auntie' me," Prudence said. "And answer that damn phone." Pru reached across the table to slide the phone to the girl.

Entitled. As much as she hated the word and did not want it in the house, the way Benita glared at her tonight, the way she said Rosario's kiss triggered her—triggered her—only made Benita out to be a privileged child. The very thing they fought so hard to end.

Nurse darted into the room. Gave them all a stern look. "We are calm, right? No blood pressure rising, no angry shouting?"

They quieted down and stared at Nurse.

"Benita was just sharing the news," Rosario said. "She has been commissioned to create a mural in the sky. Who is that, Benita?"

"The Museum of Digital Stories," Benita answered.

"Sige, call me if you need anything, Ate Prudence. Watch your blood pressure."

◆

Years ago, Prudence got stopped at ORD by the TSA coming back from the PHL that very JUL. It was the year President No-One-Names rejected six Muslim nations from entering the country.

"Hold your hand out," said the guard.

She offered her palm, etched deep with wrinkles—lifelines, heart lines, money lines. The guard swabbed her hand. "I have to go through your bags," he said.

He rummaged through all of them. Pulled her books out, splayed the bindings open, exposed the words under fluorescent lights. She watched each book run through the X-ray machine:

Radical Hope

On Tyranny

We Should All Be Feminists

Create Dangerously

We Gon' Be Alright

Her Wild American Self.

"What are these for?" he asked her.

"Reading," Prudence answered.

"Don't be smart. You're already on the edge, lady."

And her journals. Pru had been traveling for weeks and she had three fat handwritten journals. Each entry had been scribbled in dark blue pen on recycled paper. Her letters scored every line as deeply as the wrinkles of her palms. The guard ripped pages from the binding, held them up. "What language is this?" he asked.

"What's it matter to you? My words. My thoughts. Private."

Hank, her husband, a silver-haired man with translucent skin, looked over her shoulder and said, "Are you kidding me? That's just bad penmanship!"

"Calm down, sir," said the TSA man at the conveyor belt. "Just a routine random check."

Hank huffed and sighed. "You know," he reasoned, running his hand through his hair, biting his lip as he did, "even if she was Muslim, which she is not, you have no right!"

The TSA called for reinforcement. They called for translators. They brought in German shepherds with their black snouts and their perky ears.

A female guard pulled her aside as security scanned the lines of Prudence's poetry. Each letter moved—fell into backbends, spun in wild circles, soaked in ink and bleeding through the page.

"What is this?" they demanded.

"Do you have a bona fide relationship with the United States of America?"

"If so, prove it. Read these pages out loud."

"For God's sake!" said Hank. "She's an American citizen! You've got her passport!"

She refused to read to them.

The lady guard said, "I will touch you now. First, your arms."

Prudence held her head up, raised her limbs like wings.

The gloved hands patted her arms.

"Now your torso."

Rumpled her breasts. Cinched her waist.

"I will touch your back now."

Tap-tap-tapped her shoulders, her lower lumbar, her ass.

Pru held her breath.

"Spread your legs," said the guard as she ran her hands down Prudence's legs.

She looked past the guard, at a sign that read "Recombobulation Area."

"Now my hands will go between your legs."

"Is that necessary?" shouted Hank.

She shut her eyes. Refused to cry.

"Perhaps," said the male guard who began the inquisition, "she is not who she says she is. Perhaps this," he held up her U.S. passport, "is fake. Where are you really from? Vietnam?"

She looked down at her feet. They were bare. The red nail polish chipping, the skin on her heels, flaking. She wanted her sandals back.

"Answer us!" said the guard. "Or we will call the FBI!"

"The FBI?" yelled the husband. "Come on!"

Pru shot him a look, hushed him.

"Get this line moving!" yelled another passenger. "We have a flight to catch!"

◉

Prudence waved her hand, signaling for more wine. Benita poured. The rush of the pinot noir filled the glass.

"Ate Pru, that time you got stopped by the TSA?"

"Yes."

"What did you feel at that moment?" Rosario asked.

"What do you mean? I didn't feel anything. I was pissed."

"Oh, I see where you're going," Benita said. "Her feelings of anger led her to action."

"The Story Revolution," Rosario said.

"My feelings did not make me do anything," Prudence said, downing her wine all at once. "More," she told her great-grandniece. "Don't tell Nurse."

◉

Prudence was held for three days in a room with other persons the TSA deemed dangerous. Other so-called Muslims. Hank charged off to retain a lawyer, to call on Congress, to write his senator.

Her one phone call went to a sister-friend, Zara, the Arab American poet from Michigan. She was an organizer. An activist. The sister-friend notified their people—emerging writers and poets of color. And they called on writers from an Asian American Pacific Islander NGO, and they brought in visual artists, musicians, and DJs from the Black and Latinx communities. These storytellers as well as poets and songwriters from the Indigenous tribes sat their asses down and wrote. They enlisted creatives from the LGBTQ and nonbinary communities. They fought President No-One-Names on his terms. But they used bigger words. They argued complicated thought patterns that threw President No-One-Names off his game. The journalists joined the army of Word Warriors. Even Fox News fell in line. Right. Fox was not always progressive, so back then it was a big deal. Instead of insults, they hurled:

Truth.

Facts.

Evidence.

Law.

Patience.

Forgiveness.

Understanding.

"I never should have had children," Prudence said. She rolled her chair to the window, searching for the moon in the chaos of wind, cloud, rain.

"You didn't," Benita said. "You are not my mother."

"Benita," Rosario said, rising. "That's no way to speak to Ate Pru."

"I fight my own battles, Rosario," Prudence said. "I am your elder, Benita."

"Ageism."

"Benita!" Rosario snapped.

"Forgive my bratty thirty-year-old triggered niece, Rosario. It seems I have spoiled her."

"You hypocrite, Auntie!"

"It seems she has forgotten where she has come from," Prudence said.

"Makes no difference where we come from. Hasn't mattered for years!"

Benita grabbed an empty bottle of wine, poured into the air all the nothingness of it. Stormed off, her slippers slapping at the marble floors. She shook her head as she walked away. She sighed.

◊

Benita tossed the glass bottle down the recycling chute, waited for the bottle to hit the receptacle underneath the building. Echoes of the ocean rose from the chute.

The kiss was innocuous and if it were up to her, she'd have stayed silent. Gone invisible. She did not want to draw attention to the kiss or Ate Rosario. She loved her mentor. But her agent kept calling. *You have to do something.* And then her followers. *#NoKissingBenita! #JusticeforBenita!* Lola Auntie had no idea how one wrong tweet could cancel her forever. How silence could work against you.

Benita stomped her way to the wine cellar, dashing down a flight of stairs, hand on the rail, hair flying in her face. The heat of the alcohol flushed her skin, exacerbating her irritability.

She nearly waited too long to say anything. Her sky murals were finally being noticed—not just by the international art scene, but the digital platforms too. Her images were trending. Social media was like a mumu under her bed, keeping her from a good night's rest. In the end, she knew Ate Rosario would understand.

In the wine cellar, she ran her fingers along the shelves— cabernet, malbec, zinfandel. She pulled a pinot noir off the shelf.

Before tonight, she might have changed her mind. Found a way to play the diplomat. But Lola Auntie was so fucking bossy. Every time Lola Auntie told her what to do, Benita did the opposite. She couldn't help it.

●

In those days, "a bona fide relationship with the United States" was code for being a fifth-generation American citizen of Northern European ancestry. People were divided among themselves, and wars erupted over issues like God and unborn babies and the right to choose who to love.

It was impossible for people like Prudence Mercado to prove she had a bona fide relationship with the U.S. because she was Brown. Because even if you carried your papers, you could be stopped, jailed.

"Give her time," Rosario said. "She'll come to it on her own."

"We took it too far."

"What would Zara advise?"

"Zara?" She imagined her sister-friend and her frenetic mane of curly black hair, standing before the crowds of writers and poets at open mic protests, fist pumping the air, poems streaming from the speakers, the crowd chanting pantoums alongside her. "She hated public displays of affection," Prudence said, finishing off her glass of wine.

Tonight, she could not look directly at the girl. Too mad. Instead, she examined the skies through the glass. She wanted to stop fighting. To love the girl. To thank Rosario. To enjoy their dinner. But she was so mad. She felt neither love nor forgiveness and it was a relief.

When Benita returned with a new bottle of wine, Prudence ignored her. Benita stood, waiting to be acknowledged. Prudence continued to gaze out the window, examining the reflection of her great-grandniece.

⬦

The Story Revolution took off, at first. Poets, writers, digital storytellers typed and keyed and posted and swiped their stories all hours of the day. Testimony, the first-person kind, was read by and processed by almost everyone. People began listening. Reading. Not because they wanted to learn, but because they wanted to know, *and then what happened?*

But not even three weeks in, writers' block descended on the word warriors. The artists got bored and distracted and went out for coffee. A lot. Publishers lost their criteria since everyone's story mattered. Bad poetry was published. The writers, also readers, stopped reading other people's stories and only read their own, out loud and in public.

The nonreaders—the game show junkies and reality show mavens—lost interest. Who cared what happened? Nothing was at stake.

Story armies went AWOL.

Baseball season began. The country divided itself up by teams— the Brewers, the Yankees, the Red Sox.

Prudence lost heart. Almost quit.

"No," Zara told her. "It's part of the journey. Don't quit."

Then the libraries closed. No one had access to words bound on paper. Librarians digitized everything. Books were no longer printed but evaporated into a cloud. And the cloud was locked. And the password was forgotten.

Worst of all, the people stopped listening. Reading.

Reluctantly, Prudence began posting selfies and memes and writing poems in the form of tweets, calling everyone back. She and some of the Story Revolutionaries, the true believers, wrote through the dismal nights, never stopping. They workshopped their stories, editing them, rewriting them, copy editing them before posting. The community bonded.

There was some traction, but it seemed everyone was watching the playoffs, donning ridiculous hats, wearing matching jerseys.

And then the World Series.

On the night of the final game in a series between the Los Angeles Dodgers and the Miami Marlins, the players took off their caps during the national anthem and never put them on again, not that night. They took the singer's mic captive. Instead of swinging a bat and hitting a ball, the players stood at home plate, mic in hand, and shared their stories.

There was booing. Heckling. The tossing of empty plastic cups. But the stories were so real.

And then, after each player, each Rodriguez, Aguilar, Jimenez, each Ito, Galang, Jackson, each Harris spoke, the stadium began to cheer. One section raised their arms and all the sections followed, roaring as the fans participated in the longest-running stadium wave ever.

"Who else knows this story?" Manny Garcia yelled.

Pandemonium.

All the writers banged on their keyboards anew. Conducted searches. Reopened libraries and touched books once more.

●

"That story is so old," Benita said. She took a swig of her pinot noir. "Why must you tell it over and over? What is baseball, anyway?"

"This has become too abstract," Rosario said. "Your generation does not know and cannot feel what it was like."

"Well, wasn't that the point of your Story Revolution?" Benita asked, rolling her eyes. "To eliminate injustice?"

Prudence wiped the windowpane with the sleeve of her sweater. The storm outside was abating. She could make out the fronds of her coconut palms. She took a deep breath and blew on a smudge and wiped it clean. The family resemblance was strong.

What was the point of the Story Revolution?

The wind swept through the garden and leaves spun up and into the night sky. They sailed off the balcony. She wished her mother were here. She missed her so much. Benita was among the few descendants left.

"Come here," Prudence called to Benita, raising her arms.

Benita exhaled long and then walked up to her. Prudence watched as her figure came closer in the reflection, waited as Benita stood behind the wheelchair. Benita leaned forward, and stooping, she wrapped her arms around the old woman.

"Yes, Lola Auntie?"

Prudence closed her eyes. No hugging. No touching. No kissing. She pulled her great-grandniece close and felt Benita's body, wiry and lean, against her own small shape. "I suppose I will have to cancel you now?" Prudence whispered, sniffing at Benita's skin.

"You better not," Benita said.

Prudence felt a rush of energy coursing through her. There would be no changing of minds. This great-grandniece was too much. The point of the Story Revolution disarmed Pru. Calmed her. Gave her all the feels.

Imelda's Lullaby

Imelda lies on a cot at the foot of the old woman's bed. The air con hums just under la Doña's snoring respirator. Across the room, the curtains blow just high enough to reveal a sliver of the moon. Imelda squints, wishes Manila were outside that window, not Miami.

La Doña is thick-boned and fat and so still. Imelda rises, just to check. She places her small hand on the old one's belly, lets it rest until she feels the fall and rise of la Doña's breath. Asleep like this, dead like this, there is something beautiful about the old one. The lines on her face smooth away like creases on silken sheets and the cheekbones slope high like soft hills. The mouth, hidden under the mask, sets in its eternal pout. La Doña insists on lipstick. "What if there's emergency in the middle of the night? Y mi cara? Fea." Even sleeping she is difficult, Imelda thinks. Plastic rollers and thick black bobby bins circle the old woman's face, a magnificent pink halo.

Awake the old woman's fea comes out. She screams fast Spanish, swallows her consonants, and spews bits of chewed-up food at Imelda. La Doña, widow malcriada, living at the edge of the Gables, her children scattered like seed—New York, San Francisco, Chicago. Not a single one fallen close to this old tree. This vieja reminds Imelda of her auntie Remedios, the family spinster unable to keep her nurses. They run away on her. Climb the iron gates and slip across borders like butiki in the night.

"Tao yoon," she told her auntie once. Why make them sleep on floors?

They are help, her aunt answered. "Hindi pamilya. Hindi kaibigan. I pay them to work. Beds are for guests."

●

Imelda wipes la Doña's brow. At least you give me a cot, she whispers. A breath escapes the old woman, deep and low like a secret. On nights like these, Imelda thinks about Manila, where it is daylight and the city is thick with traffic. There, cocks crow and everyone wakes to their melody. There, sunlight surrounds the houses, fills them with the city noise.

Back home, Imelda was the youngest of three daughters. Her mother taught the sisters how to direct the cook, the labandera, the katulong who scrubbed the floors. She went to all-girl convent schools and never talked to boys, though she knew they were watching. And when she was twenty, she married Armando Chin, a businessman who owned a screw factory. He was ambitious and worked long hours. He gave her a house in Makati with marble floors and terraces filled with sweet sampaguita blossoms. They raised a beautiful family. He gave her everything. I was always too nice, she thinks to herself.

La Doña spits up thick mucus and Imelda leaps to her bedside, holding the mask off the bitter face and gently washing with a damp towel. The old body seizes then crumples up like used tissue.

"Leave me, China!" she shouts.

"Espera, señora," Imelda says.

"Para!" Her arms lift up. The hand sprawls, fat and lush. The red fingernails try to dig into Imelda's light skin.

"Tranquila," she tells the old woman. "Or I will sing."

Imelda holds her breath, but the sour smell of the dying soaks into her own skin. And still, she washes little rivers of vomit that have trickled down la Doña's chin. Wipes the perspiration from her own brow.

"Did my son call?" asks la Doña.

"No, señora."

"¿Y mi hija—Ninguno de los dos?"

"No, señora."

La Doña might have been an old spinster. The phone in the house never rings.

"What do you know," la Doña says. "You're not even a nurse."

"No, señora, I'm not. But I am all you have."

"Cheap help."

"Your only help."

"Illegal help, China."

Imelda ignores the insults, though her Spanish is nearly excellent. Instead she thinks, Holy Mary, Mother of God, pray for us. She sings to the old woman. And that's when she sees la Doña has wet her bedding.

❦

When Imelda found the letters, she threw his things out the balcony—didn't even bother to bag the laundry, to box the toiletries, to unplug his clocks and stereo and speakers. Those things she yanked from the walls and hurled onto their terrace patio to crash and scatter.

He cut her off. He cut the children off. He told her she had grown soft and plain and matronly. "What did you think I would do?" he asked her.

How could she have missed this? Fifteen years.

She found a job in the Ayala Museum and fed the children herself. She spent money on them as if he were still in the house. Margarita went to the beauty parlor twice a week to have her coarse hair blow-dried for one thousand pesos each visit. Jun-Jun partied with his barkada at swanky clubs and hotels in Makati. She held onto the help.

"Mahirap kami," she told the cook. She paid her a little less and started washing dishes.

"Please, ma'am. Don't. Nakakahiya."

"Please. Kitchen ko. I am the one who is embarrassed."

She gave the maids weekends off and learned to wash the laundry.

❦

"Don't handle me like that, China," snaps the old lady. "I'm not a baby."

"Permiso, señora," she answers, head bowed, eyes down. But inside she thinks, and yet you soil yourself as if you are.

Imelda must bend her knees and take a breath to roll the old woman to her side, to pull the sheets out from under her, wash her backside dry. "Let me clean you first and then we'll sit up."

"It's the middle of the night, China."

"Just for a while. Until I change the bedding."

"You'd think they'd check on me—just once or twice. Me estoy muriendo."

"You are not dying."

"¿Eres médica?" Silence. "I didn't think so, China."

It isn't just the urine, the pale yellow of human stink rising from wet sheets, it's the smell of decay, of breath fermented by the night. Imelda rolls the body bit by bit, singing softly to herself, turning the backside, the torso, the shoulders. She washes the vieja with her right hand, with her elbow, with her whole body and with the other arm, she holds her up.

"China, you're too small to handle this."

"I do, don't I?"

"Faster, China. I'm cold."

La Doña's body is a loaf of unbaked bread, oozing from her frame, and under this moonlight it appears to be rising fast. Imelda closes her eyes.

❦

Because she loved her children more than anything, because she couldn't let them know the truth—they were poor and their father had abandoned them—because there was nothing else to do when Jun-Jun showed up bruised and begging after weeks of gambling, she borrowed four million pesos to pay off Jun-Jun's losses, to afford Margarita's lifestyle at the Rockwell, to pay for her tourist visa and to arrive here in the United States of America as Mrs. Armando Chin. She let her visa lapse. Went into hiding and waited.

When she heard about la Doña she considered the job a blessing, a secret to fix her problems. Dollar to pesos, she'd make the money back in months, she thought. She considered the alternatives—to turn to Armando and beg; to admit defeat to her elders; to marry a rich old White tourist; to sell everything they owned; and worst of all, to refuse Margarita and Jun-Jun—but none of it made sense to her. Always too nice, is what Auntie Remedios told her.

"You let those children walk all over you. You spoil them."

"I love them, Auntie. It's not their fault."

Imelda was different than her sisters. Her sisters married well too, but they never befriended their katulong. They never apologized for anything. Once, her ate invited her husband's kerida to their eldest daughter's wedding.

"Why not," her ate told her. "She has a husband too. And a reputation. Why make a scene."

●

"Cuidado, China! I am old. I'll break!"

Imelda lifts the old woman from the bed, heaves her gently onto two feet, and shifts her into the wheelchair. "This will only take a moment," she says.

"I am not a baby," says the old woman, struggling as Imelda straps her in and places a soft flannel blanket over her knees.

"Do you want to fall?"

"Are you never in a bad mood?" When Imelda doesn't answer, the old woman snorts. "Me molesta, China."

"Do you want to sleep on dirty sheets?"

She peels the soiled linen from the bed, her hands gracing the wet stains. The smell suffocates her. The curtains blow up. The glittery moon—thin like a fingernail, hooked like a sly smile—is running fast away from her.

"What happened to your husband, China? To your children? Why aren't you with them?"

"Can't you see I'm working? Your children treat me well."

"They pay you well, you mean. You don't fool me, China. Something bad happened. No?"

"You and el señor left Cuba."

"We had no choice."

"So then, we are the same, ma'am."

"Maybe you are running."

◉

Every minute since she arrived, her life with la Doña is a series of castigations, war dances, word battles of the mind. It doesn't matter, Imelda thinks. La Doña's old and she has no one else. Even though she's figured it out, she won't turn Imelda in.

Every month, Imelda wires money to the children. Some of it for their living expenses, some to pay off the loan. She sends the money to Jun-Jun and in this way, she makes her way home little bit by little bit. Five years now and it seems the U.S. dollars are barely making a dent, but she keeps working.

She takes a deep breath and hoists la Doña back into her bed. She takes the curlers out of her hair, one by one.

"But it isn't daylight," says the old one.

"You should rest now, with your head on a pillow." She brushes the brittle curls out and runs her fingers through the old woman's scalp. She sings just under her breath.

"Louder," says la Doña. "If you're going to sing, then sing."

The melody comes out of her like waves pushing gently through the ocean. The stars come out like children, watching the old woman waft into a deep sleep. This is the song she sang to her own boy and girl, cradled in her arms, dancing in the middle of the night. La Doña's eyes close. She takes a deep breath, and slowly sleep comes.

◉

The morning is dark. The moon lights through the window. The phone rings and wakes Imelda out of the first moment's rest she's had. The voice at the other end of the line, distant and cutting in and out, is crying. There has been a death.

"Paano?" she asks.

"Is it for me?" calls the old woman from the bed.

Imelda holds her breath. Listens. "He lost all of it?"

"Is it my son?"

She cradles the phone in her neck. She brushes the tears away. "Sige," she says. "I have to go."

And when she returns to the old woman, she tells her it's nothing. She fluffs the pillows and straightens her comforter. "Wrong number," she says.

And when la Doña's eyes close again, she slips out of the house and sits under the waning moon, deep in the green of la Doña's tropical garden. She listens to the palm trees rustling—hush, hush, hush. She inhales air, humid and soft like home. She understands now she can never go back.

Labandera

Washing

Malaya squats at the bottom of the hill, a plastic tub of dirty linen flush against her thighs. Seven a.m. and a jackhammer rips the sky open, grates against the bellow of jeepney horns. This early in the morning and trucks belch diesel fumes. Water spills from the tub, cooling her calloused feet. She looks over her shoulder to a row of cardboard houses and aluminum rooftops. She eyes her shanty. A bed sheet flutters light as butterfly wings. She squints, searching for her granddaughter.

"Are you ready, anak? You'll be late."

She yanks at the collar of a white cotton shirt. Lipstick bleeds from its corners. She wonders who has done this, the Sir's wife or the Sir's mistress? She thinks about the stories behind the stains, imagines the way people dirty garments. The sun heats the sidewalk. Vendors pull their bushels of fruit out into the open—and mangos, bright bananas, and light green santol pop against the gray polluted air. From where she sits, she sees bundles of lychees, red and ripe, hanging by their branches. She glances at the stack of clothing next to her and calculates how long it will take her to finish the work.

Mang Tomo calls to her, pushing his cart of corn up the narrow hill. He waves, and from under the brim of his straw hat she sees his smile, wide and gummy with gaps between his teeth. "Kumusta ka, Lola?" he asks.

She nods, says, "Good, good." Handsome, she thinks, not bad for his age. He winks at her and all the lines of his face collapse like the folds of a Spanish fan. "You will be home later?"

"Sa gabi," she tells him, after her work is finished and dinner has been cleared away.

Then moving past her, he hawks his wares, crying, "Maís! Maís!" She watches his body moving slowly, the calves of his legs bulging from all the years he's spent pushing that cart up and down the streets of Metro Manila. Nakú, she thinks, ang hirap ng buhay.

Her mother named her "freedom" and she understands that this is not the life God meant for her. "I was at the wrong place at the wrong time—what can I say?"

She calls again to her grandchild, thirteen-year-old Filomena. Lola often catches the child daydreaming, dancing and staring at the sky. "Hurry up, anak. Do you want to be a labandera like me? Hurry up!"

Lola washes each garment and thinks of her apo, the troubles of their relationship, the future Filomena could have if only she'd behave. Something different than this, she thinks, rubbing her forehead with her forearm. She could have a better life. People skirt about the lola. They cover their mouths with kerchiefs to keep the waste of diesel from their lungs. Somebody bumps her. Lola loses her balance. Soap suds crash like the Pacific at high tide. Dirt streaks her legs. Lola pushes herself back up, her arms waving like grasshopper legs. Her joints ache. She feels old.

Looking up, she sees the perpetrator, a young woman in a cotton housedress bearing a child on one hip, dragging another at her side. The woman moves away, indifferent to the effect of her actions. Children in white and blue uniforms run past her. "Respect your elders," she calls after her. "Watch what you do!" A jeepney of twenty riders zooms past Lola, drowns her voice. Turning to the shack, she shouts, "Move, anak!"

♦

Lola scrubs the blood from a pair of white pants. The blood is thick and has hardened like mud. She looks up from her work and tells one of the children on the street to call her grandchild. "Tell her I mean business." She wipes the sweat from her brow. The humidity clings to her body. A shadow creeps over her, and for a moment the sun is gone. The lola keeps scrubbing.

"That's sickening, Lola," Filomena says. "How can you touch that?"

Filomena stands behind Lola, waiting. The old woman dips the pants back under the basin of water, rubs vigorously. The suds tumble onto the hot pavement, turn everything white. Finally, the child says, "Aalis na po ako." The old woman nods. She reaches into her pocket and hands the girl five pesos and Filomena leans over to kiss her.

Lola looks into her granddaughter's face. The child bears the same jaw, lips, soft as petals, and a tiny black mole at the tip of her left eyebrow. Like Malaya, Filomena speaks her mind. Too often, Lola thinks, and sighing, she leans into the girl and sniffs. Her apo smells like a baby, with talcum powder showering her neck and back. Ang sarap, Lola thinks. How delicious my girl.

"Dahan-dahan, ha?" the lola warns Filomena. "Ingat ka. Stay out of trouble."

♦

When Malaya was fourteen, her mother sent her to the market to buy a sack of rice. "Be quick," said her mother, kissing her on the forehead. "Dahan-dahan." There were rumors of war, of soldiers, and fighting. "No more playing around, just get the bigas and come home right away."

She walked the back roads, watching a sky full of orange light. The cicadas seemed to have gathered on all the branches of the magnolia trees, whirling their song to the setting sun. The sound mesmerized the girl, made her feel like she was floating into the purple red sky. She didn't see them coming, didn't hear them. A jeep full of soldiers rode past her, backed up. Called to her. But she was gazing at the trees, looking for cicadas, wondering how they found this perfect pitch. In a moment the soldiers had taken her away. Six little men, sallow as overripe bananas. Noisy and abrupt. Speaking words that were not words.

Hanging

Lola Malaya pulls a rope across the patch of dirt behind squatters' row. Her oldest friend, Lola Ime, sits on an empty crate, watching her tie the rope onto a street lamp and the other to a sickly looking palm tree.

"Did you hear?" Lola Ime asks.

"Gossip again!" Lola answers. "I'm not like you. I don't have time for gossip."

Lola Ime shoos her words away. "This affects you, Lola. Listen," she says.

"Do I have a choice?" She glances at Lola Ime, a gray-haired woman, a toothless woman, round as a mushroom with fat hands and feet. Imelda crosses her arms, closes her eyes. After a long moment she points her finger; she castigates Lola.

"No matter how old you are, I am still older than you. Still your ate. You should not talk to me like that," scolds Lola Ime.

"Artista!" Lola says. And after a long moment she gives in. "Sige," she says, "ano? Tell me na."

Imelda leans forward, slapping her knees. "The police want to tear down the shanties. Where are we going to go?"

"Rumor," says Lola.

"Truth," answers Lola Ime. "Talaga, Lola."

"So what," Lola says. She picks up a shirt, wrings it, shakes it. The sleeves sail open like wings. From her pockets she pulls wooden pins, hangs the laundry. "Where did we go when the lahar hit?" She pictures Mount Pinatubo erupting, black snow showering her village, burying her house in ash. "Where did we go when our families sent us away?" She bends over and grabs another garment. "No problem."

"Your mother," Lola Ime corrects. "My husband."

"Same thing. We survived."

"How can you talk like that, old woman?" Lola Ime holds an open palm to Malaya and closes it swiftly into a fist.

"What's the use, Ime? You can't change it, no matter what. Stop worrying, na."

The noise from the street clutters the air with horns and bells. Traffic must have halted, she thinks. The sharp ping of a rock hits the white sheet she has hung, leaves a black mark. Nakú, she thinks, not this again. Soon a battery of rocks come flying over the rooftops of the makeshift houses, and the cries of children pitch insults at the old women. "Tira!" she hears them caw. "Tira ng Hapones!"

Lola Ime curls her arms up around her head, folds her feet up close to her tummy. Shuts down. The taunting continues. Lola Malaya runs around the corner of the houses, picking up rocks as she goes, tossing them as she runs.

"Demonyo!" she screams. Her heart thumps and fills up her chest. "Pambihira!" she says. "Show your faces, you little bastards!"

◆

At their age, she was living in a war-torn chapel with fifty other hostages—girls and young women stolen from their families.

What do these devil children know of this life—to spend your nights lying in makeshift cubicles, your legs spread so far apart you fear your limbs will snap. She was taken before she had desire, before she understood the difference between love and sex, before she knew the art of flirting. She was taken before she understood the beauty of men. She did what she did to survive. And what would they have done?

The soldiers stood in line, like waiting for a bathroom stall. The pews had been removed and bed clothing hung like laundry in narrow rows to give the men some privacy. They used sheets taken from house raids. Curtains or bedspreads—sometimes dirty laundry—divided the garrison into space just large enough to fit one cot, one girl, one soldier. Sometimes a girl next to her would claw at the curtains, or kick at her stall. Hands and feet would punch the way the unborn kick inside their mothers' bellies. Then came the sounds of bayonets ripping into flesh, and the noise would end. This was how she learned not to fight back.

Perhaps the devil children are right. Tira ng Hapones. So what about it? Even if it's true, what does she get for surviving it? By the time she gets to the street, all she hears are echoes of laughter.

When she returns to the line of laundry, Lola Ime is sobbing. "Ay nakú, ang hirap ng buhay. Hirap na hirap." She rubs her chest. "Ang sakit sa puso."

"Stop it," Lola says, tearing down the newly soiled wash. "You make it worse."

"Ay, Lola, ang tigas ng puso mo."

But Lola knows better. Her heart isn't hard, just practical. "You can't let them get to you," she tells Lola Ime. "Ignore them."

"You don't ignore them. You chase them and they laugh even harder," Lola Ime says.

"Don't you let them get to you, I mean. Don't let them see."

Lola Ime shakes her head, beats her chest with the fist.

She spends the rest of the morning re-washing the garments that have been marred with dirt, re-wringing the sheets, re-hanging everything. Above, the sun continues to burn through the haze. The women are silent. The heat from their bodies intensifies like a halo of white.

Ironing

She stands in Ma'am's kitchen, underneath the air con's blower. This steady wind dries her damp skin. All day, the heat. No respite, no breath. Until now she thinks, sighing. Steam floats white and breathy from the mouth of an iron. On hot days like this, she looks forward to pressing laundry, eating the family's leftovers, having afternoon meryenda, while Emma the housemaid teases her about Mang Tomo. The white tile feels cool against Lola's tired feet.

"Nakú, Emma," she sighs. "Ang hirap ng buhay." She flattens a range of creases and darts the iron's nose against the shirt's button-down chest.

"A man of commerce," Emma says, clicking her tongue. "Not bad, Lola." Emma stands at the kitchen sink, cleaning milkfish and bitter melon.

"A corn vendor," Lola corrects. "Mabait siya."

Just beyond the kitchen, they can hear the children chasing after Hollywood, the family dog. While they continue their tasks, the two make chika-chika, and nibble on rolls of pan de cocoa. Emma pours cold glasses of calamansi juice.

"It's tart," she warns Lola.

Lola is fast with the iron. In this light, against clean white cotton, her hands look hard as earth, with blue mountains tunneling just beneath her skin. She presses wrinkled limbs and torsos, flattens darts that shape slight curves at the hips and bust of skirts and blouses. She places the ironed clothing on golden hangers wrapped in silk. She folds linen in perfect rectangles and stacks them in a basket made of bamboo.

Ma'am charges into the kitchen, past the white double doors with a newspaper rolled up in her hand. She waves it at Lola like a wand.

"Kita mo, Lola?" she asks. "Did you see? Wowee naman!" Ma'am's hair falls straight across her shoulders and collarbone. Smiling, she winks at Lola. "Ang litrato ni Lola sa front page," she coos, holding the paper up in front of the women.

In the photograph, Lola and her kumare hold up picket signs before the president's motorcade. In the foreground a blur of big black cars with red lights. A smattering of Philippine National Police dots the photo in white helmets and blue short-sleeved shirts. An officer stands just to the left of mga lola, his white teeth popping out of the shadow, his arm waving at the camera, cheering.

Purple scarves wrap the old women's shoulders and cover their thinning scalps. They hold their free hands up, shape them like the letter "L." The hand-painted signs read "Justice" and "Laban" and "Never Again."

Lola studies the photo and smiles. The faces of her fellow survivors scrunch up and all the wrinkles in their skin make them look mean and old. Warriors. Their graying brows rise up in reprimand. The mouths have been caught in the midst of their battle cry, "LABAN!" You'd never know, she thinks, how weak the hearts, how fragile the bones. In the middle of the photo, she casts her arms like swords, the purple scarf swiping the sky a brilliant lavender.

"Lola," Ma'am says. "Your granddaughter must be so proud."

Lola only smiles at Ma'am, as if she's lost her words.

"Let me see," Emma says, peeking over the young housewife's shoulder. "Wow, Lola," she sings. "Movie star."

●

Every time Lola shows up on television, or on the front page, or every time some American comes to interview the lola about the war, Filomena stops eating. She stops speaking. Sometimes she goes about her business as if her grandmother weren't around at all. Her face takes on the look of the lost souls. No expression. No reaction. No life. Silence enters their home, a breeze through the window, a little draft from impending monsoon rains. She'd rather Filomena scream at her. Thinking of her apo, a chamber in her heart closes up. She presses her iron heavy on the dress.

How will I make Filomena understand my actions? Sometimes when the child sleeps, Lola studies her face, the slope of her cheeks and the dark lashes resting like tired butterfly wings. She traces the little mole, rising like a star upon Filomena's brow. How easy to mistake the child for Malaya as a girl. Because Filomena shuts Lola out, the old woman waits for night to close the distance between them. She whispers stories into the child's hands, into her ear, telling her, "I do this so you will never have to, anak. I do this so never again. Never again."

She cannot sleep at night. Even after fifty years, the nightmares keep her awake. Each night the soldiers come to her, and she remembers the nights, the shadows looming over her, blocking light from stained-glass windows. The soldiers overlook God's mother, tucked in the corner of the church, leave her standing. She beseeches Mama Mary to give her strength.

She has forgotten the blur of faces—or maybe Mama Mary has saved her from seeing them. What stays with her is the stench of death and war painted on men's bodies—hot sweat, fresh blood—hers, or his, or maybe some dead American soldier's. What stays with her are the sounds in the church. The echoes of other Filipinas begging for grace, the calling out at night. What she hears even now are the voices of the men. "Kura! Kura!" Garbage words. Angry nonsense words. The groaning of their bodies. The howling.

●

"Talaga," Ma'am is saying. She spreads the paper down on the kitchen table, her painted fingers gleam pearly pink, her rings shimmer gold. "You are so courageous, Lola. Think of what you're doing."

Ma'am pulls a sack of clothing out of a cupboard and hands it to her. "These are dresses," she tells her. "For Filomena, Lola."

The dresses are fancy linen cut sleek to fit the body. Light colors—pale yellow, pinks, and baby blues—they'll pick up dirt too easily. "I've grown too fat," Ma'am tells her. "Such a waste to throw them out."

Lola nods, whispers a thank-you, irons a cotton camisole a little more vigorously.

From the other room, Ma'am's children yell at one another. Hollywood barks. Something crashes. Ma'am stands up and sighs. "Ay, Emma, can you stop them? Did you bathe Hollywood today?"

"Not yet, Ma'am," Emma tells her.

"Wash the dog," she tells her.

"Yes, Ma'am," Emma answers.

"And don't forget to dry him really good—so he doesn't smell."

"Opo, Ma'am."

Lola hangs a child's dress on a silk-covered hanger. She thinks about that spoiled little Hollywood. Washed every day like a baby, then blow-dried like a beauty. What a life, she thinks.

Gathering

She makes five hundred pesos at Ma'am and Sir's house. Closing the gate, she slips the money into her pocket, pulls out a bamboo fan. She whips the pamaypay open and cools herself. "Nakú," she utters. "Init."

She walks among the people, keeping one hand in her pocket, clutching the fist of pesos, while the other hand gracefully flutters her fan. She steps around children, past hens and kalabaw, in between parked motor trikes and stalled jeepneys. Now and then she spits on the ground, relieves her mouth of diesel fumes.

When she arrives at Santa Maria she walks to the back and steps into another kitchen. This one, hot and filled with steam, thick with cooking grease and the aroma of freshly cooked rice. She walks past Manang Tess, who fries fish for Father Anacleto. Manang Tess sings loud and off-key.

"If you're hoping to woo the young priest that way, Manang," Lola says, "forget it."

Manang Tess raises the volume of her song and her voice cracks above the popping grease. When it's clear that she's not interested in speaking, Malaya asks her, "Is his laundry ready?"

"Sa hallway," Manang Tess answers, pointing her finger to the door.

Lola steps out of the kitchen and walks down a long marble hall. On the wall, portraits of Santa Maria pastors hang. She glances up at the photos, walking past black-and-white and sepia-toned priests—some of them American, some Spanish, some Filipino. At the end of the hallway she winks at the portrait of Father Anacleto. His image lives within an ornate golden frame. His black robes flow from a tall and lean body, and she must crane her neck to see his beautiful young face, his large eyes, high cheekbones. His thick hair has been carefully combed back with pomade. Gwapo, she thinks. He would make a good lover, a good one for a beautiful young dalaga. A girl with equally long legs. They could have beautiful children. Too bad.

She spies an open door and peeks into a bathroom where every surface is marble—the floors, the walls, the ceilings. And every fixture, gold. Walking over to the toilet bowl, she fingers the handle. How beautiful, she thinks. How nice to flush waste away with gold. She pushes the bowl's gold lever and watches the water swirl in circles. How nice.

"Afternoon, Lola Malaya," calls a voice loud as God's.

She looks up and the young priest stands at the doorway with his hands folded under his arms. He wears a Coca-Cola T-shirt and running shorts. He looks too young, she thinks. Just a boy.

"I'm sorry I couldn't make the rally, La," he says.

She walks past him and gathers five plastic grocery bags of laundry.

He tells her they prayed for all the lola in mass today.

"S'okay," she says, picking up the bags. "Is this all of it?"

He nods.

"How was it?" he wants to know. And she tells him about the farmers, workers, and squatters gathered for miles down Commonwealth Avenue. She saves the "comfort women" for last. Banners skipped over their heads—red and purple flags, yellow and green.

"Many people," she tells him, "looking for justice." The lola waited for six hours without the shade of a tree. Some of them took to bickering with one another. "You know mga lola," she tells him. "Always tsismis, too much gossip!" When the president drove past, it seemed the motorcade sped up. Father Anacleto shakes his head, clicks his tongue.

"Is that any way for a priest to dress?" she asks him.

"Exercising, Lola," he says. "Alam mo na."

He walks her to the front door, makes mano, placing the old woman's hand to his forehead.

"Nakú!" she says. "It's me who should be paying you respect!" She waves her free hand at him and begins walking down the gated yard to the streets.

She wonders how Father Anacleto grew to be beautiful, kind, and spiritual too. How did his mommy do that, she wonders. Filomena has potential, but she's so masungit. A child should never be that mean. Laging kontrabida.

She walks to two other homes and gathers dirty laundry, placing plastic sacks in a large duffel bag she has sewn from old sheets. She swings the bag over her shoulder, bends at the waist, and walks toward home. Maybe, she thinks, I will bring her Jollibee for dinner. Hamburger and rice. After all, Lola thinks, didn't Ma'am just pay me? We will start over, she thinks, start happy. She digs into the bag Ma'am gave her, wonders if the dresses will fit her apo, if she will like them at all.

When she gets to the corner, she weaves her way among the parked cars. The bag weighs heavy on her back and she must be careful to bend her knees as she climbs the curb. She pushes her way through the glass door, wondering where the security guard who usually greets customers is. Nakú, she thinks, if something happens, where is he? The burger joint, with its red and yellow walls and giant bumblebee, has little room for Lola and her sack of dirty laundry. She must shove her way through people who seem planted to their spots. No one moves out of her way. She finds a place in line and waits like all the others. When she gets to the counter, the girl in the baseball cap and polo shirt smiles, looks past the lola, and says, "Can I help you, sir?" Lola turns and sees a young man in a blue suit and wire-rimmed glasses pulling out his wallet.

"Excuse," says Lola to the clerk. But the young man has stepped forward and is trying to get around Lola's sack. "Excuse me," she says a little louder, swinging her sack of dirty clothes. "Young lady, I was here first." She blocks the young man. "Take my order."

Outside, she balances the laundry on her back, clutching a white paper bag of french fries, rice, and burger. She walks in the shade of the alley, stepping around old bottles and discarded paper cups. The air smells of rotting vegetables. Dogs run past her, chase one another for leftovers from nearby garbage cans. Near the end of the building, behind the dumpster, she sees the back of the Jollibee security guard leaning on a schoolgirl. He must be twice her age, she thinks. His arms are spread wide, and he holds her down against the brick. Her head is thrown back and she cannot tell if the girl enjoys this or is being held against her will. The brim of his hat covers her face. His rifle has fallen to the ground, rests next to her stack of books. Lola sees schoolgirl shoes and the gleam of white anklet socks. The girl places one foot firmly on the ground and the other she presses against the wall. Her skirt—blue and black plaid—rises up. Her leg is lean and beautiful in the light. No wonder, Lola Malaya thinks, he was not at the door. He's taking a break pala! As Lola nears the two, she turns her gaze to her feet.

⚇

The memory recurs in the way her flesh aches. When her husband was alive, the nightmares began each time he drew himself in and out of her. Though he was gentle, her skin remembered. It took her body a very long time to learn that acts of kindness included kissing and touching, appeared in the chaos of arms and legs gripping one another.

She was too small and the soldiers had a hard time entering her. They'd get mad at her. Hit her. Shout words like thunder. When they grew frustrated, the soldiers spat on her. They took knives and flames from matches and scarred her navel, the nape of her neck, the inside of her thigh. One soldier branded the soft flesh of her breast, marked her for life.

⚇

Lola cannot help it. She walks past them and she glances their way, wants to know if the girl needs help. Not that there is much she can do. The girl moans and Lola's heart beats fast. "Nakú!" she yells, running at the two. She yanks the girl by the hair. "This is how you behave?" she says. She knows this girl. "Have you learned nothing?" she asks Filomena, who is screaming now and pulling herself away from Lola.

"Pick up those books," the lola tells her granddaughter. "Pull down your skirt."

The guard zips up his pants, straightens his hat, grabs the gun. He turns away from the women, like he is not a part of the scene.

"Let me go," Filomena says.

"Never," Lola answers as she gathers herself, the sack, the laundry, the girl, and carries her burden across Manila.

Sorting

The clothes lie in piles across straw mats. Lola has ordered her granddaughter to sit in the room and listen. She goes through the bags of dirty clothes, counts the number of shirts, mga kamiseta, the socks, mga pantalones.

"In broad daylight?" Lola says.

Filomena draws her legs up, pulls her T-shirt over her knees. A trail of smoke curls its way up into the stuffy house. She holds the cigarette loosely between her slender fingers.

"Is there no shame?" Lola asks her. Talagang walang hiya. She tosses a dark pair of socks into a pile. "Has my life meant nothing to you?"

She glances over her shoulder at the girl. Filomena's eyes are wide open, round saucers, polished stone. Vacant as a doll's. Lola tosses Ma'am's hand-me-downs at Filomena. "For you," she mutters, not looking at her.

"Do you understand," Lola asks, "Napakahirap ng buhay." She waves at her apo. "Talagang walang hiya!"

"Shame?" Filomena says, "Ano ba yan? You should be ashamed! Not me. You're on the streets every day, shouting your trauma to anyone who will listen!" The girl stands now, pacing the small room.

Knocking into things. Her arms, gesturing at her lola. "At ang nanay ko? Where is my mother now? She has left you too. You embarrass us!"

❦

Lola Malaya considers her name. Freedom. Considers her life. Considers the child. Her heart weakens. The tears fall. A pain shoots through her and she has lost her breath. Outside she hears the rooster crowing. She takes the beads from her nightstand and storms out of the house.

On a rock, Lola settles herself and conjures Mama Mary up— her serene face, her full lips. This Blessed Mother is the Pinay version of the Mother of God and Lola sees the dark grain of mahogany that is her very complexion.

Filomena yells through the window, cannot stop now that she's begun. Cannot understand how airing the past can bring Lola justice. "What makes you think those politicians even see you?" she calls. "Why can't you stay quiet?" she wants to know.

Lola sits under the Manila sky, utters Hail Marys and dreams about another life.

❦

After three months, rebels from the mountain snaked into the garrison and killed all the guards. The women lined up, weeping silently, and tiptoed out of the church. Lola found her way to the house where she was born, but when she got there, the door remained locked. Her mother called from behind a screen. "You are dead, iha," she said. "It's better to go to the city, start a new life."

That first night, Malaya slept at the foot of the door, waiting. She woke to the sound of dirt hitting aluminum, to a shower of earth falling upon her. She looked below, down the ladder that led to their nipa hut, and a group of men called to her, threw fistfuls of dirt at her. "Tira," they chanted. "Tira."

Her father came to the door and shook his head. She saw his tears. "Go," he said. "We will never have peace, and you will always have shame unless you go."

The sun has stained the sky red, purple, and vibrant orange. The cityscape mars a beautiful sky and brings Lola Malaya to the streets again. Mang Tomo makes his way down the hill, a sack of corn at his side. He waves at Lola Malaya, begins to run to her.

The sight of the old fool only makes the pain worse. Her tears fall and do not stop. He nears her, smiling wide and toothless. Stretching, he offers the gift. "Tira lang," he tells her. "Still fresh today, but tomorrow no good." He takes a handkerchief out of his pocket, wipes the tears from her face. "Okay lang," he whispers. "S'okay." Her hands shake. The rosary rattles like wind chimes. He takes a seat on the ground next to her and covers her free hand with his.

"Ay, Tomo," she whispers. "Talagang sobrang hirap ng buhay ko."

The prayers wash over the old couple. She circles the rosary in her hand three times, fifteen decades of Hail Marys before the moon illuminates the skyscrapers and the sound of car horns blink like stars. She stretches her fingers and curls them over Tomo's battered hand. Like this they point to the constellations, twinkling in the night like hope.

ISLA OF THE BABAYLAN

•••

Isla of the Babaylan

Once long ago, in the western Sulu Seas, I ruled an island. I am Kapwa, first daughter and queen, descendant of Malakas and Maganda. My children, the twins Pakisama and Pakiramdam, were born on the night of the new moon. They came into this world with powers babaylan receive only after years of apprenticeship. My husband, Lambing, was an excellent cook. He knew how to read the tracks in the forest, how to harvest fruit from trees, and how to cull medicine for the tribe. He had a gift for naming all the living things on earth, for writing the names on bark, on bamboo, on banana leaves. In this way we passed down all the things we learned. Too bad no one can read his writing.

I see you, worry yoked to your shoulders, fear feeding your dreams. You have forgotten. You have turned away. You don't even eat our food anymore. Not with your hands. Not on leaves. Not with white rice.

I come to you in your dreams and you don't recognize me. And still you wonder, what will you do now? Won't you let me show you? Remind you? School you?

You think all our people do is sing and dance and tell bad puns. All we do, in times like this, is cook and feed one another. Make biro-biro and laugh inappropriately. As if the answer is in chicken adobo. As if pansit, with its uncut noodles, will really give you long life. You think what we do is play. You, my darling, have no idea.

●

Even as a child, Pakiramdam had a voice more beautiful than the maya bird. Every morning, upon waking, she'd poke her head out the windows of our hut, and sing. Her chanting rose above the pitch of insects buzzing, above mourning doves cooing, above the whistling of north winds. She hummed, woke the vibration of the primordial earth, and then she opened her mouth.

On this morning, as Pakiramdam sang, she danced. Lambing and I lifted Pakisama onto his feet.

"Wake up, boy," I said.

"Gentle," Lambing told me. "He may be dreaming."

Pakiramdam's voice split into three-part harmony. She summoned the village to rise. We could feel a rush of wind as the doors of huts opened. Pakiramdam thumped the earth with her bare feet, a sound heavy as drums.

My family climbed our way down the ladder, past the magnolia tree, through the palms of coconut. We ducked under branches of the mango tree, slipped beneath the banana's purple heart, and stepped onto the lush tropical soil.

And when my daughter's song was done, the whole tribe squatted, sat low to the ground, eyes closed and listening.

The earth sent sparks of energy through the bottom of our feet, like bees buzzing in the soles. Wind hurried through the branches of the trees. Sunbeams skipped around the palms.

●

Are you listening? We wasted our mornings? We did not have pressure the way you do? These rituals. This earth. Those animals who sat with us in silence. This way prepared us, this way of being. For what? Wait.

●

I squatted to the ground, my knees pointing at the sky, my palms pressed together in prayer. I listened. The earth shifted, left, then right. Pakisama leaned on me, but I pushed him gently away. "Shhh," I told him. "Quiet."

A noise came to us from the west. A different kind of music. The current from the sea sent cold winds through the village, carried with it strange smells.

Pakiramdam began singing once again. This time her melody was minor. The beat of her words fell more softly to the ear. She slowed down.

I could hear the voices of the women in the trees. They were restless.

Lambing and I went to work. I visited villages in the east, I cared for the elderly, the sick, the women ready to give birth. He traveled south, to the rainforest to see about gathering fruit, herbs, sap from trees.

At noon, when the heat consumed everything, the women grilled seven milkfish, wilted green kangkong leaves, sliced sweet mangos. They steamed pots of hot white rice. They cracked coconuts and took the water from the husk and filled clay jugs and placed them on the altar.

We tossed rice wine to the ground. We gave thanks. Invited the ancestors to join us. I prayed for wisdom and words to calm the women. When we sat to eat the food, each woman placed a red gumamela on a tray before me.

"There is talk," said a young mother.

Said another, "Not everyone is sharing the workload."

I listened. I looked at them.

"And why is that a problem?" asked an old woman.

"Some of the men are lazy."

"Their wives are disgusted. What kind of society makes one gender work more than the other?"

"I heard Kontrabida yelling all night long. Her husband is good for nothing!"

"You must do something, Kapwa."

"Not everyone has a husband like Lambing."

I closed my eyes. Kontrabida stirred a pot of soup. She sewed stories, working herself up, starting fights between lovers. In the distance, a monsoon approached, but I could feel it was not rain, not a storm.

❋

Why was that an issue? When there is sorrow, everyone holds the broken one. When there is sickness, we all heal the wounded. Men wear flowers. Women carry spears. We share the load. We let women be the boss. We let men too. Everyone shares the work.

❋

The next day, I took Pakiramdam and Pakisama to see Kontrabida. We hiked to the farthest eastern mountain on the island. I could hear her shouting as we climbed.

"I want you to watch," I told my children. "Observe."

Kontrabida was a small woman, with eyes dark as rosewood, mouth stained red with betel nut. Her skin had many piercings. The tattoos on her body recorded heartbreak and illness. She was very beautiful.

Her house was noisy with children.

She offered me a red gumamela.

"Thank you," I said. I put the flower behind my ear. "Give me your hands," I said. She offered her brown fists and I opened them, examining each palm. They were scarred and rough. The fingers had dirt under their nails. I held her hands. Closed my eyes.

"You're angry."

"The men are not holding up the other half of the sky."

"Some men are."

"Some men say they are."

"You stir trouble," I said. There were halos around her body, lights the color of fire. "You're making other women upset too."

"They're tired. They ask their husbands to wash their children. They say, please bring in wood while I cut up these vegetables. And the men say, 'In a minute. In a minute.'"

"Where is Mabait?"

"Fishing. Again. He goes for days at a time, and when he returns he is too tired." She brushed her hair to the side. Her face flushed and beads of sweat, tiny as grains of sand, rimmed her hairline.

"He's a good man," I told her. "He will bring you a school of fish tonight."

Her children chased one another. Screamed. Laughed. Pakisama and Pakiramdam sat among them, still, quiet, listening while the children crawled over them.

"He's been gone for three days," Kontrabida complained.

I smiled. "Will you take a breath with me?" I asked.

"I have to cook, Kapwa."

"You must breathe," I said.

She turned to the children.

"See how restless?" I looked into her eyes. I inhaled deeply. So did she. "Now let go." The wind blew through the trees. "Let go," I said. I watched her shoulders relax. The trees swayed. She closed her eyes. Went silent.

◉

At the shore, Pakiramdam, Pakisama, and I waded into the sea. Watched the sun drown, turn the skies from blue to brilliant orange. From my pouch, I took a handful of red hibiscus, some crumpled from the journey, all vibrant, soft, and in full bloom. I blessed each one and offered them to the water. The tide took the flowers away one at a time, brought them back in twos and threes, then washed them all to sea. We sat on the beach. The water was cold. The sea foam noisy.

I thought you'd never ask. "Gumamela" is Filipino for hibiscus. A blossom for one day. Magnificent. But only one day. No, it isn't sad. It's beautiful. When the hibiscus falls, the next day a new one blooms.

Pakisama leaned his head on my shoulder. Pakiramdam sat on a bank of sand a few feet away, head down, surrounded by sea birds. The light receded in the sky.

"My feeling is," Pakiramdam said, "she misses her husband."

"She wants to be with him," Pakisama answered.

"What about today," I asked.

Pakisama closed his eyes. His hair, long and free in the wind, danced around his face like a song. "She liked when you held her hand."

"She was relieved," Pakiramdam answered.

"But not because you were with her," Pakisama said.

"Because she came to herself," I answered.

◆

I sent the children to visit Mabait, the husband. They met him in his dreams.

Yes, it is possible to visit people when they sleep. Yes, I visit you all the time. No, you never remember. That is why I am here now.

The children went to him and found him walking up the mountain with a dozen milkfish on his back. He was tired from the journey. Pakiramdam said his heart was swollen from longing. He had left a part of his soul at the hut.

Pakisama blessed him. Pakiramdam chanted a hymn. They brushed his skin with a small bag of rice and salt. Slipped a round prayer stone into his pocket. Told him how lucky he was to have such a family.

The fisherman nodded. "I know," he answered. "I give thanks all the time. Even when she is in a foul mood."

Pakisama gave Mabait a vision of his children sitting around a fire, waiting for Kontrabida to sit with them, to close their eyes, to listen. In the vision, the husband and wife made a fish stew with greens and eggplants, with onions and sour tamarindo. The family ate from the same cast iron pot. "Right," Pakisama said, "even when she's angry, love her. Anger is her nature."

"Sadness is her nature," Mabait answered.

"Good," I told them when they returned. "Now do the same with her."

❋

Where is this going? What does this have to do with your restless soul? With your rejection of sleep? Come home, anak, come home. The day is hot. The night is cold. You will see that once I was like you.

❋

In the days to come, a monsoon wrapped its wings around our little island, winds blowing so strong the palm trees bent their faces to the ground, the old banyan tree in the center of the village cracked and fell into pieces.

As if this was not enough, Kontrabida lost her soul. The Conquistador enchanted her with promises he could not keep. Where did he come from? The west. He was the storm I had been sensing, weeks before his arrival. Typhoon winds brought the Conquistador and his ships from Iberia. All those months on the water toasted his white skin orange. He infiltrated the village with a spell. "Te quiero, linda. Te adoro, cariño," he whispered. "Ven aquí."

He was tall, this Conquistador. His hair was the color of the sun. His eyes like seawater. His skin leathery, the color of overripe mango. Layers of fabric stitched in gold threads draped his body.

"Qué quieres, mi amor?" he asked her.

Kontrabida told him she wanted a partner to hold up the other half of the sky. An equal.

"My husband is beautiful and strong, but he is never here. I do all the work."

"I can do that," he lied. "I can carry the entire sky, if you like."

"With those soft hands?" She laughed. "No. Half the sky. No slacking."

The Conquistador took her when Mabait had gone fishing. And he stayed.

❋

Yes. The children went to Kontrabida. Yes. The children blessed her, washed her skin with rice and salt, planted prayers into her tattooed skin. But they were not specific. When Kontrabida said she wanted a man to hold up half the sky, they gave her this man, this Patricio from Spain. They should have named Mabait. It was a mistake.

Patricio was so malambing at first. So kind. And after seven nights, he asked Kontrabida to gather women whose husbands also left their huts—the hunters, other fisherman, the Babaylan who traveled other islands. He sent a soldier to each of their huts. They divided our tribe.

●

Was I mad at the children? No. How else would Pakisama and Pakiramdam learn? They had to make their own mistakes. Did I feel guilty? I did not.

I did. What happened the day the Spaniards took my island, my people lost our souls. I lost my own. I let my thoughts overtake my heart. I let my fear become the whole of me. Still, Pakiramdam chanted in the mornings, and at first, I'd take my body to the earth. I sat myself down. I pretended to listen.

All the while, I thought of strategies. Ways to retrieve our souls. To take back our village. But the men had weapons we had never seen before. Carried gold crosses. Spoke in curses we could not understand. Their souls arrived black as midnight. I could not enter their dreams.

I went about the day on the outside, the queen. The angel of the island, fixing little traumas. But inside, a part of me was missing. I could not heal this big trauma. My husband, Lambing, washed my skin with rice water, with gumamela flowers. He tattooed my body with sacred poetry. But I was lost in my thoughts. How could this be happening?

Meanwhile, soldiers from another sea lived in our huts. They used our women. They used our men. They cut our trees. Ripped gumamela from the ground. They offered everything to their god.

Forbid us to gather, to feast, to make offerings. They tore the sky, shredded all that blue. Left only night. Stole the stars. Our people went hungry. Our dying left their bodies without ritual. Nothing could I fix.

I lost myself to myself. The days were hot. The nights were cold. I could not sit still, nor could I listen. I had to act. My soul traveled to the gods, to our ancestors, begged them to help me find a way.

They sent me back. How else would I learn? I found myself squatting. The sun heated my face. I planted my feet onto the earth. The wind ran through my hair. I came to myself, breathing. I sat still. I felt the walls of my heart. I looked for light. I inhaled. I exhaled. Still, still, very still. I listened. I came back to myself.

♦

You must breathe. You must inhale, exhale. Listen. You must be still. Kontrabida, you can change the world only if you come to yourself. Honor yourself. Be yourself. Do not let the orange men steal your soul. You can right this. But first come home. The days are hot. The nights are cold. Come home.

ACKNOWLEDGMENTS

In the summer of 2022, while on a visit to my mom in Wisconsin, the owner of the nail salon she frequents asked me how long it had been since my dad had died.

"Four years," I told him.

"Sometimes," he said, "when your mom get her nails done, I see his shadow over there." He indicated the chairs by the window. "Just waiting for her like he used to. Sometimes, he nap."

Whether or not my dad's shadow is actually there is irrelevant. What is relevant is that I can imagine him there. That his life is still a presence in our lives. That he could be among us, waiting as we go about our daily business—that is what matters. That he may communicate to us in story, in dream, in music. That is what matters. That there may be others.

So many of the stories in this book imagine the dead moving among us, communicating to us from the other side. So many of the stories are about the legacy of family, the future of our kin. I begin this litany of thanks by acknowledging my ancestors. My father, my cousins, both sets of lolo and lola, and my great-grandparents. All the aunties and uncles. Those blood related and those family by affinity. For with them are the seeds of story. Because of them and my desire to know them and pass them on to my nephews and nieces, my parents' apo, I write. Salamat po.

These narratives are spun from myths told to me as a child, discovered in books and inspired by researchers like Leny Strobel,

Virgil Apostol, and other Babaylan scholars. They are not meant to replicate original creation stories as much as they are a re-envisioning and response to them. Thank you to those culture bearers for your influence. Salamat, Grace Nono, for your inspiration and support. And a special note of gratitude to Datu Migketay Victorino Saway, tribal custodian of the Talaandig Ancestral Territory in Songco, Lantapan, Bukidnon, for his leadership promoting rights of indigenous peoples and their culture in Mindanao. I thank you for your wise words that begin the pages of this book.

Several of the stories in *When the Hibiscus Falls* have been published in other iterations. I thank the fiction editors at *The Rumpus, The Miami Rail, riksha—Asian American Arts in Action, Prairie Schooner, Calyx,* and *Flyway,* and the editors of the anthologies *Kuwento: Lost Things, 15 Views of Miami, Immigrant Voices: 21st Century Stories, Pinay Power: Peminist Critical Theory,* and *Screaming Monkeys: Critiques of Asian American Images.* Thank you for inviting me to write.

These stories exist because of my community of editors—Denne Michele Norris, Karissa Chen, Patricia Engel, Nicole Sumida, Beverly McFarland, Hilda Raz, Lis P. Sipin-Gabon, Rachelle Cruz, Lynne Barrett, Achy Obejas, and Melinda L. de Jesus.

Special thanks to Edwidge Danticat and to Julia and Ligaya Galang. Your critical and supportive eyes and your generous spirits have helped to shape this book. And to Rachel Christmann for "checking in." Special thanks to my cousin, Michelle Galang, for your expertise in Tagalog and Kapampangan.

Thank you to the crew at Coffee House Press—to Anitra Budd, Erika Stevens, Lizzie Davis, Daley Farr, Marit Swanson, Abbie Phelps, Annemarie Eayrs, and Christina Vang—for your passion, dedication, and good works. Christina, the cover you designed is stunning! And to Allan Kornblum, Coffee House Press founder and ancestor. I hear you talking in the edits all the time. Thank you! The world needs editors like you, Allan, open to all things, and in all voices.

Salamat to Michelle Blankenship, publicist and friend, for believing in the work, and me.

To my Miami literary community for creating this vibrant writing scene—to Chantel Acevedo at the University of Miami, Mitchell Kaplan at Books & Books, and Deborah Briggs of The Betsy Hotel, thank you, thank you, thank you.

To my students, especially spring of 2022 English 390, who passed an early draft of the book around the workshop circle to invoke their good energy into the pages, thank you. You inspire me.

In gratitude to the University of Miami for the numerous hours you have gifted me in the form of summer awards and fellowships. Not everyone has a research institute supporting them to steal an hour or two from researching *(Lolas' House)* or writing novels (*Angel de la Luna and the 5th Glorious Mystery* and *Beautiful Sorrow, Beautiful Sky*) to write these stories.

Thank you to my VONA community for holding space. The mission is everything.

Great thanks to my mother, Gloria Lopez-Tan Galang, my most avid reader and critic, for your patience and your love and support. You have always understood this need to write. Salamat, Mommy.

And to my husband, the journalist and book critic Chauncey Mabe. You are my best reader, most honest editor, most feisty literary debate sparrer, and supporter in all things—literary and life.

Coffee House Press began as a small letterpress operation in 1972 and has grown into an internationally renowned nonprofit publisher of literary fiction, essay, poetry, and other work that doesn't fit neatly into genre categories.

Coffee House is both a publisher and an arts organization. Through our *Books in Action* program and publications, we've become interdisciplinary collaborators and incubators for new work and audience experiences. Our vision for the future is one where a publisher is a catalyst and connector.

LITERATURE
is not the same thing as
PUBLISHING

FUNDER ACKNOWLEDGMENTS

Coffee House Press is an internationally renowned independent book publisher and arts nonprofit based in Minneapolis, MN; through its literary publications and *Books in Action* program, Coffee House acts as a catalyst and connector—between authors and readers, ideas and resources, creativity and community, inspiration and action.

Coffee House Press books are made possible through the generous support of grants and donations from corporations, state and federal grant programs, family foundations, and the many individuals who believe in the transformational power of literature. This activity is made possible by the voters of Minnesota through a Minnesota State Arts Board Operating Support grant, thanks to the legislative appropriation from the Arts and Cultural Heritage Fund. Coffee House also receives major operating support from the Amazon Literary Partnership, Jerome Foundation, Literary Arts Emergency Fund, McKnight Foundation, and the National Endowment for the Arts (NEA). To find out more about how NEA grants impact individuals and communities, visit www.arts.gov.

Coffee House Press receives additional support from Bookmobile; Dorsey & Whitney LLP; Elmer L. & Eleanor J. Andersen Foundation; the Gaea Foundation; the Matching Grant Program Fund of the Minneapolis Foundation; Mr. Pancks' Fund in memory of Graham Kimpton; the Schwab Charitable Fund; and the U.S. Bank Foundation.

THE PUBLISHER'S CIRCLE OF
COFFEE HOUSE PRESS

Publisher's Circle members make significant contributions to Coffee House Press's annual giving campaign. Understanding that a strong financial base is necessary for the press to meet the challenges and opportunities that arise each year, this group plays a crucial part in the success of Coffee House's mission.

Recent Publisher's Circle members include many anonymous donors, Kathy Arnold, Patricia A. Beithon, Andrew Brantingham, Anitra Budd, Kelli & Dave Cloutier, Mary Ebert & Paul Stembler, Eva Galiber, Jocelyn Hale & Glenn Miller Charitable Fund of the Minneapolis Foundation, William Hardacker, Randy Hartten & Ron Lotz, Dylan Hicks & Nina Hale, Amy L. Hubbard & Geoffrey J. Kehoe Fund of the St. Paul & Minnesota Foundation, Kenneth & Susan Kahn, the Kenneth Koch Literary Estate, Cinda Kornblum, the Lenfestey Family Foundation, Sarah Lutman & Rob Rudolph, Mary & Malcolm McDermid, Daniel N. Smith III & Maureen Millea Smith, Robin Chemers Neustein, Alan Polsky, Robin Preble, Rebecca Rand, Grant Wood, and Margaret Wurtele.

For more information about the Publisher's Circle and other ways to support Coffee House Press books, authors, and activities, please visit www.coffeehousepress.org/pages/donate or contact us at info@coffeehousepress.org.

M. EVELINA GALANG is the daughter of Filipino American immigrants who first came to the United States in the mid-1950s. Born in Harrisburg, Pennsylvania, she is the eldest of six. By the time she was twelve, she had moved to seven cities before her family settled in Milwaukee, Wisconsin. Galang is the author of two novels, two story collections, and a work of nonfiction, and is the editor of *Screaming Monkeys: Critiques of Asian American Images.* She draws from the stories she grew up on and the research from a Fulbright Senior Scholar Award as well as numerous grants and fellowships from the University of Miami. Galang has been recognized as a Dayton Literary Peace Prize finalist and as a Zalaznick Distinguished Visiting Writer at Cornell University, and is the recipient of the Gustavus Myers Outstanding Book Award. The American Library Association named Galang's *Angel de la Luna and the 5th Glorious Mystery* among recommended feminist literature for ages zero to eighteen. She lives in Miami, where she teaches creative writing.

When the Hibiscus Falls was designed by
Bookmobile Design & Digital Publisher Services.
Text is set in STIX Two Text.

CPSIA information can be obtained
at www.ICGtesting.com
Printed in the USA
JSHW081724150723
44759JS00001B/2

9 781566 896795